HOT SUMMER NIGHTS

"What's wrong?" he stopped and asked.

"Nothing. Everything's right."

He kissed her again, keeping his head close, rubbing their noses. "Stay with me tonight."

His whispered words came out in a sensual tone that tickled her ears. She wanted him to make love to her so bad, it clouded her thoughts. "I don't know."

"Bobbi, I can't wait no more. All I want to do is make love to you. I tried to wait until summer school was over, but I can't. Whenever I look into your eyes, I see our future and our great romance."

"One of the world's greatest romances, right?" She mocked something he'd told her once.

"That's right."

BOOK YOUR PLACE ON OUR WEBSITE AND MAKE THE ARABESQUE ROMANCE CONNECTION!

We've created a customized website just for our very special Arabesque readers, where you can get the inside scoop on everything that's going on with Arabesque romance novels.

When you come online, you'll have the exciting opportunity to:

- View covers of upcoming books

- Learn about our future publishing schedule (listed by publication month and author)

- Find out when your favorite authors will be visiting a city near you

- Search for and order backlist books

- Check out author bios and background information

- Send e-mail to your favorite authors

- Join us in weekly chats with authors, readers and other guests

- Get writing guidelines

- AND MUCH MORE!

Visit our website at
http://www.arabesquebooks.com

HOT SUMMER NIGHTS

Bridget Anderson

BET Publications, LLC
http://www.bet.com
http://www.arabesquebooks.com

ARABESQUE BOOKS are published by

BET Publications, LLC
c/o BET BOOKS
One BET Plaza
1900 W Place NE
Washington, DC 20018-1211

All Kensington Titles, Imprints, and Distributed Lines are available at special quantity discounts for bulk purchases for sales promotions, premiums, fund-raising, and educational or institutional use. Special book excerpts or customized printings can also be created to fit specific needs. For details, write or phone the office of the Kensington special sales manager: Kensington Publishing Corp., 850 Third Avenue, New York, NY 10022, attn: Special Sales Department, Phone: 1-800-221-2647.

First Printing: March 2003
10 9 8 7 6 5 4 3 2 1

Printed in the United States of America

To Terry, for all your patience and support, I love you.
To Shirley and Jan, for putting up with me.
To my mother, father and brother, with all my love.

One

In the dark movie theater Bobbi Cunningham shook her head in disgust at the screen. "This is ridiculous, don't you think?"

"Shh." Her best friend, Roz Fisher, held a finger over her lips. "I am so into this." She never took her eyes from the screen.

"You would be," Bobbi said with a twist of her lips. Roz had always been a romantic at heart. Bobbi grabbed a handful of popcorn and shoved it into her mouth. She cringed throughout the rest of the movie without saying another word. Romance pictures were so sappy.

As the credits rolled and the house lights came up, Roz emerged from her trance. "That was such a cute picture," she commented as she stood to let the couple next to them out.

Bobbi stood halfway letting the couple by as well. "It was just another remake of Cinderella. You knew she'd get the guy and they'd live happily ever after."

"Yeah, but it's the fact that it was a period piece, and how well the roles were portrayed that made it so good. I loved the costumes and the—"

"And the whole fairy tale." Bobbi grabbed her purse and followed Roz down the steps. "Can't you see how damaging pictures like that are?"

Roz stopped at the bottom of the steps and looked back up at Bobbi. "Damaging to whom?"

"Young girls." She reached the bottom of the steps and they walked out into the lobby together.

"Girl, you're trippin'."

"No, I'm not. If they keep making movies about some white knight coming along and sweeping you off your feet, we'll wind up with a society of women unprepared for the real world." Bobbi tossed her empty popcorn box into a nearby trashcan.

"Tell me you wouldn't like some man—say a black knight—to come along and sweep you off your feet?"

"It doesn't matter if I'd like it or not; it just doesn't happen in the world we live in. The picture's sweet. I just don't care for brought-to-life fairy tales."

"So we can expect a lukewarm review in this weekend's paper?" Roz asked.

She held the door open for Roz as they left the theater. "I'm not saying it was a bad movie, so I won't let my personal opinions get in the way of the review. I just want to see more realistic stories about relationships."

"Like what? You want to see movies about men cheating and women gaining weight, with a lot of fussing and fighting."

"It doesn't have to be like that. Hollywood should portray the real deal. These young girls coming up today already think the way to a man's heart is through his pants. Whatever happened to filling his stomach first?" She opened the car door to her used Honda Accord.

"Well, I agree with you in some respects. Young women are faster today, but I'm still holding out for my knight in shining armor." Roz climbed into the car smiling.

"You're hopeless," Bobbi commented, laughing.

She drove the fifteen minutes to the apartment they

shared. Neither of them could afford to live alone, and considered themselves lucky to have found each other. It had taken Bobbi a year after moving from Douglas to Macon, Georgia, to find Roz and the apartment. She was far away from her family and their drama, but not too far away for a quick visit.

Roz was the perfect roommate. She kept to herself most of the time, and enjoyed the free movies courtesy of Bobbi's job as a reviewer for the *Telegraph,* Macon's local newspaper. Bobbi was the chef, and Roz was the organizer; together they made a perfect team.

"What you gonna review tomorrow?" Roz asked, as they pulled up to the apartment and got out.

"A horror flick. Want to go?" she asked, perking up.

"No way. Free movie or not, you know horror pictures keep me up all night."

"It's better than some mushy romance picture." Bobbi climbed the stairs to the second floor ahead of Roz.

"Yeah, I hear you saying that, but I remember when you sat up all night watching *Untamed Heart* and cried at the end."

Bobbi stopped at the front door and spun around. "That's because Christian Slater died at the end! It wasn't mushy, it was tragic."

Roz took the key from her hand and opened the door. "Yeah, right."

Once inside, Roz dropped her keys on the dining room table and picked up a stack of mail. Bills, bills, advertisements, and—

"Anything for me?" Bobbi asked, walking by on her way to the kitchen.

"Yeah—this." She held out a letter with a red ink disclaimer stamped across the front.

This correspondence is forwarded from an Alabama State Prison. The contents have not been evaluated, and the Alabama Department of Corrections is not responsible for the substance or content of the enclosed communication.

Bobbi took the letter and held it for a few minutes before looking up at Roz. She took a deep breath and tried to smile.

"You haven't gotten a letter from him in a while." Roz shrugged.

"I know. I should throw it in the garbage can."

"Don't do that. Trust me, you'll regret it one day." Roz dropped all the bills on the table and walked away.

Bobbi flipped the letter over and ripped it open. She hoped it wasn't another portrait from prison. Inside was a single sheet of paper with a short note. She pulled out a chair and sat down.

Dear Bobbi,
   I tried to call you twice last month but you weren't at home. I trust you can find it in your heart to forgive me. Although I haven't seen you in such a long time, you will always be my baby. I never meant to hurt you or anyone else. All I'm asking for is a little of your time, we really need to talk.

She stopped reading, folded the letter, and shoved it back into the envelope. So now he wanted to talk. No way. If she never talked to him again, it would be too soon. He'd made his bed; now he'd have to lie in it.

Roz came back into the dining room. "You all right?"

"Yeah, I'm fine. He wants to talk to me. Says he tried to call."

"What you gonna do?" Roz asked, leaning against the entrance to the kitchen.

Bobbi hesitated for a moment; then jumped up. "I'm gonna change clothes, fix myself something to eat, and start on that review." With letter in hand, she walked down the hall to her bedroom.

"That girl suffers from a bad case of avoidance."

"I heard that, and no I don't," Bobbi yelled down the hall before closing the door to her room.

Quentin Brooks completed another successful pitch, and picked up his biggest bread-and-butter customer since moving to Macon. "Well, that concludes my presentation. I believe I can save the Crown Plaza some money and keep your system running smoothly." He picked up his samples and slid them back into his briefcase.

"Mr. Brooks, I think we've got a deal. Those layoffs in the data center are killing us. Your services will be right on time."

Quen stood and held out his hand. "Thank you, Mr. Parker. It's going to be a pleasure doing business with you."

Quen strolled out of the hotel office feeling confident and a little more secure. He held his chin up toward the bright Southern sky, and put on his shades.

Walking out to his car, Quen checked his cell phone for messages. He had two callbacks, and one message from his sister. He rang Evette back.

"Hello."

"You rang." He hit the key remote on his car, then opened the back door.

"Quen, how fast can you get up here?"

"Why, what's wrong?" He pitched his briefcase into the backseat and closed the door.

"Mama's done lost her mind. That woman went and hired some bum off the street to do some work on the house. I told her to ask Robert, but I don't think she can find him."

Quen buckled his seat belt as he cursed his older brother under his breath. "Where's Robert?"

"I don't know. He's probably working on some business deal out of town. I haven't seen him in about a month. He drops by Mama's house periodically on his way in or out of town. He's never around, and she won't listen to me. You're the only one she listens to."

"What's she hired this guy to do?"

"Some painting, yard work, and other stuff like that. She kept the baby for me yesterday, and I saw him leaving. He looks like he'd cut your throat if you're not watching him. You've got to get up here."

He let out a deep sigh. "I've got a class that starts tomorrow night, but I'll give her a call. I thought I hired somebody to take care of the yard for her?"

"I think that little guy moved. And you know how your mother is, she won't call nobody and let them know she needs anything."

About as stubborn as you, he thought. "Okay, Evette, do me a favor. Call a lawn service and set something up for me. I'll pay for it; just get them out there. Then call that guy she hired, and let him know he's no longer needed. Don't tell Mama, just do it."

Ever since Quen had moved his mother from their old home on the South Side of Chicago to her new home on the West Side, he'd been taking care of most of the bills. His older brother, Robert, traveled weekly for his job, and seemed to forget about the family for months at a time. Evette lived in one of Quen's rental properties on the South Side, and fought with their mother constantly. Whether she'd admit it or not, she was a carbon copy of the woman.

"I'll try, but I think you need to get up here. There's no telling what else she's trying to do."

"Maybe I can get away this weekend." He started his car. "I'll let you know after my class tomorrow night." If it wasn't one thing, it was another. He ran back and forth to Chicago a little more than he wanted to these days. Thank goodness this trip would only constitute a brief visit.

"Marcus, I don't have time for this." Bobbi looked down at her watch. Her night school class started in one hour, and this call was going to make her late.

"Bobbi, you've got to help me. Look, don't call Ma, just come get me."

"Come get you? Where are you?" she yelled, becoming more irritated with her little brother.

"I'm in jail!"

"What! In jail! Where at, Marcus? What happened?" Her mind was racing along with her heartbeat.

"I'm here in Macon. And if you don't get down here in thirty minutes they might change their mind and keep me. Please, Bobbi, I can't spend the night in jail."

"Don't move. I'll be right there."

"Trust me, I'll be here."

She ran out to her car and drove as fast as she could without attracting the police. Marcus had no business in Macon during the middle of the week, and what had he done to wind up in jail? He'd been hanging out with a bad crowd lately. She prayed drugs weren't involved, like the last time he'd gotten in trouble.

Thanks to an ex-roommate's night of wild partying years ago, Bobbi know exactly where the Macon County jail was. She picked her roommate up out front, never having the pleasure of venturing inside. This evening, the pleasure would be all hers. Twenty minutes later, she entered the parking lot, backed into a space, and looked down at her watch again. If she hurried she might still be able to make it to class.

Once inside, she was told she'd have to wait a few minutes because Officer McManus wanted to speak with her. Alongside the wall was a bench she made her home for the next thirty minutes. She didn't have time for a lecture about her brother; she just wanted to see Marcus and smack him upside his head.

A tall middle-aged white man graying around the temples approached her and held out his hand. "Ms. Cunningham, I'm Officer McManus."

Bobbi stood and shook his hand. "Hello, I'm here to pick up Marcus." She noticed the officer had a Michael Douglas dimple in his chin.

"Yes, and thank you for waiting. If you've got a minute, I'd like to speak with you."

"Sure." She shrugged. While he looked around for a place for them to talk, she glanced up at the clock on the wall. She'd never make it to class before it was over, so she stopped stressing herself.

"We can talk over here." He held out his hand and motioned toward a vacant desk across the room.

Bobbi walked in the direction he'd given. This was her first time inside the station, and she was surprised at how quiet it was. No loud-talking tough cops. No bad guys sitting around in handcuffs, like on television. All she saw were several middle-aged black and white men, talking on phones.

"Have a seat." McManus sat behind an old steel desk, and Bobbi took a seat next to it. He moved his chair around closer to hers.

"Ms. Cunningham, I'm letting your brother go because I don't believe he did anything. He—"

"Then why is he in jail?"

"He hasn't been arrested; we're just holding him. Marcus rode up here from Douglas with some men who stole a car tonight. Luckily for your brother, they dropped him off at a party before their joyride. And several people backed the fact that he never left the party. However, he did ride to Macon with these men, and no doubt he would have been involved in whatever else they were about to get into."

Bobbi shook her head. What was happening to Marcus? Since he'd graduated from high school last year, he'd been going downhill.

McManus continued. "When we locked those men up, Marcus asked to call you to pick him up."

"Thank you. I'll see to it that he gets home and stays out of trouble."

McManus stood and pulled a business card out of his pocket. "I want to give you the name of someone who runs a program for young men in Douglas. You might want to talk with your parents and get Marcus in there. It could change the direction of his life."

She stood up and took the card. That's exactly what Marcus needed—some direction. "Thank you, I'll make sure my mother gets this."

"You need to stop a young man his age from getting into any more trouble, before it's too late."

Bobbi shook her head and took a deep breath. "Well, I appreciate this, and we'll see to it that he stays out of trouble." Bobbi put the card in her purse. She was mad at Marcus and concerned about him at the same time.

McManus led the way back across the room, then went to get Marcus.

When her brother walked into the room, Bobbi rolled her eyes at him and stalked out the front door. He ran to catch up with her.

"Bobbi, wait up. I know you're pissed."

She stopped and spun around with her finger pointed and her nostrils flared. "You'd better be glad you didn't pull this in Douglas and embarrass Mama."

Marcus opened his mouth to say something, but Bobbi rolled her eyes at him again and stomped over to the car. She unlocked the door, pulled it open, and threw her purse inside. She cut her eyes at Marcus before getting in.

He lowered his head and climbed into the passenger seat. He turned up the radio the minute she started the car.

Bobbi pulled out of the police station and started down the road before she couldn't take it any longer.

"Who the hell were you with anyway?" she asked.

"Huh?"

She leaned forward and turned off the radio. "Who did you ride up here with?"

Marcus sighed and sank lower into his seat. "Peanut and his boys," he said, barely above a whisper.

"Peanut!"

"I know what you're gonna say."

"Does Mama know you run around with that bum? Does she even know you left Douglas?"

He looked out the window, but didn't answer her.

Bobbi clutched the wheel and gritted her teeth. She looked at Marcus, but he kept his head turned, looking at the houses as they passed. She wondered what went on inside his head.

"Marcus." She controlled the rage in her voice. "Did you know they were going to steal a car?"

"Of course not," he said and looked at her sharply.

"You know Peanut has a police record. He'll probably end up in prison."

"I don't know anything about them taking that car." He gave a dismissive gesture.

"What's going on with you? Talk to me. You take off in the middle of the week and come up here to a party with a bunch of car thieves and drug dealers."

"We wasn't doin' no drugs."

"Oh, stop it. I know Peanut's a drug dealer. Everybody in the county knows that. And you have no business around him."

"Peanut's cool." He reached for the radio knob.

Bobbi swatted at his hand. "He's old enough to be your father, boy."

"Yeah, well." He threw his head from side to side as he talked. "Just look where my father is." He grabbed the knob this time and turned the radio back on.

This time she let him. He leaned back on the headrest and stared up. She looked over at him and saw the pain in his eyes.

TWO

Marcus camped out on Bobbi's couch after spending most of the night, and much of the morning, watching television. She took off work early Wednesday to drive him back to Douglas, Georgia.

As soon as they were on the interstate, Bobbi took the opportunity to try and get through to her brother. She knew he didn't want to be lectured, so she treaded lightly.

"Marcus, are you and Melinda still together?"

He looked at her with furrowed brows. "Why?"

"I'm just asking."

"No."

"What happened?" Bobbi knew they'd been dating on and off since the eleventh grade.

"She moved to Detroit with her sister."

"Well, you need to find something to do instead of hanging out with Peanut. Marcus, he's going to get you killed if you aren't careful."

He laughed with a snort. "I can take care of myself."

"You're seventeen years old. You're not ready for the type of trouble Peanut lives with. I'm telling you, he's on his way to prison." She glanced at him with concern. "And I don't want you to end up there."

He shook his head before crossing his arms and reclining back in his seat. "I'm not gonna do anything that'll get me locked up. The police knew I had nothing to do with stealing that car; that's why they let me go."

"Marcus, you're lucky that girl said you weren't with those guys. If not, you might be sitting in jail with them right now."

"Believe me, I know that. But I don't want to think about it right now."

"Then think about this: It's not too late for you to register for community college this fall. You had good grades, so I'm sure you could get in."

"And who's going to pay for it?"

"Apply for financial aid, or save your money. That's what I did."

"It's easy for you. You make more money than I do."

"Marcus, how much do you think the *Telegraph* pays me? That's a small newspaper. I don't make a lot of money, so I live on a budget. I can help you set up one if you want to try and go to school."

"I'll think about it." He closed his eyes and drifted off to sleep.

Bobbi hoped his brush with the Macon police had scared him into straightening up. Since graduating from high school, he'd been picked up twice before by the police. Both incidents had something to do with drugs. If he didn't find his way in life soon, she knew he'd repeat the same vicious cycle as their father. She prayed that wouldn't happen.

As she pulled into her mother's driveway, Marcus stretched and looked around, realizing where they were. "We here already?"

"Yep." She drove around to the back entrance, which was the center of entertainment for the Cunninghams. A large seating area, complete with a picnic table and an old-fashioned swing, sat beneath a large shade tree. Surrounding the yard was her mother's flower bed. The shade tree next to the swing created a perfect place to relax and read a book, which Bobbi did often.

Her mother stood in the back door with her hands on

her hips. "Looks like somebody is here to greet you." Bobbi gave her brother a crafty smile as she parked the car.

As Wilma Cunningham stepped out of the house, Marcus sat up and cursed under his breath. "When did you call her?"

"Last night, while you watched television," Bobbi confessed. "You knew she'd be worried about you." She gave him a stern glance before jumping out of the car.

Mrs. Cunningham came down the back sidewalk in her white nurse's aide uniform, scowling at her son as he prolonged his exit from the car.

"Hi, Mama." Bobbi greeted her mother with a big hug and kiss. From the look on their mother's face, Marcus was about to pay dearly for this little stunt.

"Hey, baby." She returned Bobbi's hug. "Thanks for bringing that boy back down here." She looked around Bobbi at Marcus. "Come on in here," she called out with impatience creeping into her voice.

"Where's Aunt Alice?" Bobbi asked.

"She's upstairs in her room."

Bobbi knew her mother and Marcus were about to get into it, and she'd witnessed enough of their battles. "I'm gonna run up and say hello." She looked back over her shoulder at Marcus edging away from the car. "He's all yours," she said wearily.

Mrs. Cunningham started in on him. "Boy, what in the hell were you doing in Macon?"

After visiting with her great-aunt, Bobbi found her mother in the kitchen cooking dinner.

"Hmm, something smells good." She took a seat at the breakfast bar overlooking the sink.

"It's smothered chicken. You staying for dinner?"

Bobbi straightened up. "Of course. You don't think I

made that trip just for Marcus, do you? I could have put him on the bus. I wanted some of your home cooking."

"Uh-huh, well, make him give you some gas money. Did you make it to class last night?"

"No. And that reminds me of something." Bobbi found her purse on the kitchen table and fished a business card out. "The police officer gave me this card to give to you. It's some program for troubled kids." She handed the card to her mother.

Wilma wiped her hands off on a towel and read the card. She shook her head. "Marcus just needs a good whippin'."

"And who's going to give it to him? He's too big for you to whip," Bobbi pointed out.

"He's never too big. I've given him six months to get his act together, or he has to move out. Either he goes to college, gets a better job, or goes into the service."

"Mama, what's happening to him? He's not dumb."

"It's those drugs. I know he smokes that stuff, I can smell it on him."

"What stuff?" Bobbi knew what her mother was referring to. She liked to laugh as Wilma stumbled over the correct word choice.

"Those reefers, joints, or whatever you call them. Funny cigarettes. He comes in here at all hours of the night eating everything in sight. Then he goes to bed and sleeps most of the day away. Reminds me of your daddy."

"Let's not go there. I thought Marcus had a job?"

"He does. But he doesn't have to be there until two—that is, when he goes to work."

Bobbi shook her head. "I've tried to talk to him."

"I know. We all have. Don't worry, things are gonna change around here real soon. Just wait until Alabama gets a hold of him."

Bobbi's eyebrows shot up in surprise. "What are you talking about?"

A loud crashing noise came from behind them. Bobbi jumped off her stool and followed her mother as she ran into the dining room. Aunt Alice stood next to the table in her bare feet, looking down at the broken dishes. Her long gray hair was tied back into a ponytail that rested on her shoulder.

"Alice, why didn't you call me?" Wilma hurried over and took the tray from her, careful to step around the dishes. "You know this tray is too heavy for you. You should have grabbed Marcus."

"I had it just fine. Besides, he's in his room blasting that music, and I wanted to see Bobbi again before she left." She took a step forward.

"Alice, no. Let me get these dishes up before you step on something and cut your foot." Bobbi guided her great-aunt around the mess and helped her into a seat as Wilma returned from the kitchen with a broom and began sweeping up the mess.

"I'll get this up. You guys go ahead and visit some more."

Bobbi took her great-aunt's hand and escorted her out to the backyard for a stroll. "Auntie, we need to chat. Mama's talking about Alabama again. What's going on?"

Alice looked back over her shoulder before whispering to Bobbi, "He's coming back."

On Thursday evening, Bobbi hurried to the Macon State College campus. She didn't want to miss anything else since summer school moved at such an accelerated pace. Surely she was already chapters behind since missing the first night.

When she entered the classroom, students were mingling about and taking their seats. She grabbed a seat in the middle of the room and waved at a few students she recognized from previous classes.

A tall black man walked in, grabbing her attention as he closed the door behind him. He looked to be in his early fifties, with gray hair and a thick mustache and long sideburns sprinkled with salt and pepper. In his short-sleeved shirt and bowtie, he reminded her of Papa Joe, her grandfather. He plopped his briefcase on the table at the head of the class and picked up a marker.

"For those of you who missed class last time, here's some vital information you will need before this semester is over." He turned to the board and wrote his name, Professor Harold Jennings, and his phone number.

Bobbi wrote his information down on the inside of her tablet. If she was lucky, she could breeze through this class without making a single call.

The door opened with an annoying squeak. Bobbi frowned in its direction as a few more students slipped in. The door started to close, only to be pulled open again. This time, a piece of metal from the bottom of the door scraped across the floor, causing Bobbi to cover her ears. She looked up as a tall handsome black man eased through the door.

"Nice, very nice," Bobbi caught herself whispering almost too loud. She quickly glanced around, then thanked God no one had heard her.

She lowered her hands and watched him weave his beefy body between the chairs to a seat two rows over. Like Prudential, she thought—solid as a rock. Brother man was built like a boxer—more Muhammad Ali in his heyday than a Mike Tyson type. He had nice broad shoulders and chest, thick arms, and a nice rear view. His mustache and goatee connected in a precision trim. Even his close-cropped haircut looked as if he'd just left the barber.

When her eyes traveled up from his feet to his face,

brother man smiled at her. Embarrassed that he saw her looking at him, she cut her eyes to the front of the room and Professor Jennings. She grabbed her ink pen so fast it flew right out of her hand onto the floor. Casually, she picked it up and lowered her head to doodle on the paper.

Sociology 341 had begun.

"Okay, if everyone will move into their respective class societies and let's stay in these groups for the duration of the course. I'm expecting your final presentation and oral report to be given from the group's perspective. For those of you who missed class last night, come see me and I'll let you know where you've been assigned."

Bobbi made her way to the front of the room. Professor Jennings explained to the small circle around his desk how the semester would be conducted. Each society had been given their final examination topics. Other classwork would have to be completed alone. He read off their assignments and they went to join their societies.

Bobbi hung back after the others left. She had a problem already. "Excuse me, Professor Jennings."

"Yes, Ms. Cunningham?" He sat on the corner of his desk, giving Bobbi his undivided attention.

"Are you sure I'm in the prison society?" She bit her bottom lip with her teeth, hoping he'd made a mistake.

He looked down at his paper, then up at her. "That's correct. Is there a problem?"

"Well, I don't know anything about prison, or jail, or anything like that, so I was kind of hoping I could switch to another society." She gave him a pleading half smile.

He looked her over, nodding. The expression on his face was stern and fatherly. She sensed he was in deep thought, and she was in deep trouble.

"You've just given me justification for keeping you in the group. College is all about learning, Ms. Cunningham. If you don't know anything about prison life, then that means you'll learn something, and I will have fulfilled one of my duties as a professor."

Crap. So much for this class being a breeze. "Yes, sir." Her smile faded as she turned to join her peers.

Each society had a sign taped to the wall, and students gathered in their respective groups. When she saw the sign labeled PRISON, brother man was sitting there watching her walk his way. Now she had to work with him. *Oh, how lucky.*

Two other students were in her group: a slim white woman with long brunet hair, who had that cute Meg Ryan smile going on; and a white guy who resembled Brendan Fraser in the movie *Still Breathing,* when he had that absentminded look on his face. *There I go doing that again.* Relating everyone she met to a movie character or actor was an occupational hazard she had to get rid of. She took a deep breath and pulled a chair over to join them.

"Hello, I'm Bobbi Cunningham. Guess I'm your new society member." She held her hand out to the woman first.

"Hi, Bobbi, I'm Monica. Nice to meet you."

"I'm Gregory." The Brendan look-alike shook her hand.

Then, brother man shook her hand. "So you're our missing link? I'm Quen."

Bobbi thought he held her hand a little too long. "That's me, the missing link. Hope I didn't miss much."

"Only a bunch of reading," Monica volunteered. "Read the first two chapters and you'll be all caught up."

"Thanks." Bobbi looked around as if she didn't notice Quen staring at her. She glanced at him, but made it a point not to hold eye contact. His eyes were coal black, and his skin was a rich smooth chocolate, like a fine piece of Godiva, she thought. His khaki slacks and fitted T-shirt showed off his muscular body well. He even had on summer sandals, and she loved a man who wasn't afraid to show his toes. So, she'd give him a few points for being well groomed. A small smile crept onto her face before she tried to suppress it.

Quen liked the new addition to their society: Bobbi, the cute brown-skinned honey with big brown eyes that spoke to him. She had a small mole on the bridge of her nose that caused him to look straight into her eyes when he greeted her. It was sexy—like her full lips with a hint of lipstick. He liked everything about her so far.

He also liked the topic of their final exam, a study of prisons in the Georgia system. His volunteer work with ex-convicts at the Lean On Me Agency would hopefully provide them with a leg up.

Professor Jennings let each group decide on what aspect they would focus. They were to narrow their topics down to a title, on which he would give final approval. Before class ended, he gave each group time to start their projects.

"I don't know much about prisons, but could we start off with a tour of Macon County Prison to get a feel for it? What do you guys think?" Monica offered the first suggestion.

"I don't see why we have to go out there so soon," Bobbi spoke up. "Can't we decide what direction we're going in first? Then we may discover we don't need a visit after all."

"At some point we'll have to visit the facility," Quen added. "But I agree with Bobbi. We need to decide which aspect of prison life we want to focus on first. I don't think we'll have any problem getting approval for a visit."

"Okay, that makes sense," Monica said.

Quen consulted his tablet. During the lecture, he'd thought about how his volunteer work could help the whole group. "I've also got a suggestion I'd like to throw out at the group."

"Let's hear it." Monica glanced from Gregory to Bobbi. They nodded in agreement.

"A couple days a week I do volunteer work, helping ex-convicts through the Lean On Me Agency. We can focus our project on how they cope with life on the outside once released. If so, I'm sure I can get a lot of material and firsthand information for us."

"Yeah, I'd like to know what kind of head trip they go through before getting out," Gregory commented. "And, yeah, how that affects them once they're released into society."

Quen looked at him. "Yeah." He nodded and gave a heavy sigh.

Bobbi listened to them as if she weren't a part of the group. Her thoughts had slipped back to the letter she'd received earlier in the week from the Alabama state prison.

Class ended with the group agreeing on the title, "The Long-term Effects of Prison Life After Release." Bobbi reluctantly agreed so as not to rock the boat. As she picked up her purse to leave, Quen approached her.

"Are you always this quiet?"

She grabbed her tablet before looking up at him. "No, not usually. I just wish we had another topic. I thought this was sociology, not criminology." She shrugged and gave a helpless gesture.

"Sorry, guess I'm partly to blame for that. Criminal justice is my minor, and I more or less talked the group into choosing the prison topic. I thought my knowledge in the area would help."

She slowly walked out of the room, with him following. "I guess I did miss something the first night. I wanted to spend my summer studying something fun, but there's nothing fun about prison." She looked over at him walking in stride with her.

He shrugged. "That's true."

Quen held the door open for her as they exited the building. "I'll look forward to seeing you Monday night. Maybe I can make this project a little fun for you."

She shook her head. "I don't see how. We're going to study murderers, drug dealers, child molesters, the scum of the earth. Very few of them get rehabilitated anyway. And some are worse when they get out than when they were sentenced. Come to think of it, that's what we should do our study on."

Quen dropped his head. "Hmmm . . . now I see why you didn't want to study prisons." He cut his eyes up at her. "Not all prisoners are bad guys; cut them some slack. A few of them are even innocent. And don't forget women are in prison, too."

She took a deep breath and glanced away. "I know, but they're there for some of the same reasons." When she looked back at him, she could tell he didn't share her feelings regarding prisons. "I realize not everyone in there is guilty, but most of them are."

Quen crossed his arms and smiled as he changed the subject. "What's your major?" he asked.

"Public services."

His eyebrows shot up in surprise. "And you don't think learning anything about prison or prisoners will help you?"

Bobbi relented. "I'm sure it will. I just have a hard time with it." She wasn't about to explain her situation to a complete stranger. Her last statement should have been enough for him to back off.

"Trust me, this class will come in handy in the future." Quen looked around as more students exited the building.

"Well, I've gotta run." She pulled her car keys from her purse. "Nice talking with you. Guess I'll see you on Monday."

"Yeah, I'm looking forward to it." He backed away, watching her head for her car.

Three

Saturday morning Quen stepped off the plane and hurried through Chicago's busy O'Hare Airport to the car rental counter. As eager as he was to see his daughter, Kristy, he was just as eager to get back to Macon. Chicago held painful memories he didn't care to relive, and as soon as he finished his business, he was out of there.

He drove for several blocks along Lake Shore Drive before heading south to his mother's house. One thing he loved and missed about Chicago was the beautiful lake view.

Just as he'd thought it would be, Evette's Toyota Camry was in their mother's driveway. Undoubtedly, his sister was inside driving their mother crazy. They bickered like sisters instead of mother and daughter.

He parked behind Evette's car and grabbed his overnight bag from the trunk before he headed to the door.

"Well, it's about time." A heavyset Evette beamed at her little brother from inside the doorway, with her braided hair pulled into a ball at the nape of her neck.

Quen entered his mother's ranch home, giving his sister a hug. "Hey, I told the pilot to step on it, but you know how slow planes are," he said jokingly.

She playfully hit him on the arm before closing the door. "You look good, man. What ya been doin'?

Working out or what?" She made a gesture from his head to toe.

"Working out a little." He didn't want to insult Evette, so he didn't mention her added weight. "What did you do to your hair?"

She smoothed a hand over her braids. "You like them? Lisa braided it for me. It's just for the summer."

He nodded, setting his overnight bag in the foyer. "It looks good. Where's Ma?"

"She's in the kitchen. I hope you brought some work clothes, because she's got a job for you."

"Don't worry, I made some calls and got somebody to help her out." He moved through the house toward the kitchen. "Did you take care of that other guy?"

"Of course, and she's still mad at me for that. But I told her it was all your idea."

He shook his head, but kept walking. "Thanks, Evette." The smell of his mother's cooking filled the air. He detected bacon, scrambled eggs, biscuits, and possibly fried ham.

Sue Brooks stood at the kitchen sink raking leftover food into the garbage disposal. She turned when she heard her baby's voice approaching.

"Quentin, what a nice surprise. Come on over and fix yourself something to eat."

They exchanged a warm hug and kiss before she put her plate into the dishwasher.

He looked over at the food on the stove. "Ma, from the looks of things you were expecting me for breakfast."

"I didn't know what time you'd get here. We'd hoped you could make it for breakfast, or else Evette and I would have to eat all this food. She eats like she's eating for two anyway," Sue joked.

Quen stepped into the guest bathroom and washed his hands. "Maybe she's pregnant," he said, loud enough for Evette to hear. He remembered how they used to tease one another when they all lived at home, and he missed it.

Evette sat at the kitchen table finishing her breakfast. "Screw you. You're always picking on me. I've gained a few pounds, so what." She shrugged nonchalantly. "And I'm not *pregnant.*" She yelled loud enough for Quen to hear down the hall, with a loud emphasis on *pregnant,* then continued eating.

"Hmm, everything smells good. I miss your cooking, Ma, that's for sure." He grabbed a plate from the cabinet and emptied the skillets onto it.

"So," Sue joined them at the table with a fresh cup of coffee. "You haven't met anyone to cook breakfast for you yet?"

Quen shook his head. "Right now, I'm becoming a breakfast expert. My pancakes are the bomb."

"Maybe Arlene will take you back." Evette stuck her tongue out at him, laughing. "Payback is a mother, huh?"

Quen stopped chewing, and looked from Evette to his mother, attempting to hold in a smile. "What's wrong with your daughter? You let her swear in the house like that." He nodded at Evette as if to say *good one,* then continued eating.

"I talked to Kristy yesterday," Sue informed him. "She's doing wonderful. She said, 'When's my daddy coming? I want to see my daddy.' When you pick her up, bring her by. Ms. Arlene doesn't let her visit enough."

"As soon as I take care of your new gardener, I'm running to get her. Is it okay if she stays the night?"

"You know it is; you don't have to ask. Now, tell me why I need you to hire me a gardener? What was wrong with the man I had?"

"I told you she was mad." Evette jumped up to put her plate into the dishwasher.

"Be quiet, Evette." Sue crossed her arms. "Let him explain."

Ever since Quen's father had died when Quen was in high school, his mother had handled her own business. When she needed her children's help, she asked, and they always came through for her. Quen wasn't surprised she questioned him about the gardener, but lately she'd become a little too trusting for her children's taste.

He put his fork down. "I know some men who work for parks and recreations, and run a lawn service on the side. They guarantee everything they do, and personally I trust them since they're bonded. I'm paying for everything in advance so there won't be anything for you to do. Mama, Evette and I are just watching out for you. Robert would agree if he was in town."

Sue accepted the idea, and thanked them for thinking about her.

After Quen took care of the gardener situation, he went by to pick up Kristy. Mother and daughter lived in an upscale condominium on the upper north side of Chicago.

Quen had met Arlene the day he joined BellSouth. After graduating with a degree in information management from Roosevelt University, he'd started as manager of their data center. He'd met friends at a North Pier nightclub to celebrate his first big job, and Arlene happened to be a friend of a friend.

Six months later, she was pregnant. Quen had always wanted to be a father, and had actually been happy. At twenty-one, he'd been willing to get married like any self-respecting young man should do. However, at twenty-three, Arlene had told him she wasn't ready to be a wife. She had her whole life mapped out, and she wasn't ready for a child and husband. She'd planned to continue her education and get a law degree.

After Kristy's birth, Arlene had told Quen he wasn't good enough for her, or her overbearing Pops. He'd stayed on the South Side and she'd stayed on the North Side while they'd raised Kristy together. Things had been going along fine, until Arlene's new boyfriend had entered the picture. Quen had disliked him the moment they were introduced. If her Pops hated him, Arlene was determined to get involved with him. Quen suspected that's why she'd gotten involved with him and had Kristy. He'd never measured up in her Pops's eyes, and having a baby was one aspect of her life that her Pops couldn't control.

Although she wasn't born under ideal circumstances, Kristy was Quen's heart. From the moment he'd laid eyes on her in the hospital, he'd been in love. He'd dedicated his life to taking care of her.

Once in the lobby of the swanky condominium, he rang the bell.

"Hello," came Arlene's professional voice through the intercom.

"Arlene, it's Quen," he said. He heard the buzz as she let him in.

"Come on up."

Quen and Arlene had always had an amicable relationship. He wasn't good enough to marry, but he was good enough to be Kristy's father. She'd never denied him access to his daughter, or asked him to pay child support. He'd kept Kristy often while Arlene attended law school, giving him time to bond with his daughter. Unfortunately, he'd never been able to bond with her mother.

He got off the elevator on the fourteenth floor and noticed since his last visit, a large gold mirror had been hung on the wall opposite the elevator. A gold statue sat on the table next to a vase of large white flowers. He wondered how much Arlene paid for this overpriced apartment. The two homes he owned on the South Side probably cost less, and had more square footage.

Before he reached the front door, he heard it open. He smiled when he saw his baby's head peek out the door. She looked taller than she had six months ago at Christmas. He half expected her to run out and into his arms like she used to, but then realized she was growing up.

"Who's that grown woman disguised as my baby?"

With one hand on her hip and the other on the doorknob, she let Quen in, smiling. "Hey, Daddy."

"Hey yourself, big girl." They exchanged kisses and he gave her a bear hug.

"Did you come to take me to Georgia with you?" she asked, after he released her and she closed the door.

"Not this time, pumpkin." He ran his hand down the back of her head, feeling her long silky hair, which grew faster than she did.

"Daddy," she whined as she pulled away from him, as if she hated to have her hair touched. Then she grabbed his hand to squeeze it while they walked into the living room.

Arlene peeked out from the kitchen. "Hello."

Her long hair hung past her shoulders, almost as long as Kristy's. Quen smiled and saluted her, something he had done ever since she'd told him her father was an army sergeant.

"Mama, I'm going back to Georgia with Daddy, right, Daddy?" Kristy swung their hands through the air playfully.

Arlene gracefully strolled into the living room like a swan, thanks to her years of ballet. With a mug in her hand, she gave them a sideways glance, then arched a brow at Quen. "Oh, she is? And when was this decided?"

Before she got her feathers all ruffled, Quen cleared

things up. "She's just spending the night at Mom's. But before the summer's out, I'd like for her to come down. Do you think you can squeeze it into your plans?"

"I'm sure she can find some time." Arlene sipped from her mug.

Kristy nodded wildly. "Right after my last dance class, I want to spend the rest of the summer in Georgia. Is that okay, Daddy?"

Before Quen could answer, Arlene did. "Honey, Daddy's in school. You can spend a week or two at the most. Remember, we're going to Las Vegas to visit your uncle Curtis before school starts."

Excuses, excuses, excuses. Anything to keep Kristy from spending too much time with me, Quen thought. God forbid she might enjoy herself. "Well, I wouldn't want to keep her from Vegas. How's Curtis these days?"

"Wonderful. He built a new house and they have a new baby."

"That's great." Her brother was the one member of her family he got along with.

Kristy had released Quen's hand and moped over to the couch to sulk.

Quen hated to see her so sad. "Come on, baby, what you doing? Get your bag and let's go. You're all mine until I leave tomorrow night. And we can talk about your visit in the car." He turned to Arlene and nodded as if to say *okay.* He saw the hint of a smile on her lips and knew everything would work out.

She shrugged and made a helpless gesture.

Kristy rose from the couch and slouched off down the hall.

While Kristy gathered her overnight bag, Quen and Arlene worked out a date for Kristy's visit. But Quen didn't tell Kristy until they were in the car.

"Daddy, can I live with you?"

Quen looked over at his baby, stunned; she'd never

asked to live with him before. He imagined Arlene had a pretty tight rein on her. "What's the matter? Is your mother giving you a hard time?"

"She won't let me do nothing," she grumbled, twisting around in her seat.

"Kristy, you're thirteen. What is it you want to do?"

"My friends went to see Ja Rule last week, and I've never been to a concert before. Mama wouldn't even let me go."

He glanced at her again, as if seeing her for the first time. She *was* growing up, and entirely too fast for him. "What are you doing listening to Ja Rule in the first place?"

"He's off the chain, Daddy."

Her eyes sparkled, and her smile was angelic—yet slightly suggestive. Quen ran a hand over his face and took a deep breath. "The next thing I know you'll be telling me you're dating."

"Huh, I don't like any of those stupid boys at my school."

Thank goodness. "Kristy, first of all, you're too young for dating or concerts. Don't worry; by the time you're old enough, Ja Rule will still be around. Look at Michael Jackson. He's still performing and I was a fan of his when I was your age."

"But I don't want to wait until I'm old before I go to a concert."

"Ouch." He could explain to her about staying power, but decided to let her discover it the same way everyone else did. All things came with maturity.

"Daddy, you just don't understand." She crossed her arms and leaned back into the headrest.

"Naw, I guess I don't. But you'll be coming to visit me next month, and they have free concerts in the park all the time. Maybe I'll take you to one of those."

"Mama said I could come?" She perked up.

"Yeah, before you go to Vegas you can visit for a week."

"Great," she said, before leaning over to kiss him on the cheek. "Mama's so strict. It's like being in prison up in there," she said with a twist of her lips, then slowly looked up at her father. "Well, sort of."

"Baby, I doubt that it's that bad. Your mother loves you, and I'm sure she's doing her best. Cut her some slack, okay?"

"Okay," she huffed, opening her purse for a tube of lip gloss.

Quen shook his head. She was growing up. They drove along in silence with Quen thinking about how his baby was gone, and this teenager had taken her place. He missed his baby, but looked forward to spending time with his teenager.

"Are you still seeing Dr. Minter?" he asked, as he pulled into his mother's subdivision.

"Yes," she answered in a soft voice, avoiding eye contact with him.

"How's it going?"

Kristy shrugged. "Okay, I guess. I don't go that much anymore."

"Yeah. Does your mom go with you?"

"No, she just drops me off. She said I don't have to go anymore once school starts back."

He pulled into the driveway.

"What about you, Kristy, do you want to stop going?"

"Yeah, I guess," she replied absently as she looked out the window. When she saw her grandmother standing in the doorway, she lowered the window. "Hi." She waved. "There's Mama Sue." Excited, Kristy quickly gathered her things as Quen turned off the ignition.

Before she jumped out of the car, Quen stopped her. "Baby, if you ever decide you want to go talk to Dr.

Minter again, or any other doctor, just let me know, okay?"

She nodded, then leaned over to kiss him on the cheek before bolting from the car.

The sight of her cheerful and happy put a smile on Quen's face. If her therapy sessions were just about over, he'd have to discuss it with Arlene before leaving Chicago.

Four

On Monday evening, Bobbi left the *Telegraph* excited about class that night. She'd just written a review for a deeply thought-provoking foreign film that had her reflecting on her life. What she needed now was more stimulating conversation. Also, Quen had said he was looking forward to seeing her. She smiled. Why, she didn't know, because he wasn't interested in her, although he smiled at her often.

As Bobbi walked across campus, she looked around and enjoyed the beauty of her surroundings for a change. The campus was a luscious green with blooming flowers everywhere. She'd come this route hundreds of times, not once noticing how beautiful it was; nor had she thought about how fortunate she was to be here. She was the first in her family to attend college, and she was proud of herself. After a quick glance at her watch, she realized she had a few minutes before class, so she stopped at a nearby bench to enjoy the view. Her mother would have a field day pruning and trimming all the flowers in the campus gardens. The blooms gave off a sweet fragrance and the colors were a treat to the eyes. She sat there thinking about her life, her family, and her future.

It was that damn foreign film, she told herself. Every movie she watched seemed to have some effect on her. This one had her feeling soft inside, and evaluating her life.

She closed her eyes and enjoyed the gentle breeze that blew by. She'd never been one to meditate, but that's what she felt like doing right now. Meditation was good for the soul, she'd heard. She opened her eyes and looked around.

Unable to resist the urge, she bent down and unfastened her sandals. One at a time, she slid them off and eased her toes into the cool grass. A scene from the movie came to mind as Bobbi stood and walked in a little circle with her eyes closed. She took several deep breaths to relax and open her mind.

"Got yourself a new study technique?"

Bobbi opened her eyes to see Quen standing next to the bench, smiling at her. Embarrassed, she stopped, walked back to the bench, and sat down.

"No, I was taking a break before class." She casually bent down for her sandals. Oh, how she wanted to burrow through the ground and come up at home, away from him. She probably looked ridiculous.

"So, what's that little walk you were doing?" He pointed his finger with a circular motion toward the grass.

She fastened her sandals and looked up at him. *Of all people, why did he have to come along? I probably look like a nut to him.* "I was trying to cool off. Haven't you ever done that before?" She grabbed her books and avoided looking at him as she headed toward their class.

"You know, I don't think I have. A glass of ice water usually does it for me." He snickered and stepped in beside her.

She waved him off. "Forget about it, will ya?"

They approached the building and Quen reached around to open the door. "Sure. I just never met a woman who meditates, chants, or whatever that was you were doing. Are you into psychic stuff, too?"

"No. And I wasn't doing anything like that." She tried

to smile so he wouldn't think she was being rude. She'd have to stop taking those films so seriously.

They walked down the hall in silence until they reached the class.

Inside the classroom, Quen chose a seat a couple of rows behind Bobbi. She tried not to think about her embarrassing moment before class as she concentrated on Professor Jennings's lecture.

An hour later, they stopped for a break. When Bobbi stood to leave, Professor Jennings called her.

"Ms. Cunningham. May I see you for a moment, please?"

Oh, no, what had she done now? She made her way to the front of the room. Her professor had on another bowtie, making him look like her grandfather. She hoped he wasn't about to ask her if she was learning anything.

"Yes, sir."

"Do you feel any better about working with the prison society?"

She looked up at the curious smile and raised brow he gave her. He was in her corner, she could tell. His gaze resembled the way her aunt Alice looked at her, with hope for the whole family.

"Not actually, sir," she admitted, lowering her eyelids with a half smile. "But we just started, so I'm sure I'll manage."

"Not only will you manage, you'll excel. Mark my words. Anytime a person tackles a subject he has little knowledge of, he can't help but learn from it. If you have any problems, come see me. That's what I'm here for. But first, use the resources within your group. The objective here is to learn as much as possible from one another."

She nodded her head. "I'll do that. Well, I better try and run to the ladies' room before the break's over." She dashed off so she could get back without missing anything.

For the second half of the lecture, Bobbi fought to stay awake. She'd had a long tiring day. When Professor Jennings ended the lecture in order for society members to meet, Bobbi heard him, but she was too drowsy to move.

She jumped when someone tapped her on her shoulder. She turned around to see Quen sitting in the seat behind her.

"Care to join us?" he asked, pointing to Gregory and Monica, who had gathered in a back corner of the room.

"Oh, I'm sorry." She quickly gathered her belongings.

"Didn't wake you, did I?" he asked jokingly.

Still a little sleepy, she stood to find him laughing at her. "No. I wasn't asleep. I was resting my eyes. Haven't you ever done that before?" she asked with a trace of sarcasm.

"Sure, just like I walk around in the grass barefoot to cool off," he shot back.

She gave him a quick roll of the eyes before joining the rest of her prison society members.

Quen followed with his pad open, ready to start taking notes.

"Are you going to be our recording secretary?" Bobbi asked.

"Uh, guess I am," he said, with a flick of his pen. "Unless, of course, you'd like the honor?" He held his pen in midair.

"No. You go right ahead. You've got the gold Cross pen and everything."

He winked at Bobbi, making her want to roll her eyes again, but she resisted.

"Okay, now that you two have that settled, I guess we can get started," Monica declared.

"I brought some information that should help us get started." Quen handed everyone a sheet of paper.

Bobbi read over the title, *Concerns for the Ex-convict*, then frowned. Number one on the list was *family communication*. She stopped reading and dropped the paper.

"I thought we chose to deal with the problems related to finding employment and housing first?" She looked around at her society members for support.

"Doesn't make any difference to me," Gregory spoke up.

"We could start with those aspects if that's what you guys want to do," Quen said.

"It doesn't really matter to me, either; but I like what Bobbi said. It sounds like that would be a little easier to research. We need to create an outline so we don't lose focus," Monica added.

"That'll work." Quen agreed, nodding his head. "Just keep the paper I gave you. It'll come in handy later."

"Okay, we've got two months to pull this together. When and where are we going to meet?" Monica asked.

The roles of the group were being defined. Monica had established herself as the leader, Quen as the recording secretary, and Gregory an innocent bystander. Bobbi wasn't sure where she fit in.

As a group, they agreed on Saturday mornings at eleven o'clock. The next fifteen minutes were spent working out research assignments.

As they discussed the project, Quen took charge and made sure no one had too much work. He even agreed to lead the final presentation. He'd asserted himself into the lead position. Bobbi liked that.

While he gave out assignments, she looked him over again. He was a nice-looking man with plenty of sex appeal. However, he wasn't exactly her type. Her dream lover would be Casanova charming, exude sex appeal, and every time he smiled at her, he'd cause her heart to skip a beat. Most of all, he'd simply adore her. Maybe he'd look like Morris Chestnut, or Michael Jai White from the movie *Spawn*. She'd never met a brother that fine in Macon—until she'd met Quen.

"Oh, Bobbi," Quen sang out to get her attention.

She shook her head, pulling herself out of the daydream. "I'm sorry. What did you say?"

"Asleep again?"

Smart-ass. She uncrossed one leg and crossed the other. "No. I was thinking about something. What did you say?"

"This Saturday we'll start at ten, an hour earlier if that'll work for you?"

"Sure. I'll be there," she agreed. Again, Quen gave her a smile that reminded her of Denzel Washington. Just for that she could forgive him for being so smart.

"If anyone needs help, let me know. I can get more information," Quen assured the group.

After project discussions were complete and Bobbi was on her way out the door, Quen caught up with her.

"I hope I didn't embarrass you earlier about being asleep."

"No, don't worry about it. I was taking a little power nap." She laughed.

"Uh-huh, I thought you were. You must have been up late last night?"

"Believe it or not, I went to bed early. I don't know why I was so sleepy in class."

"Professor Jennings has a rather monotone lecture voice. I'm surprised more people weren't asleep."

"Me, too. We're in for a long summer quarter."

"True. But he's a good guy, and he knows his stuff."

Bobbi nodded in agreement and kept walking.

"Did you get a chance to glance over the handout I gave you?" he asked.

"Just the title. I thought we weren't going to work on that right now?"

"We aren't, but take a look at it anyway. I know you're

not all that excited about our topic; but after you read my handout, you might have a change of heart." He held the door open as they left the building.

"I'll look at it." She didn't want to talk about prisons or criminals. However, she was interested in learning more about Quen. He carried himself like an older man, although he didn't look much older than her.

"How did you get involved in working with ex-convicts, anyway?" she asked.

"I met one of the counselors at a party, and he told me about the agency's desperate need for volunteers. Back then I had more free time on my hands, so I signed up."

"And now you don't?"

He shrugged. "Not as much. I run a little computer business out of my house."

"What kind of computer business?"

"I design websites for corporations. I also do a little consulting in disaster recovery and security, which I seem to be doing more of lately."

"Sounds . . . interesting." She wrinkled up her nose.

Quen laughed. "Is that your way of saying boring?"

Bobbi crossed the parking lot and wondered if Quen had parked in the same area. She liked it when he laughed. He had a great smile. "Well, it sounds like you're stuck in front of a computer all day."

"It's not really that bad. Besides, I enjoy what I do. It's challenging."

"Yeah, right." She picked up her step once she saw her car. "Love a challenge, do ya?"

He looked over at her. "I do, how about yourself?"

She caught the playfulness in his eyes. He probably thought she was referring to her, but that couldn't be further from the truth. "I post my movie reviews on the web. I also do some research for work, but that's about as challenging as I like my computers."

"Well, for this class project it looks like we're all

going to spend more time on the Internet. Got any ideas where to start your research?"

He should have already known the answer to that one. "I don't have a clue. I'm going to pick a search engine and start throwing darts." She waved a hand through the air. Her pace slowed, then stopped when she reached her car. "Unless, of course, you've got some great sites in mind?"

"I think I can come up with a few to help you."

She held her tablet to her chest as if holding onto a security blanket. "Why don't we just pay you to do the whole report? You seem more than qualified with all your volunteer work."

"I don't think Professor Jennings would like it if he found out."

"Who's going to tell him?" she asked, holding up her right hand, palm out. "Not me."

Quen let out a hearty laugh.

She was glad he realized she wasn't serious. "I'm just kidding. I know we can't do that. Besides, he told me I couldn't change societies because I'm supposed to learn something."

"When did you ask to change?" Quen asked, looking more serious.

"My first night. I'm telling you, I really don't care to delve into the life of an ex-con. As long as they stay away from me, everything will be all right." She leaned against her car.

Quen backed up against the car parked next to hers.

The look on his face made Bobbi wish she hadn't said what she had. Obviously, she'd offended him.

"I'm sorry. I don't mean to sound so harsh. Working with ex-cons is obviously something you like doing and I didn't mean to disrespect that."

"It's okay. Since I'm responsible for you having to deal with this subject, I'll have to make it interesting for you. I'm sure you'll learn some things that will surprise you."

"What about you? How can you learn anything when you already know most of this stuff?"

"Oh, I don't know as much as you're giving me credit for. That's why I'm taking the course."

She acknowledged what he'd said and went on to indulge her curiosity. "I bet you've heard all kinds of prison life stories, haven't you?"

He nodded, but didn't elaborate.

"What are they like? I mean, are ex-cons bitter and mad at the world?"

He set his books on the trunk of the car parked next to hers and crossed his arms. "Let's see. Of course, not all of them are mad. Most of the men I deal with just want their lives back. Not that anyone can give them to them. For those who've been away a long time, life is so different they don't know which way to turn first. That's where I come in."

"Sounds like you're very sympathetic toward them."

"I understand them, and I'm willing to do whatever I can to help."

Good-looking and compassionate. Bobbi had never met a man who did volunteer work on a regular basis. He wasn't a bad guy, she'd concluded. "Do you think you make a difference?"

"I hope so. Isn't that why anyone volunteers—to make a difference? Have you ever done any volunteer work?"

"Once. When I was a freshman I taught adults to read." She shrugged, knowing her efforts didn't compare to his.

The sound of a woman clearing her throat came from behind Quen. A young woman approached with keys in hand.

"Excuse me." He grabbed his things and moved away from the woman's car.

Bobbi jumped at the opportunity to make her exit. "Well, thanks for walking me to my car. I'd better be going."

"Sorry for holding you up."

"No, I enjoyed talking to you. And don't forget I need those websites you're going to look up for me."

"Yeah, I'll pull some sites together. I can bring it to the next class."

"Thanks, I appreciate that."

"Okay, until next time." He bowed his head and walked away.

Bobbi watched him as she climbed into her car. He had parked across the lot from her. Interesting, she thought. There was more to him than good looks and muscle.

Later that night, before Quen climbed into bed, he received a call from Arlene. She wanted to talk about Kristy, among other things. Since she seldom called, he lay across the couch listening to her. But he found his thoughts drifting.

He hadn't meant to run off at the mouth like he had. He had wanted to walk Bobbi to her car, say good night, and leave. Instead, he stood around like some schoolboy who'd just discovered the joy of girls. He had to admit, she was a very interesting woman, and he wanted to know more about her.

"Are you listening to me?"

"I'm sorry, I was looking at something on television. Say that again." Quen look at the big-screen television that sat turned off in the corner of his den. He'd almost forgotten Arlene was on the other line. Right now he had Bobbi on the brain.

"I asked if you were sleeping any better? The last time we talked, you mentioned you still weren't sleeping through the night."

"Well, nothing's changed. But that's okay. When I'm up I do most of my homework."

"You wake up at around three in the morning and do homework?"

"That or watch television. Since I'm up I try to do something constructive."

"And you're worried about Kristy seeing a therapist, when you're the one who needs to see somebody. When's the last time you had a good night's sleep?"

He thought back to a time when he didn't have so much on his mind. Right now he had so much bottled up inside him, it was hard to get a good night's sleep. His mind never stopped racing.

"It's been a while since I've had a good night of . . . anything." He took a deep breath and exhaled. Arlene had never been this interested in him before. "But I'm sure you didn't call to talk about me. When's Kristy's last counseling session?"

"Next Saturday. Her grades have improved and she concentrates better. Overall, she's doing good."

"What happens if she relapses, say a couple of months from now?"

"I take her back. It won't be a problem. Quen, the doctor agrees that Kristy's fine. Trust me, I wouldn't stop her sessions if I felt like she needed them."

"Yeah, I'm sure you're doing the right thing. I want her to be well adjusted and . . . and I don't know." Living so far away from Kristy frustrated him at times.

"She's going to be your typical teenager and she's going to drive us crazy."

He laughed. Arlene knew how much he worried about his daughter. "Thanks, Arlene. I'm really concerned and I still feel so responsible for everything."

"Quen, you need to let it go. Let's all live our lives and not dwell on the past. Kristy's fine, I'm fine, and you're going to be fine. Call somebody and see about getting into a sleep program. If anybody needs therapy, it's you."

"Gee, thanks." *I know what I need, and it's not therapy.*

Five

Quen quickly showered and dressed before going downtown to the Lean On Me Agency. Having his own business afforded him the flexibility to volunteer at different times of the day. However, he hoped to one day work full-time for the agency.

He'd signed up to work four hours this Tuesday morning. One appealing feature of the work was that each day was different than the one before. He aided ex-convicts with housing, government assistance, and the perplexing job of securing employment. He enjoyed the challenge and the gratification he received after the men returned to thank him.

The agency shared an old brick renovated warehouse downtown with another nonprofit organization. The parking was free, the atmosphere congenial, and he felt right at home.

Once inside, Quen greeted Olivia, the agency's motherly secretary, with a nod as she worked her jaws over the phone. Maybe this morning he could slip past her desk without an early dose of gossip. He waved and kept walking.

"Girl, hold on a minute. How you doin' this morning, sugar?" she called out to Quen, before he could disappear down the hall.

He stopped and flashed her a polite smile. "I'm fine. How about yourself?" All hopes of escape vanished.

"I'm good. I just wanted to warn you that your *buddy,* Perry, is here this morning." With pursed lips, she winked at him.

Buddy was not the term he would have used. With arched brows, he stroked his goatee. "Thanks, Olivia. Why he can't sign up like everybody else, I'll never know."

"If he signs in, everybody will know when he's working. Nobody wants to work with him, and he knows it." She stood and peeped down the hall to make sure they were alone, then added in a conspiratorial whisper, "He's trying his best to get a staff position around here, but you didn't hear that from me." She winked again and waved before returning to her phone conversation.

Quen shook his head, thinking about the person on the other end of that phone line who'd probably heard every word of her conversation. He took in all she'd said while making his way to the small back room office the volunteers shared. He didn't think Perry was qualified to hold a staff position, no matter how much kissing up he did. One of the qualifications was a college degree—something Perry didn't possess.

When Quen entered the room, he found Perry relaxed with his feet up on the desk, working the phones. He spent a lot of time at the agency, he dressed nicely, he even appeared intelligent in his horn-rimmed glasses; however, he didn't know the difference between *for profit* and *nonprofit.* The thought of him having any say in running the agency made Quen nervous.

He nodded hello before taking a seat behind an ancient wooden desk. After Quen picked up a folder to see who was scheduled for the morning, Perry hung up.

"Hey, college man's here. How was your weekend, buddy?" Perry dropped his feet and rested one elbow on the desk.

Quen shook his head. "I had a good weekend, Perry. How about you?" he managed to respond.

Perry's bulldog-like attitude made him sound powerful over the phone; however, Quen recognized it as a front for his small stature and lack of education.

"Lovely, just lovely," he said.

"I didn't know you were scheduled for today. What's up this morning?" Quen asked, glancing up as he finished his cup of coffee.

"I've been working with this guy who has an interview today. He wanted to come in early and practice a little bit. So I thought, what the hell, I'll help the guy out."

"That's mighty big of you." Thanks to Olivia, Quen now knew why Perry gave more than the ten hours a week the agency asked for.

Perry pointed toward Quen. "Now, if only this dude would dress right for an interview. If he comes in here in a pair of jeans, or a warm-up suit, I'm through with him."

"Morning, gentlemen." Donald Stewart, the agency director, entered the office.

Quen turned in his seat, and Perry jumped to his feet as Donald walked across the room.

"Good morning, Mr. Stewart." Perry practically climbed from behind his desk to greet Donald.

"Morning, Perry." All six feet and four inches of Donald towered over Perry. His eyes moved from Perry to Quen. "Quen, how's it going this morning?"

"Just fine," Quen replied, reaching out to shake his hand.

Donald gave the room a sweeping glance. Quen followed his gaze, not sure what he was looking for. Donald nodded as if he'd made sure everything was in its place.

"I just wanted to stop in and personally thank you guys for all your help. We really appreciate everything you do around here."

"No problem. We're just glad we have something to contribute," Quen answered for the both of them.

"That's right, Mr. Stewart," Perry jumped in. "I've placed a few guys with a new fast-food restaurant. And I'm thankful for the opportunity to give back. If I can help out in any way, just ask and I'm—"

"Thank you, Perry. You're doing enough right now. I appreciate the heart you put into your work." Donald smiled at Perry until he returned to his seat.

"Gentlemen, if you need anything, don't hesitate to ask. Not that we'll always be able to get it, but we'll try. I'm going to be out of town for a few days working on more placement opportunities, which should help out."

"That's great," Quen remarked. "Securing full-time employment is the hardest part of the struggle."

Donald gestured to Quen. "Quen, if you have a few minutes, I'd like to talk to you about the proposal you turned in a few weeks ago."

"Sure." Quen stood to follow Donald back to his office.

Just as they started out, a young man came in. "Hey, Mr. Stewart." The young man, no older than thirty, had on black denims, a white V-necked shirt, and a pair of white leather sneakers.

"John, it's good to see you." Donald stepped into the hallway as they exchanged greetings. Quen looked back over his shoulder at Perry, who'd bounced his pencil off the desk by the eraser, then leaned back in his seat, arms crossed. The frown on his face told Quen that Perry's interview client had arrived.

After a brief conversation with the client, Donald led Quen up the hall to his office, across from Olivia's desk.

"Have a seat and make yourself comfortable," Donald said, taking off his suit jacket. He hung the jacket across the back of his grayish-black leather chair before sitting down. The chair, like most of the furnishings at the agency, had seen better days.

Quen sat across from him in a smaller metal chair with a cement-like cushioning. Donald's office couldn't compare to the executive offices of Quen's BellSouth days. However, the emotional rewards in nonprofit work outweighed the financial ones.

Donald leaned back in the seat and crossed his legs. "Olivia gave me a copy of your proposal to have college students teach soft skills to our clients, and I liked it. I realize we should do more in that area, but can't due to a lack of resources. So, tell me more about your plan."

"Sure." Quen leaned forward, welcoming the opportunity to bounce his idea off the decision maker of the agency. He'd submitted the proposal after a brainstorm one day, but hadn't been sure if anyone would consider it.

"I propose we use graduate students from Macon College to help teach things like office etiquette, business casual dressing, even answering the phones—assuming it could be part of the school's intern program. I'm sure the college would welcome it, and all at no expense to the agency."

A small grin turned into a broad smile, as Donald nodded his head. "I like it. That's a great idea, and it saves us money. But why not have some of our volunteers teach those skills?"

Quen cleared his throat. The thought of some of the volunteers teaching soft skills scared him. Some of them needed to brush up on their phone etiquette themselves.

"Most of our time is spent chasing employment, helping with financial assistance, and whatever other urgent needs they come in with. Also, I'm not too sure how qualified we are to handle it. Graduate students are in the job market and are trained in how to find jobs. Who better to teach it?"

"Hmm, sounds like a win-win situation."

"Yes, sir. I think it is. I'm surprised no one thought of

it sooner." That proposal wasn't Quen's only idea for improvement, but he thought it best to wait until he held a position before making too many suggestions.

"Well, thanks for keeping an eye out for us. I'll look further into it." Donald grunted a few times before continuing. "I've got some other news that may not be so good." Donald stroked his chin in a characteristic gesture.

"There's been a slight change in plans, and I don't know if it's going to have an effect on hiring or not. We may only get funding for one new position for the fall, instead of two."

Quen sat up in his seat, ears perked.

"I know you were promised a counseling position, but we're going to have to wait and see which one they let us have: a counselor or an administrative staff person."

A staff person! Olivia's gossip about Perry rang in Quen's ears.

In the midst of Bobbi's recurring dream about her perfect lover, a loud knock came at the door. She eased up on one elbow, thinking for a second that the sound was a part of her dream. Some nights she dreamed about Prince. Last night, it was Will Smith. Could that be Jada at the door, coming to get her man? No way, Bobbi decided, lying back down.

After another more persistent knock, she threw the sheet back and climbed out of bed. Maybe Roz would beat her to the door. Then she could climb back in and get a few more winks. Instead, the knock turned into banging and she hurried out of the room.

A quick peek in Roz's bedroom confirmed she'd already left for work. Bobbi yanked the front door open and found her sister, Gigi, on the other side smoking a cigarette. Her smoky eyes and long auburn hair with intense red highlights was enough to wake Bobbi. A suitcase—too small for a long stay, and too big for overnight—was by her side.

"Damn, girl, I didn't think you were at home." Gigi took one last drag from her cigarette, then dropped and stepped on it, leaving the unsightly bud in the doorway.

Bobbi didn't know whether to smile or frown. Her big sister was notorious for pop-in visits. You never knew when she'd show up, nor whom she'd bring with her. Why did Gigi have a suitcase when Bobbi hadn't talked to her in more than two months?

"I thought the complex was on fire the way you were banging on the door. To what do I owe the pleasure?"

Gigi grabbed her suitcase and strutted in, giving Bobbi a quick hug. "Girl, I just had to get away. I knew you wouldn't mind, so I hopped a bus and headed on down."

"You couldn't have found a phone anywhere between Chicago and Macon?" Bobbi closed the door behind her.

Gigi rolled her suitcase over beside the couch and flopped down. "I started to call, but I didn't want to wake you."

"Thanks for the consideration," Bobbi said, as she wiped the sleep from her eyes. "What's going on?"

Gigi pulled off a pair of black ankle boots, stood, and stretched. "What you got to eat? We can talk about it over breakfast." She found her way into the kitchen.

Bobbi hoped this little visit wouldn't be as eventful as the last one. Last Christmas Gigi had shown up with a new boyfriend and his two rambunctious children. Afterward, Bobbi swore she'd never be anybody's mother.

Bobbi left her sister to shower and dress. When she returned, she found that Gigi had helped herself to breakfast. The smell of eggs and bacon filled the room.

After filling a teapot with water, Bobbi joined her big sister, who looked like she didn't have a care in the world, at the table.

"So, tell me why you're here."

After a long sigh, Gigi pushed her plate aside.

"I caught Roger with this broad from his band."

"Why do you keep dating musicians? You know how they are." Bobbi felt more like the big sister today.

Gigi slumped over, resting her forehead in her palm. "I can't help it. I'm just drawn to them," she mumbled over the table.

"What about Mason? He wasn't a musician, but you two seemed to hit it off" Bobbi had liked Mason. He was older and more mature, just what her free-spirited sister needed.

"I loved Mason. There was only one problem. His wife!"

Bobbi's eyes widened. "He was married?" she asked.

"For over five years."

"Gi, why would you do that?"

"I didn't know until after I fell in love with him. That's another reason I'm through falling in love. Men lie too much."

The teapot whistled and Bobbi went to fix a cup of tea. "There are good men out there. You keep looking for some Prince Charming to take care of you the rest of your life. You need to be prepared to do that yourself."

"I can take care of myself, but I want my sugar daddy. I deserve to be taken care of." She reared back in her seat and flipped her long red hair over her shoulder.

Bobbi laughed and turned back to take her seat at the table. "And the sad thing is you always seem to find some poor soul who has nothing better to do with his money."

Gigi put her plate in the sink. "Girl, most men are looking for a woman to take care of. They like it when you're depending upon them. It gives them a sense of power, and makes them feel needed. You're too damn independent, that's your problem."

Bobbi twitched in her seat to keep from jumping up. She and Gigi were miles apart in their views of men. Most of the men she met were looking for women to take care of them.

"Gi, let's change the subject."

Leaning against the sink, Gigi let out a deep sigh. "You're right. I came here to get away from drama. Let's talk about Auntie's birthday party. Who are you bringing? And don't say nobody; you've got to be seeing somebody by now."

"I'm not taking a date to Auntie's party. It's a family affair."

"Oh, bring somebody. She'll love it."

Bobbi shrugged. "I don't think so, but don't let that stop you."

"I did meet this cute guy who reminds me of Daddy. He's so handsome. You should meet him."

"If he reminds you of Daddy, I don't think so."

"Oh, cut the man some slack; he's still your father." *Okay, time to change the subject again.* "How long did you say you were going to be here?"

"That depends on how long you and Roz let me crash."

"What about work?"

"I'm unemployed at the moment, but I've got a line on something at Vibe magazine. They're looking for a new photographer, so I'm expecting a call any day now. I hope you don't mind that I gave them your phone number."

"You don't have a cell phone?"

"If I did, I would have called you last night."

"Okay." Bobbi shook her head, laughing. "God, Gi, you and Marcus are just alike."

"And you and Aunt Alice are just alike, always hating on Daddy." She pulled away from the sink and walked down the hall.

Bobbi sat there, sipping her tea. It didn't matter how

much she loved her siblings; they were freeloaders. Gigi called herself a freelance photographer, but to Bobbi that meant she worked when she wanted to. Marcus was reluctant to grow up and out of his mother's house. Instead, he opted for hiding out in his room, occasionally going to work. Maybe her father's work-on-work-off-again habits had affected them. Could it possibly be her job to set a positive example for the future Cunningham family? If so, she was up for the challenge.

Six

Bobbi pulled up to the campus library Saturday morning twenty minutes after ten. She'd fooled around with Gigi, causing her to be late.

The minute she walked into the library, she spotted Quen. He'd taken a seat directly across from the entrance, which made it easy to find him. She crossed the room, looking at him in his warm-up suit, sneakers, and baseball cap. How a man could look sexy in warm-ups she didn't know, but he did. His long legs were stretched out beneath the table as he read a book.

"Is this where the prison society meets?" she asked, dropping her tablet on the table with a loud thump.

Quen sat up so fast the book fell out of his hand and onto the floor.

He'd been asleep. "Oh, no. Was somebody sleeping?" she teased as she sat across from him.

He shook his head and reached down to pick up the book. "Okay, you caught me." He shrugged. "What can I say?" He looked down at his watch. "I've been waiting on you guys for over twenty minutes now." He wasn't smiling.

"Hey, I'm sorry, I got held up. I'm a whole twenty minutes late; sorry to wreck your morning." Brother man wasn't looking so good right now. Was he the same nice guy who'd walked her to her car the other night?

Quen readjusted his cap and took a deep breath before

relaxing back into his seat. "I've just got a hard stop at 11:30, and I'd like to get started. Everybody agreed to ten; now where are they?"

He looked at her, and she stared back at him. Did he actually think she knew where the rest of the group was? She held up both hands, palms out. "I have no idea."

He gave an irritated look toward the library entrance. Bobbi opened her tablet and created a sheet for project notes.

"I'm sorry." He reached across the table, stopping her from writing.

When he touched her, she went warm all over. She looked at her hand as a tingling sensation ran up her arm.

He continued, "I didn't get much sleep last night, and I'm afraid I woke up a little cranky. Don't take it personally." He pulled his hand back.

"Okay. I was just proud I'd caught you sleeping. I didn't expect to get my head bit off. You must have been up really late."

"Try *all* night."

"You pulled an all-nighter?"

He nodded. "And I wasn't studying for a test. Just couldn't sleep."

"At around two or three this afternoon you're going to pass out somewhere. That's when it hits you. Trust me, I used to pull all-nighters studying for exams."

"Well, if it'll put me in a better mood, I'll welcome it. I don't like having a jacked-up attitude, especially toward you." He gave her a sheepish grin.

No, he wasn't trying to apologize. She would have called him on it, but she let it go. "Flattery will get you nowhere, Mr. Brooks. What about those websites you promised me? Did you bring them?"

He flipped open his tablet without taking his eyes

from her. He took a sheet of paper off the top and slid it across the table. "That should get you started."

She took the paper and glanced over the websites listed. Over the top of the paper, she could see Quen looking at his watch again. Lack of punctuality was obviously one of his pet peeves.

"We did all agree to start at ten o'clock, didn't we?" he asked. Signs of irritation were all over his face.

Bobbi nodded. "Sure did, but I don't remember whose idea it was to move it up an hour."

"It was Monica's." He snorted. "And look, she's not even here."

"Now what do we do?" Bobbi asked.

He shrugged as if he'd given up. "I guess we can go ahead and start without them. Monica did say her man was in town today. She's probably forgotten about us. And who knows where Gregory is."

"Well, looks like it's just me and you. Where do we start?"

When Quen took off his cap, he looked at her as if he was seeing her for the first time. His eyes had a sudden spark to them, and a renewed focus. He was fully awake now. The hair on her arms stood up.

"So, where's your man?" he asked, with a slight nod of his head. He leaned forward, resting his forearms on the table.

"Who said I had one?"

"You look like the type of woman who's taken. You're probably engaged." He reached out for her hand again. "But I don't see a ring. So that means he hasn't proposed yet. But he will. You're too beautiful to let get away. You'll get married, have plenty of babies, and live happily ever after."

Did he just say she was beautiful? What had gotten into him? She pulled her hand back and started laughing. "What are you, clairvoyant or something?"

"Am I right?" he asked, arching his left brow.

"No. You couldn't be further off base."

"So, there's no man?"

She shook her head. "No, there isn't."

"There isn't a woman, is there?" he asked with a frown.

"What do you think?" She crossed her arms and leered at him.

He shrugged. "Hey, I don't know. You said I was way off base."

"I meant, I don't believe in happily ever after."

Quen frowned and sat back, giving her an I-don't-believe-you smile.

He was studying her, and Bobbi knew it. She didn't like being stared at so intently. "I don't mean that exactly, it's just that society fills young girls' heads with so much nonsense. Most women today live vicariously through romantic movies. It's like this movie I reviewed last week, another Cinderella story told with a twist. You know, the white-knight-in-shining-armor-saves-the-day story." She uncrossed her arms and twisted in her seat, crossing her legs.

"What's wrong with that?"

"Those men don't exist. Not in today's society anyway. I'm a realist. I know happily ever after doesn't live in my neighborhood. Finding a good man is like . . . finding a four-leaf clover. You spend hours searching through the grass, and never get lucky."

"Or you give up."

"Who wants to waste her life searching?" she asked with an attitude.

"It's not wasted if you find what you're looking for," he shot back.

She laughed. "Well, have you found your four-leaf clover? It sounds like it."

"No." He leaned closer, striking a challenging pose.

"But I don't intend on giving up so easy, like some people I know."

Quen had gotten under her skin again. He had a way of irritating her. Cranky or not, she didn't like him this morning.

"Spoken like a true believer in fairy tales." She lowered her voice, noticing they'd attracted some attention. "Looking for the girl who fits the glass slipper?"

"No. That would mean I'm a prince. And believe me, I'm no prince. But we all need to believe in something. Why not fairy tales?"

"That's where stuff like that happens—only in fairy tales. It leads to false hope, which turns into failed marriages."

"Well, now I've heard it all. Fairy tales lead to failed marriages. Sounds like you've got a self-fulfilling prophecy going on if you're not careful. Whenever you find your four-leaf clover, I hope you don't step on him."

Her eyes narrowed as she crossed her arms protectively. Their conversation had taken a dangerous turn. Who did he think he was?

His wicked grin made her feel naked for everyone in the library to see—like he knew some secret about her that no one else knew. She wracked her brain for a good comeback. She couldn't let him have the last word. He loved a good challenge, and she wanted to give him one.

"Hey, guys. Sorry I'm late."

Bobbi and Quen looked up as Monica stood at the end of the table. She pulled out a chair and sat down.

"So, what did I miss?" she asked, looking from one to the other.

Quen took a deep breath and stretched his arms over his head. "We were just getting started," he said, not taking his eyes off Bobbi.

Speechless for what must have been the first time, Bobbi brooded to herself and vowed to get him back.

Quen rolled over and looked at the illuminated clock on his nightstand; 3:45 A.M. and he was wide awake. He clasped his hands behind his head as he lay back in his king-size bed and stared up at the ceiling fan. He didn't want to do homework or surf through infomercials for something worthy of the hour. Instead, he ran the scene from the library over in his mind again.

His conversation with Bobbi had turned into a sparring match. It hadn't helped that he hadn't been in the best of moods earlier. He always woke up around three in the morning, did a little homework, then fell back to sleep. Why couldn't he have done that last night? He hoped she'd forgive him the next time he saw her.

He closed his eyes and could picture her across the table from him with her big, beautiful brown eyes. At ten on a Saturday morning, she'd taken the time to apply makeup. Her luscious, full lips had been covered by a hint of brown lipstick that, in his opinion, she didn't need.

The morning hadn't been a total mess. He had managed to find out that she wasn't involved with anyone. Not that her single status would do him any good, especially after he'd pissed her off. But he couldn't help himself. She'd sounded so down on relationships, and he hated to see that.

He, on the other hand, wanted a relationship like his parents'. His father had swept his mother off her feet. Robert had been a soldier and Sue a bank teller. Their whirlwind courtship had lasted six months before they were married. Even after three children, the crazy love they had for one another had been strong. Quen also remembered how affectionate they'd been toward each other. If he were lucky, maybe one day he'd have a love so rare.

* * *

By Sunday afternoon, Gigi had made herself at home. Roz didn't seem to mind her crashing on the couch. And overstaying her welcome wasn't anything Bobbi worried about. She knew one day Gigi would pick up and leave as mysteriously as she'd arrived.

"Chef Cunningham, what's for dinner?" Gigi asked, following Bobbi into the kitchen.

"Grilled salmon."

"Hell, I can cook fish."

"Then why don't you?" Bobbi gestured to her side, motioning Gigi toward the refrigerator.

"Girl, you know you're the one who followed Mama around the kitchen, not me. I'm surprised you haven't landed a husband yet with your fancy culinary skills." She held up her freshly painted nails as she opened the refrigerator, grabbed a bottle of water, then took a seat at the kitchen table.

Bobbi laughed at her and pulled a brown package from the refrigerator. "I'm fixin' to put this fish on the grill. The only person I'm 'bout to impress is you, because you know you can't grill fish," she said in her most Southern voice.

"Girl, anybody can grill fish. I would cook, but I'm your guest. Besides, my nails are wet."

"Yeah, right." Bobbi loved her sister, but Gigi was the laziest and luckiest woman she knew. She didn't cook, clean, or have any money; yet she always managed to land a man to care for her.

The front door opened and Roz walked into the kitchen. "Hey, ladies, what's up?"

"Roz, am I glad you're home." Gigi pushed back the other kitchen chair. "Have a seat, hon; we need to talk."

"Oh, no. Sounds like I'm about to get myself into

trouble." She eased into the seat, dropping her purse on the floor.

Bobbi couldn't protect her. She opened the package and proceeded to clean and season the fish.

"What you doing tonight?" Gigi asked.

Roz shrugged, "I thought about going back to church, but I don't have any plans . . . or do I?" she asked, leery of the answer.

The telephone rang.

"You do now. We can drive to Atlanta and go out." Gigi leaned back in her seat and crossed her legs.

Bobbi dried her hands on a towel and reached for the phone, but Roz had already picked it up.

She held the receiver to her chest while staring at Gigi. "Atlanta! It's Sunday night," she said, shocked.

"Roz, watch out. She'll have you in New York before the night's over," Bobbi joked.

"Hello," Roz answered the phone, laughing and pointing at Bobbi. "Your sister's a trip, do you know that?" she whispered, with her fingers over the receiver.

Roz froze. "Uh." She bit her lip and looked up at Bobbi.

What? Bobbi mouthed after noticing the funny expression on Roz's face.

"It's for you. I think you know who it is." She held out the receiver.

Bobbi stared at the phone, unable to move. *Not again. Why won't he just leave me alone?* She shook her head.

Gigi, after witnessing this awkward moment, reached for the phone. "Who is it? I'll handle it."

"That's okay." Bobbi took the receiver from Roz and held it while Roz sat back down.

"Hello."

"This is the Alabama Department of Corrections with a person-to-person call for Bobbi Cunningham. Will you accept the charges?"

Bobbi turned her back and closed her eyes. She hated the cold tone of the operator's voice, which always made Bobbi feel like she'd done something wrong. When she looked back at the kitchen table, Gigi gave her a big-sister protective stare. She looked like she was ready to beat up somebody for her.

Bobbi picked up the base of the phone and stepped out of the kitchen and into the little dining room. "Yes," she whispered.

Seven

Bobbi passed through the little dining room into the living room, to get out of earshot of the kitchen.

"Yes, it's good to hear your voice, too. I've just been kind of busy with school and all." Bobbi stared at the ceiling and swallowed hard.

"Baby, did you get the pictures I sent you?" he asked.

Her father didn't sound like the same cheerful man she remembered, who always quoted some saying or phrase. He was always the life of the party, and her parents used to have plenty of parties.

"Bobbi?"

"Uh, yeah. I got the pictures." She lowered herself onto the couch. She could hear Gigi and Roz talking in the kitchen. "I would have written back, but, uh, I, uh—"

"You don't have to explain, baby, I understand. I'm glad you came to the phone though."

Why did she want to cry? There was no love lost for this man. Not after what he'd done to them—to her. How could she even speak to him now?

"Bobbi, I'd like to see you."

Her stomach churned as she stumbled for the right thing to say. She wouldn't go see him—no way, no how. So, why should she worry about his feelings when he hadn't cared about theirs years ago?

"I'm not going to lie to you." She stood. To keep from being overheard, she decided to carry the conversation into her bedroom. She walked down the hall, keeping her voice low. "I don't want to come see you, and I don't ever intend—"

Gigi darted out of the kitchen into the hallway, blocking Bobbi's escape.

"To come . . ." she attempted to finish speaking, until Gigi reached for the phone.

"Is that Daddy? Let me talk to him."

Bobbi didn't want Gigi to know she was talking to him; but she didn't want to talk to him either. Before she could protest, or pull away, Gigi grabbed the phone from her hand.

"Hi, Daddy. It's Glenda. How you doing?" She cradled the phone between her sholder and ear, and walked into the living room to sit down.

What Gigi wanted, Gigi got, even if she had to take it. It had been like that all their lives, and Bobbi was sick of it. Gigi asserted her big-sisterness whenever she had the chance.

Right before she'd grabbed the phone, Bobbi had been about to tell him never to call her again. But Gigi had ruined all that. In Bobbi's opinion, he'd waited too late to try to be a father from prison.

"Daddy, you so crazy. I'm gonna come see you next month."

Unable to stand it any longer, Bobbi turned and stomped down the hall. As she passed Roz's bedroom, she caught a glimpse of her sitting on the edge of the bed.

Roz shrugged and mouthed, *I'm sorry*.

Bobbi didn't respond, but continued to her bedroom. She lay across the bed, thinking about the phone call. Why had he been trying to reach her so much lately? At this point in her life, she didn't need a father anyway. She'd just about grown up without him, and was putting herself through college. One thing she'd learned from her childhood was not to depend on a man for everything.

When her father had left her mother, Wilma hadn't been prepared and wound up with nothing to support her children. Bobbi was determined to get a good job and support herself.

Thirty minutes later, when Bobbi walked up the hall, she heard voices coming from outside. Roz and Gigi were on the patio, grilling the fish. She walked out to join them.

The minute she stepped out the door, Roz held out the fork. "Here, take this, I've got to get something in the kitchen." She shoved the fork at Bobbi and went back inside.

"Well, look who decided to join us. You mad at me?" Gigi asked, smiling. She took a puff from her cigarette.

Bobbi shrugged. "It doesn't matter, I didn't want to talk to him anyway." She checked the fish. She didn't blame Roz for trying to get out of the line of fire.

"You should talk to him. He's your father."

"He's *your* father. He ceased being my father the minute he went to prison."

"He'll never stop being your father, whether you like it or not. He said he's been trying to talk to you for a while."

"I guess." Bobbi turned the fish over. She didn't want to discuss her feelings about her father. "Gi, we'll never see eye to eye, so drop it."

"He said he sent you some pictures, too. Can I see them?"

"I threw them away."

Gigi jumped up and almost turned over her ashtray. "You are so silly. I don't get it. He got caught selling drugs. It's not like he killed somebody."

Bobbi stabbed the fish, closed the lid on the grill, and spun around toward Gigi, who had put out her cigarette and opened the sliding glass door.

"Don't bring your irresponsible butt in here telling me

what I should do. You're just like him. All you think about is yourself. You have no idea, or concern, as to how your actions will affect anyone else. And in case you forgot, drugs do kill."

Gigi stopped with the door half open. "Don't you turn things around on me." She pointed at Bobbi. "Everybody can deal with Daddy's time but you. So you avoid him. That's how you've been all your life, Bobbi. For once you need to face something and stop running."

Roz returned. "Ladies, you're kind of loud, aren't you?" She walked past Bobbi and over to the grill, opening the lid and grabbing the fork. "Hot damn!" She dropped the hot fork onto the edge of the grill.

Gigi tried to slam the sliding glass door when she went back inside, but it only made a muffled thud sound.

"She drives me crazy sometimes." Bobbi turned to see Roz shaking her hand and cursing.

"I'm sorry. I left the fork in the fish."

Roz just kept shaking her head and motioned for Bobbi to pick up a plate from the table. "Why, because she tells the truth?" She wrapped a towel around the fork.

"That's not fair," Bobbi said, holding the plate.

"Life isn't always fair." Roz took up all three salmon filets. "But we have to deal with it. Unless you choose to give up and die."

Monday afternoon, Perry helped one of the counselors inside with two boxes of . . . he didn't know what. He read the labels and peeked inside, but couldn't make out the contents.

Joy Romano, a counselor at the Lean On Me Agency, instructed Perry where to set her files. "Just stack them beside the bookcase. I appreciate the help."

"No problem, Ms. Romano. I couldn't let you carry them yourself."

"I'm going to run next door a minute. Can you grab the rest of them for me?"

"Sure."

She pitched him her keys and left the office.

Perry followed the perky petite ash blond–haired woman down the hall and out the door. They parted ways, and he brought in the remaining boxes from her trunk. He unfolded the flap and sifted through the files. There was nothing but file after file of resource information. He lost interest and walked out to Olivia's desk to see who was scheduled for the day.

"The usual list of clowns," he said aloud, before looking back over his shoulder. Everyone was at lunch, including Olivia. He whistled a little tune he'd heard on the radio that morning, quickly moved behind her desk, and took a seat. The file drawer to his right held personnel information on everyone who worked there. He'd seen Olivia shove folders in there before.

"Let's see where Mr. Brooks came from." He pulled out Quen's file and laid it on the desk. He leafed through confidential information, and stopped when he found something of interest.

"Well, well, what have we here?" He picked up the personnel sheet and smiled at his cleverness. A clattering sound came from the hallway, which meant someone was on the way inside.

He folded the paper and shoved it into his pocket. "Never know when you'll need a little insurance." He closed the folder and shoved it back into the drawer. He threw his feet up on the desk, grabbed the phone, and pretended to be hanging up as the office door opened.

"Excuse you!" Olivia stood inside the doorway with one hand on her hip while pointing a finger at Perry. "Are you comfortable enough, honey?" she asked, strolling into the office.

The annoyed look on her face assured Perry she

didn't appreciate him at her desk. She'd never liked him, and he'd never cared. He took his feet down. "Sorry, I had to use your phone right quick."

She walked over, dropped her purse on the desk, and gestured for him to get up. "And what's wrong with the phone in back?"

He jumped up. "Nothing, I guess. I didn't make it back that far." He smiled at her, but got a sneer in return. That's okay, he thought. One day she'd be working for him.

"Try to refrain from using my phone in the future. And look at my desk." She pointed at the papers scattered everywhere.

The office door swung open again. Joy peeked back into the office.

"Perry, I have one more box in the backseat. Can you help me?"

He walked away from Olivia's desk and toward the front door. "Sure, Joy. I'll be right there." He smiled back at Olivia.

She waited until Joy closed the door and narrowed her eyes at Perry. He'd never called Ms. Romano by her first name before.

He looked back at Olivia, pointing to the desk. "Sorry about that, I was looking for a pen." He walked out.

"I bet you were." She sat down and looked around, expecting something to be missing.

Eight

Bobbie gathered her things and took off as soon as class ended. She had to hurry home and do something; she just wasn't sure what. As long as it kept her away from Quen, that was enough. On Saturday, after Monica had shown up, the group had outlined their project, then Quen had left. For most of the meeting, his attitude had stunk. That evening, she didn't want him walking her out to her car as if she had amnesia and didn't remember Saturday.

As she crossed the parking lot, she dug through her purse for her car keys. She climbed in and turned the key. The engine cranked as if it wanted to start, but didn't. The second time, it made a clicking noise. She hit the steering wheel with her open palm, frustrated as all get out because she needed to go.

"Come on, baby," she pleaded, gripping the wheel. "Last me a few more years, please." The third time, it sounded as if she'd broken something. She gave up. Her faithful little Honda, which reminded her of a Timex—it took a licking and kept on ticking—was having a bad day.

She reached inside her purse and pulled out her cell phone. Unfortunately, she no longer had AAA, so she called Roz. The phone rang and rang, but she didn't pick up. Bobbi didn't want to shell out the money for a cab, but perhaps she'd have to. As she got out and raised the hood, she dialed another friend. With her head buried underneath the hood, she pushed and pulled every moveable part she could find, making sure nothing had come loose.

"Know what you're doing?"

She jumped at the familiar sound of his voice. As expected, she turned around to find Quen. She hung up the phone.

"I don't have a clue. But I called a friend and he's on his way to help," she lied, holding her chin up.

Quen nodded. "Okay. I could check it out for you, but since you've got somebody on the way . . ." He trailed off, slowly backing up.

Bobbi thought about that cab fare and motioned him back with her cell phone. "Hold on. If you know something about cars . . . I, uh, I don't think it would hurt to take a peek."

He walked over and set his books on the roof of her car, then rubbed his palms together as he walked around to check under the hood. "Let's see what we've got here." After checking a few things, he turned to Bobbi. "Get in and start it for me."

She climbed behind the wheel, leaving the car door open, and turned the key. Nothing happened. After another failed attempt, she stopped and rolled the windows down.

"What's wrong with it?" she asked, calling out the window.

"I'm not sure. Turn your headlights on for me."

She flicked the lights on and off several times at his direction before he walked over to her door frowning.

"What is it?" she asked, not liking the look on his face.

He leaned over, looking down into the car at her. "It looks like you might need a battery. I can try to give you a jump, unless you want to wait until your friend shows up?"

She didn't like the look on his face when he said *friend*. It was as if he didn't believe her. She caught a whiff of his cologne mixed with the outdoors, which gave off a musk smell. Not offensive in the least, just masculine. Bobbi shook her head. "There's no telling how long he'll take, so go ahead and do whatever you have to do."

"Sure." He straightened up and backed away from the car. "You got any jumper cables?" he asked before walking away.

"Of course not."

"Luckily, I do. Let me pull my car around." He walked a few cars down and climbed into his Land Rover.

Bobbi watched his backside as she stepped out of the car and dialed Roz again. He looked good in a T-shirt that hugged his chest, a pair of slightly baggy jeans, and brown leather sandals. A smile crept onto her lips as she quickly turned away for fear he might look back and catch her. Roz still hadn't answered, so she hung up. Seconds later, Quen pulled his car up close to her hood. Thank goodness she'd backed into the parking spot.

He jumped out of his car with cables in hand and popped his hood.

"Think you can fix it?" she asked, stepping closer, examining the motor again as if this time she'd understand how it worked.

He glanced at her from head to toe. "Do you know how to jump-start a car?"

She shook her head and raised her left hand. "No. I rely on my Goodyear mechanic for everything." Then she pointed at him. "But I do know how to pump my own gas," she said chuckling.

He nodded and smiled. "That's cool. Let me show you something."

"You gonna educate me?" she asked in her schoolgirl voice.

"Oh, yeah, I'm gonna school you all right."

She crossed her arms at the seductive look on his face and twisted her lips. "And just what do you mean by that?"

"Here's how you jump-start a car." He went into detail, explaining how to tell if the battery was low, then how to hook up the cables. He broke down everything into terminology he was sure she'd understand.

She watched him work with one hand on her hip. "So, is all this going to cost me anything?" she pointed at the battery.

He looked up at her with a big grin on his face. "Let's try to start her again, and I'll let you know." He hooked up the cables.

As he walked around behind her, his body brushed against hers, causing the hairs on her arm to stand at attention. It was already more than ninety degrees, but somebody turned the thermostat up a few more notches, and she was slowly roasting.

He paused before getting into her car and gestured. "May I?"

"Sure. You're helping me—you don't have to ask."

He turned the key, but the car still didn't start. After his second failed attempt, he slid out of the car and closed the door. With his backside against the closed door, he crossed his legs at the ankle. "We need to let her set a few minutes until the battery gets some juice."

She stood still with her arms crossed, barely able to concentrate on more than his beefy body at the moment. If he could read her mind, she'd be in a world of trouble.

"Hey, about Saturday, I didn't mean to be so cranky." He shrugged and a slight smile touched his lips.

She'd forgotten she hadn't wanted to talk to him tonight because she hadn't had a good comeback after Saturday's little verbal battle. But she needed his help.

He cleared his throat when she didn't respond.

"Apology accepted?" he asked with his teeth clamped over his bottom lip.

"Oh, is that what that was?" She grinned.

"Uh-huh. I'm not on my knees or anything, but it was an apology."

When he gave her that Denzel smile again, she bit her lip to stifle a blush, but a smile escaped her lips. "Of course I forgive you," she said, looking heavenward with a slight flutter of her eyebrows. "I just hope you got some sleep this weekend."

"Yep, a little anyway."

She didn't actually know what to talk to him about. Just how long did it take for juice to run into the battery?

He walked over and grabbed a towel from his trunk to wipe his hands. "How's your research work coming along?" he asked when he returned.

"It's . . . coming," she slowly replied, while sliding her hands into her back pockets.

"Did you get anything from the websites I gave you?"

"Uh . . . I'm gonna check them out this week."

His handsome features grimaced. "You don't have that long, you know. This is *summer school."*

"I know that," she snapped back at him. "I'll have something by Saturday," she said in an assured tone.

"If you need any help, just ask." His face softened.

You can come help put me to bed tonight. She laughed inwardly for even thinking such nonsense. It looked like Quen the nice brother man had returned. She didn't know who that dude in the library was. Maybe his alter ego. They stood there through a few minutes of awkward silence.

"You must know a lot about cars," she finally said.

"I know enough to work on my own most of the time. The simple jobs anyway."

"I don't know squat about cars, and like a nut I let my AAA expire."

"In my opinion, all single women should have AAA."

"I agree, but I kept paying and paying, and maybe used their services once a year. Just my luck the car breaks down a month later."

"Yeah, that's usually how it happens. But see, if you had a man, you wouldn't have that problem. All you'd have to do is call him, and he'd take care of everything for you." He held up his hands, as if to say sorry.

She laughed. "News flash. Not all men know about cars either. I dated a guy once who had to call a buddy when we had a flat. He didn't have sense enough to keep a spare in the trunk."

"That must have been a fun date."

"Oh, it was a blast. We hadn't even made it to the restaurant yet. Everything went downhill from there."

"Do you date much?"

"No, not much. Most guys want to take me to the movies."

"Aren't you a movie reviewer?"

"Bingo."

Quen laughed and turned around to get back into her car.

"What about you?" she asked, stepping forward.

"Occasionally. But most women want me to work on their cars," he teased and turned the key. This time the car started.

She caught the subtle grin on his face and wrinkled up her nose. "You're playing with me, aren't you, Mr. Brooks?"

"Yeah, I was just kidding." He smiled as he climbed out of the car and walked around to unhook the cables.

"Thank you so much. I could have been here who knows how long if you hadn't come along."

"Sure. You might want to stop by your mechanic's and get it checked out. You probably need a new battery. That jump is a temporary fix."

"I will. So, how much do I owe you?" she asked, not expecting him to charge her.

He stroked his chin. "Hmm . . . let's see. How about dinner?"

"How about lunch?" she countered, taking into consideration her budget.

He shook his head. "Dinner."

"For a temporary fix?"

"Hey, I could have let you wait on your friend." He looked around. "Who, by the way, hasn't shown up yet."

She'd almost forgotten about that little lie. "Okay, I'm just happy my car's running. I guess dinner isn't too much to ask. When and where?"

"Tomorrow night, at Michael's on Mulberry."

She narrowed her eyes. "Can't wait until the weekend?" Michael's sounded more like a date than repayment for a jump.

"I'm starting an important project this week, so tomorrow night's the only time I'm available. Where can I pick you up?" he asked in a tone that implied everything was settled.

"I can meet you there."

He nodded with a grin. "That'll work. How about seven o'clock?"

"I'll be there with bells on."

He laughed. "Oh, I can't wait to see that."

"It was a joke," she called out as he walked back to his car.

When she backed out, Quen stood at the door of his car, watching her drive away. She should have asked him how much a battery cost, but whatever the price, she knew she'd have to pay it.

The next evening, Bobbi walked into the house and found Gigi stretched out across the couch talking on the phone. Bobbi dropped her things on the dining room table and looked over the bills Roz had brought in earlier. Unable to avoid it, she heard snippets of Gigi's conversation.

"Not until you're ready to put an end to your fling . . ."

It sounded like Gigi and Roger would be back together in no time, just as Bobbi had suspected. She ignored her sister and opened the phone bill. Undoubtedly, Gigi's phone call would show up on the bill after she left. Before Bobbi finished reading everything, Gigi hung up.

"Say, girl, what's going on?"

Bobbi dropped the phone bill and joined her sister in the living room. "It's going good, Gi. How was your day?" She wasn't sure if Gigi had gotten up for the day or not since she still had pajamas on.

"Bor-ing." She sat up and placed the remote on the coffee table. "I watched television all morning, and I hate daytime TV. But I didn't have a car to go anywhere," she said with a long face.

"Did you want to keep my car?" Bobbi asked with a raised brow.

"Yeah, if you don't mind? Tomorrow I can drop you off at work, and pick you up when you get off. I'd like to do a little running around."

"Sure. I had a new battery put in this morning, so don't run off anywhere."

Gigi stood up and stretched. "Why would I do that? Trust me, I'll be there when you get off." She pulled her head scarf off, and long red hair fell around her shoulders.

"Since I've been in all day, let's go shopping this evening?"

Bobbi hesitated. She had to meet Quen for dinner tonight. "Uh . . . I can't this evening."

"Why, what are you doin'?"

"I've got a . . . uh, I've got to meet a friend and do some research."

"Research. What kind of research?" she asked, crossing her arms.

The personal kind. Bobbi stifled a smile. "It's for school. Just some boring sociology stuff." She stood, not wanting to let Gigi know she was meeting Quen for dinner. Gigi would call it a date no matter what Bobbi said.

"Then can I take the car while you're researching?" Gigi asked, following Bobbi into the kitchen.

"Gi, I'm sorry." Bobbi turned around. "My research isn't on my computer here, it's at the library," she lied, gritting her teeth. *God forgive me again.*

"So, I'm gonna be stuck in here all day?" Gigi stood in the doorway with her hands propped on her hips.

Bobbi grabbed an apple from the refrigerator. "Roz should be in soon. She'll want to go shopping with you." She glanced up at the clock. "It's after six, I gotta run and change." She walked past Gigi, eating the apple.

"Boy, I said I wanted to get away from everything, didn't I." Gigi shook her head and strolled into the kitchen for a snack. Thirty minutes later, she sat watching the news when Roz walked in. They were in the middle of a conversation when Bobbi entered. Bobbi was decked out in all white from head to toe except for a pair of yellow-tinted sunglasses and yellow mules.

"So, what's this line you gave me about going to the library?" Gigi asked with a raised brow.

"It's hot out, so I thought I'd change," Bobbi replied in defense.

"The only thing hot out there is going to be you. I'd like to see who you're meeting at that library," Gigi remarked with her feet tucked under her. She was still in pajamas.

Bobbi let out a heavy sigh. "Hi, Roz."

Roz chuckled. "Hey, girl. You two crack me up. I bet it was a trip growing up in your household."

"It was more of a journey growing up with this chick." Bobbi pointed to Gigi.

"Uh-huh, well, you go on to the *library* and do your *research.*" She eyed her sister skeptically.

Bobbi laughed. "I'll be late if I keep fooling around with you. So, I'll catch you girls later."

"Later, hon, and don't do anything I wouldn't do." Gigi winked at Bobbi when she looked back.

Nine

Bobbi had never been able to fool Gigi, not that she ever really tried. She hadn't meant to look all dressed up either. Maybe she should have kept on her work clothes.

Just inside the restaurant's foyer, Bobbi spotted Quen sitting in the waiting area with his legs crossed and his arms spread over the back of the bench, taking up enough space for two. He noticed her, uncrossed his legs, and stood. Bobbi liked the cool and casual look of his silky slacks and light blue V-necked summer sweater. A silver chain-link necklace pulled the outfit together. He looked great.

As she walked toward him, she bit her lip to refrain from blushing. That man had a certain sex appeal about him she found almost irresistible. Almost.

"Hey, I'm glad you didn't back out on me."

"Hey yourself." Bobbi nodded. "I owe it to you."

He welcomed her with a polite smile and leaned over to whisper in her ear. "No, you don't, not really. And you look great." He planted a quick kiss on her cheek.

Surprised, she stood there with eyes large as saucers and smiled. "Thank you." What was that little kiss about? she wondered. Did he kiss all women on the cheek? He'd never done it before, and she hadn't done anything today to warrant a kiss.

"Two, smoking or nonsmoking?" the hostess asked with menus in hand.

"Two nonsmoking." Quen stepped back so Bobbi could follow the hostess in front of him.

He held her hand and helped her into the booth. She sat down and looked over the menu while they waited for the waiter.

"You look good in white," he complimented.

She glanced up from her menu. "Thank you, again." This time, she blushed.

"Did I embarrass you?"

"No, it's just that you already told me I look nice."

He shook his head. "I said you look great. Not nice."

"Okay, enough with the compliments." She put her menu down. "What do you want? Dessert thrown in with dinner?" She chuckled.

"Oh, I want more than dessert." He winked.

She crossed her arms and eyed him skeptically. After that flirtatious wink, she asked in a low suspicious tone, "Like what?"

He shrugged innocently. "Your company, for starters. I eat alone most of the time, so thanks for agreeing to dinner. A stimulating conversation with a beautiful woman is my idea of a good time."

She lowered her arms as the waiter approached, but kept her eyes narrowed. "Uh-huh." Did he expect her to believe that crock?

The waiter took their drink orders. Quen asked for a few more minutes to look over the menu.

"See anything interesting on here?" he asked.

She was still thinking about his last comment. If he wasn't the biggest flirt she'd ever met . . . He probably had all these smooth lines he ran down to every woman he took out. But then, they weren't on a date, so why was he wasting them on her?

She picked up her menu. "I'm going to have the shrimp."

"That sounds good. But I'm in the mood for some prime rib."

He would order one of the most expensive items on the menu. She nodded as if the price of the steak didn't bother her. Dinner tonight would blow her food budget for the week. Wasn't that a lot to ask, for giving her a jump? Was she crazy?

"Did you get your car taken care of this morning?" he asked.

"Yes. Thank you. I took it to Goodyear, and I did need a new battery. I was in and out before lunch." They'd also taken away her entertainment allowance for the month.

"Great, so I can expect to see you in class Thursday night?"

"God, you sound like Professor Jennings." She laughed.

"Just call me Professor Brooks." He laughed along with her. "I just want to make sure you're able to work on our little class project. It's going to be fun."

She set her menu down. "Quen, you keep saying that, but I don't see how in the world you're going to make learning about prison fun. It's depressing and sad."

"I can't change the circumstances of the situation, but what I can change is the way we research it. There's so much about the prison system that I bet you'd be surprised to learn."

She held out her hands. "Like what?"

"First off, it costs taxpayers more than fifteen thousand dollars a year to keep a man incarcerated. That's twenty-one thousand in California. And if he was the sole supporter of the family, it's an added tax burden, because the family now needs public assistance."

She shook her head and glanced over at the couple at the next table. They were holding hands across the table and the man was affectionately kissing the woman's knuckles. Bobbi turned back to Quen. "I knew that. I mean, I knew it was expensive to keep a man in prison. Maybe they should think about that before they commit the crime."

He shrugged and scratched behind his ear. "That is a problem. Most people don't think about the circumstances before they commit a crime. But do you stop and think about the circumstances when you're mad about something?"

"Yes. I do. And I'd never do anything that would land me in jail."

"Don't say that, because anything could happen. You don't know." His voice rose an octave.

"How come I don't?" she replied in a huff. "I'm smart enough to know that if I kill somebody I'll go away for a long time, and I love life too much to do that to myself."

Bobbi could see the muscles twitching in his jaw as his face hardened. It never failed. Their conversations always turned into arguments. She'd had just about enough, and wanted to change the subject.

"If some scum hurts someone very close to you, you don't know what you'd do, trust me. I've seen it before."

"Then maybe those people deserve to be in jail, or prison," she said bluntly.

He shook his head with an incredulous grin on his face. "Not all of them. Everybody's quick to throw a man in jail and not deal with the lack of resources that caused him to be there."

"Come on, Quen, they're there for one of several reasons: they killed somebody, raped somebody, stole something, trafficked in narcotics, et cetera. You pick the crime. What lack of resources can you blame for that?"

"A lack of affordable defense, for one. Innocent men are going to prison. That's reality for a black man anyway," he said. His voice had an edge to it.

"Black, white, it doesn't make a difference. If you

commit the crime, you have to do the time." She crossed her arms and fell back against the booth, smiling at him guardedly.

He nodded as the waiter returned. They ordered dinner and Quen continued.

"Okay, how about this." He leaned forward, resting his forearms on the table. "Today, close to fifty percent of the men in most United States prisons are black."

"They can't be. We're not even half of the population."

"Other than Africa, prison is another place where blacks are about to become the majority of the population. That's what's sad and depressing."

"Well, I still say some of them deserve to be there," she said in a smug tone.

"I'm not denying that. What I want is to fight for the ones who don't, or for the ones who've served their time. Bobbi, prison takes a lot out of a man mentally. Outside visits can improve the environment, but sometimes it's hard to get families to visit."

That last comment did it. Couldn't he tell she didn't want to argue about this any longer? She might as well be in class if they were going to have this discussion. She looked around, then glanced at her watch.

As if Quen sensed her discomfort, he changed the subject. "I'm sorry." He leaned back into a more relaxed position. "I'm on my soapbox again. Let's talk about something else before you walk out on me."

"Yeah, because I was about to ask for class credit for tonight."

He threw his head back and laughed. "That was a good one. I like a woman with a good sense of humor."

She tried to smile.

"Have you been here before?" he asked, somewhere between a soft chuckle and a laugh.

She let out a sigh of relief, thankful for a new subject.

"No. Have you?" Maybe the night wouldn't turn into a school lesson after all.

He shook his head and smiled, letting his eyes reveal how happy he was they'd changed the subject. "This isn't the type of place I'd come to alone. I think they have a live jazz band that plays on weekends."

"They do. I heard they're pretty good."

"Then we'll have to come back to check them out."

Bobbi lowered her head and refolded the napkin on her lap, while shaking her head. He wasn't going to play with her emotions like she was some high school girl.

"Is that a no?" he asked.

"We're just classmates. We're not dating."

"But you can fix that. All you have to do is say, 'I'd love to check out the band.' "

She looked up and gave him a twisted smile.

"Or, maybe. Or, you'll think about it. Or, 'Quen, why don't you shut up and stop making a fool of yourself?' " He shook his head.

Bobbi bit the inside of her lower lip to keep from laughing.

Two waiters arrived with trays full of food. As they placed the food on the table, Quen and Bobbi stared at each other.

What was going on inside his head? He'd just asked her out on a real date—sort of. But she didn't know whether to take him seriously or not. Goose bumps traveled up her arms, while her stomach did little flip-flops. There was something between them as he held her gaze locked into his. It was a powerful look that confirmed he was serious.

The waiter said something before walking away, but they didn't seem to hear him.

Quen reached across the table for her hands. Her stomach contracted into a tight ball as she placed both hands on the table palms up and slowly slid them across the table to meet his. He wrapped his large hands around hers and gently turned them over. He gently stroked her knuckles. She looked down at them.

"Dear Lord, make us truly thankful for the food we are about to receive. . . ."

She looked up, surprised. He was saying the blessing. She'd foolishly thought he had something else in mind. Had she misconstrued the look in his eyes, and the gentle way he caressed the back of her hand with his thumb? It all seemed more intimate than preparing to say the blessing.

She closed her eyes and joined him in prayer. "Amen."

After the blessing, he held her hands a moment longer before he slowly let them go. She was emotionally off balance and didn't know what to do next. Something was starting between them; or was she imagining the whole thing?

Quen cut his steak in silence.

Bobbi picked up her fork and attempted to eat a shrimp.

"So, what do you do for fun? When you're not reviewing movies, or crushing men?" he asked before taking a bite.

She laughed. "Reviewing movies isn't the only thing I do at work. I'm also the secretary for the research department." She twirled her fork around before directing the shrimp into her mouth.

He nodded. "Now that sounds . . . interesting."

She laughed. "About as interesting as your computer business."

They shared a knowing smile.

"I guess that's why we're in school," he summed up. "I enjoy the computer business, but I want something more fulfilling and rewarding."

"Like working with prisoners? I can understand the

rewarding part of it, once you get someone back on their feet. But it seems more frustrating than fulfilling," she said.

"Prison takes so much from a man, that giving him his self-respect and dignity back is as fulfilling as it is rewarding. Just to know that I assisted with his ability to take care of his family again makes me feel proud. You start off helping one guy, and before you know it, you're organizing programs for the entire group. Haven't you ever gotten carried away about something like that?"

"Yeah, sort of In my first position, I helped a reporter research this story about a twenty-one-year-old man sentenced to life in prison for murder. The defense's position was that he was a victim of his environment."

Quen interrupted, nodding. "Boy, I can't tell you how many times I've heard that."

"In his case, it may have been true. His parents and his siblings have rotated through jail since he was a baby. So, his mother blamed herself for his crime. She said if only she'd gotten an education, she could have given her children a better start in life. Her own mother had subsequently spent time in jail, too. It's like this vicious cycle they don't know how to break."

Quen nodded and she knew he understood where she was coming from.

"That fall, I enrolled in college. I want to help as many families as I can break the cycle of destruction."

The waiter reappeared to refill their tea.

Quen waited for him to leave. "Well, it sounds like we're in the right field. We want to help people."

"Here, here." She held up her glass and took a sip. "If anything happens in my family, it's Bobbi to the rescue. I missed the first night of class because I had to pick my little brother up from jail."

"He got locked up?"

"Not actually. His friends did. He was lucky. I drove him back to Douglas the next morning and I'm sure my mother locked him up."

"What did they do, if you don't mind me asking?"

"The guys he rode with stole a car. Not while he was with them, thank God. That's what saved his butt."

"He was lucky."

"Yeah, that's what I told him. Marcus isn't a bad guy. He just lacks direction. He graduated from high school last year, then seemed to lose interest in just about everything."

"Is it just you and your little brother?"

"No, I've got an older sister, and she needs somebody to rescue her from herself. Hey, she could be your first counseling client."

Quen laughed. "Not unless she's an ex-convict. Sounds like you have an interesting family though. How about your parents?"

She looked down at the food she'd hardly eaten before choosing her words carefully. "It's just my mom, and she's a nurse's aide. She also makes jewelry."

"What kind?"

"Costume jewelry, out of precious stones. Her jewelry's beautiful, and she actually does pretty well selling it." She felt around her neck. "I usually wear a piece, but I didn't today. Before I left Douglas, I helped her lease space in two consignment shops in town, and start a small mail-order business."

"So, I bet you get your creative flair for dressing from your mother?"

She glanced down at herself. "What flair?"

"You always come to class looking good in whatever you wear. You put together outfits a lot of women can't carry off, but they look great on you."

"Thank you. I have to admit, I am a clothes hound. Something I definitely inherited from my mother. I used

to run all over the county with her from one consignment shop to another, looking for deals."

"Well, tell your mother she's got good taste."

"I'll do that, but now tell me a little something about
your family."

When he sat back, he looked to be in deep thought.
Bobbi wondered if he was contemplating how much to
reveal.

"Okay, let's see. I have an older sister, Evette, who
lives a few blocks from my mom, and they manage to
drive each other crazy every chance they get. My older
brother, Robert's in sales and he travels so much you'd
hardly know he lives in Chicago. Unfortunately, my father was killed by a drunk driver when I was in high
school."

"I'm sorry, that's terrible."

"Thanks. Yeah, it pretty much devastated us—
especially my mom. It also forced my brother and me
to grow up real quick."

The pain of an event that happened so long ago still
showed on Quen's face. Now that Bobbi had learned a
little about him, he seemed like a nice, sane guy. She
didn't mind buying his dinner after all. They carried on
with small talk as they finished their dinners.

"So, you never answered my question. What do you
like to do when you're not working?" Quen asked.

"Um." She laced her fingers together and rested her
hands on the table. "I like to read, and I love music. I'm
just not into jazz. And I do like a little risky adventure
every now and then."

Quen straightened up. "Oh, yeah? Don't tell me I've
got a little daredevil here. How risky?"

"Not very. I love roller coasters. I especially love to
go to amusement parks."

"Well, there you go, we have something else in com-
mon. I like amusement parks, too. I thought about

taking my daughter to Disney World for a couple of days, but we never made it."

"You have a daughter?"

He nodded. "Yeah, Kristy. She's thirteen and more interested in concerts right now than amusement parks."

"Oh, I don't blame her, I love concerts, too. Does she live here in Macon?"

"No. She's in Chicago with her mother."

"Oh." She wanted to know more, but didn't want to sound as if she were meddling.

He finished his tea and continued. "Her mother and I never married. But I'm crazy about Kristy, and I thank God for her everyday. How about you, any children?"

Bobbi straightened and shook her head. "I'm not quite ready for that much responsibility. However, it does feel like Marcus is my son sometimes."

"What's he, about seventeen?"

"Yeah, but he acts younger. He should be in college preparing for his future."

"So, why didn't you go to college after high school?" he asked.

"During high school, I kind of wanted to go to college, but I knew my mother didn't have the money, so I forgot about it. Nobody in my family went to college, so I wasn't all that interested. I figured I'd get a job at Brown and Williamson or GEICO and never leave Douglas. Then I started working at the paper and my aunt Alice offered to help me pay for school, so I started saving like crazy."

"You couldn't get a grant or scholarship?"

She shrugged. "I doubt that my grades were scholarship worthy, and I think I'd waited too late to apply for a grant."

They were interrupted when the waiter appeared with the bill. Bobbi picked up her purse to pay, but Quen pulled out a credit card and sat it on top of the bill.

"What are you doing? This is supposed to be payment for fixing my car."

He laughed. "I can't let you pay for dinner."

"Why not?"

"Because I'm a gentleman. So put your wallet away."

She narrowed her eyes, then shoved her wallet back into her purse. He'd just pulled the wool over her eyes. "You never intended to let me pay, did you?"

"Nope," he confirmed, shaking his head.

Grateful, but equally puzzled, she crossed her arms and twisted her lips. "I'm gonna have to watch out for you."

He winked. "You do that."

He tilted his head and gave her a suggestive smile that set her body on fire. What a big flirt.

Ten

Quen held the door for Bobbi as she stepped out of the restaurant. He was a gentleman—she had to give him credit for that—but he was also a mighty fine con artist.

"Where did you park?" he asked.

"Over there, along the fence."

He slowly walked along with her in the direction she'd pointed.

"I hope you enjoyed your meal," he said.

"I did. But you didn't have to con me to get me here."

"Oh, I didn't. When I suggested we come back sometime, you said no. Knowing that, I'm glad I did it."

"So, is that what you are, a con artist? You took advantage of a stranded woman."

He laughed. "Okay that was wrong of me, but I couldn't believe you were willing to pay for dinner in exchange for a jump. I had to go for it."

She shook her finger at him. "I knew dinner was too much to ask for. I just knew it."

He spun around to face her midway across the parking lot. "But I enjoyed your company, so thank you."

Because of his sudden about-face she'd stopped, and her purse strap fell from her shoulder. "Since I didn't have to pay—you're welcome."

Quen took a step closer and reached for her purse strap, lifting it to her shoulder again. He ran his hand down her shoulder, wanting to feel the softness of it, wanting to know if she felt as good as she looked. Were her lips as soft as he'd imagined? He needed to kiss her. He took a step even closer when a horn blew.

"God, you're about to get me hit," she said, as she stepped around him and continued to her car.

Quen waved his apology at the driver before following her. She unlocked her car door, and he held it open for her. "Want to grab a nightcap somewhere?" he asked.

She looked around, shaking her head. "Naw, I better go on in and get started on those websites tonight. I did promise you I'd have something by Saturday." She threw her purse over into the passenger seat and stood at the car door.

He didn't want her to leave. He wanted to hear her talk some more, preferably all night. "Are you sure I can't talk you into a walk or something? It's such a nice night. My shirt's not even sticking to my back from the usual humidity," he joked.

"Maybe another time."

"Okay, I'm gonna hold you to that."

She climbed inside and he closed the door. After she started the car, she rolled the window down. "See you Thursday night," she said, as if they were going on some sort of field trip.

"I won't sleep tonight in anticipation," he said as he smiled and back away from the car.

"You're a mess." She waved and backed out.

That night, Quen took the long way home. He wasn't in any hurry to lie in bed alone and unable to sleep. He'd liked hearing stories about Bobbi's family. Actually, he'd wanted her stories to fill his head so he'd have something to dream about, instead of being haunted by memories of his past that wouldn't let him have peace.

* * *

The next day at work, Bobbi ran around her office collecting money for a coworker's baby shower gift.

"Ms. Katherine, if anybody's looking for me I'll be right back." Bobbi shoved the envelope of money into her purse, stood, and moved around her desk. Katherine, an older woman from Great Britain, sat across from her.

"Where are you going?" Katherine asked.

"To get the stroller." She slung her purse onto her shoulder.

"Oh, yeah. Well, before you run out, stop and see Rich."

"What does he want?" Bobbi moaned.

"Something about your last review."

"Crap. I didn't like the movie, so he proceeded to tell me how much his wife loved it. I suggested he let her write the review."

"Better watch it. He might take you up on that. He lets her change something every time she comes in here."

Bobbi gave her a questioning look. "You think he'll do that?"

Katherine shrugged. "You did rather get the job by default. He hired you to be a secretary. You talked your way into the added reviewer position. A smart move, if I might add."

"That's because Mary moved and he needed some-body fast. I've been a lifesaver to him. Besides, my writing skills aren't bad."

"You write wonderful reviews. Believe it or not, most of the time I agree with you. At least you can tell no-body bribed you."

"Thanks, Katherine. I think that was a compliment. I'll stop by Rich's office on my way out." She pointed in the direction she was going before turning away.

"Okay, but keep your head up. Cheers."

Bobbi raised her chin in a slow nod. She didn't really understand Katherine most of the time. She could compliment you one minute, then insult you the next, without ever realizing she'd said anything wrong.

Six months ago, Bobbi had persuaded her boss to give her the reviewer position for a fraction of the salary he'd have to pay another full-time person. After reading a sampling of her reviews, he'd given her the job.

She knocked on her boss's door, and Rich looked up and waved her in.

"Katherine said you were looking for me."

"I was. Come on in and have a seat."

She walked over and sat in the chair across from his desk. A picture of his wife, Virginia, sat on the corner of his desk. Bobbi recalled how every time Mrs. Virginia Perlman came into the office, some new policy was issued. Who ran the paper, Rich or his wife?

Rich sat behind his desk, tapping an ink pen. He stopped and slid a few pieces of paper across his desk.

"We received a letter about your last review that I want to talk about."

She picked up the letter and started reading. They'd gotten letters about the reviews before, and he'd always set them on her desk. She read on to see what was so special about this one. By the end of the letter, she understood why he'd called her in. A reader had not only insulted her, but had attempted to rewrite all her reviews, claiming to have a better understanding of film.

"When did this come in?" she asked, not sure whether to laugh or cry.

"Yesterday."

"Everybody's a critic." She dropped the letter back on his desk.

"Yeah, well, I'd like to print that one."

"What?! You can't print that."

"Why not? It's a letter to the editor. We do print those.

Besides, we don't get enough letters about the reviews, and it might be controversial enough to create a buzz."

She took the letter as an insult, and couldn't believe he'd do this to her. "Rich, printing this letter is like the paper's saying any asshole can write a review." Maybe that's how he felt about her work—that anyone could do better?

"I think you're taking this the wrong way. It's no reflection on what you write; it's just bringing in our readers' perspective."

Bobbi snatched up the letter. "No reflection on me? What about this?" She read from the letter, " 'Why don't you hire a real critic who knows the difference between a bad movie and a good one? Your asinine reviews are causing good folks to waste money.' " She threw the letter back on Rich's desk and crossed her arms. "How would you take that?"

"Okay, so we won't print that part. I have editorial control, I can print as much or as little as I like. Besides, I'm more interested in the part where he rewrote your review. It's actually not that bad. I think we can get a little mileage out of printing a letter every Sunday from a reader."

"For what purpose?" Other than to humiliate her, she didn't get why.

"To create some controversy and sell more papers. What else?"

Bobbi shook her head. "I don't think it's a good idea. What other paper prints readers' reviews?"

"We'll be the first. Later, we can even solicit reviews from some of the college kids. Maybe even give them their own section."

None of this sounded like Rich. He'd always asked her to keep her reviews to a minimum, saying space was expensive. And now, he wanted to add a college section. It didn't make sense. "Whose idea was this?"

Rich picked the letter up from his desk and glanced

at it again, stalling. "Actually, my wife, Virginia, came up with the idea. She was in here and she read over the letter. But I tend to agree with her; I think it's a brilliant idea." He looked back up at Bobbi. "I think it'll add some spark to the review section."

Bobbi treaded lightly, not wanting to insult her boss, but wanting him to realize he was insulting her. "Rich, I think people read my reviews for an objective view of the picture. They want to know if it's the type of movie they'd like. I don't think they're looking for spark. If you have a reader whose opinion is contradictory to mine, like that one"—she pointed at the letter—"your readers might not know whether to see the movie or not."

He leaned back in his seat, crossing one arm over his stomach and stroking his chin with the other.

"I understand your wife liked this movie very much, as did the reader. I seem to be the only one who didn't care for it." She'd said to let his wife write the review, and he was going to do her one better: He'd let a reader write it.

He completely ignored her. "Well, we'll run it up the flagpole and see what everyone thinks. I'll get back to you on it."

She left Rich's office on fire. Ever since his wife had retired from her real estate business, she'd been coming around the paper suggesting all kinds of changes. Rumor had it that Rich was a weak man, but Bobbi hadn't witnessed that weakness before . . . until now.

After all the commotion of the morning, Bobbi settled down to work when an unexpected call came in.

"The *Telegraph,* Bobbi Cunningham."

"Is this the beautiful young lady that does the movie reviews?"

She recognized the voice, but figured she might be mistaken. "Who is this?"

"You don't recognize my voice since last night?"

"Quen?" she asked, unable to believe her ears.

"I hope you don't mind. I looked you up."

"No, I don't mind. I'm just surprised, that's all." Her heart beat in double time.

"I hope not unpleasantly?"

"No, not at all." He was the most pleasant thing that could happen to her today. "What can I do for you?"

"Well, I lucked into a pair of tickets to the Prince concert in Atlanta Friday night. Are you a fan?"

She shot up in her seat. "Yes, who isn't? I didn't know he was on tour."

"Yeah, well, you know he's famous for popping in without much notice. He used to do that all the time when I lived in Chicago."

"How did you luck into concert tickets?"

"One of my clients brought them, but now he has to leave town tomorrow and can't make it. So, what do you say? Want to go?"

"Yes," she answered without hesitation.

"Great. We can go over the details tomorrow night in class. I've gotta run, but I wanted to ask before you made any other plans."

"Okay, and thanks for the invite."

"Sure. See you tomorrow night."

She hung up and stared at the phone a few minutes. What happened? Had Quen just asked her out? Would it classify as a real date, or did he just need to find someone in a pinch? She'd agreed to ride to Atlanta with a man she hardly knew. What had she done? Was she losing her mind? She couldn't accept his invitation, and she had to let him know right away.

She searched through the telephone book for Quen Brooks, but couldn't find him listed. She hated to wait until Thursday night to back out on him. It didn't give him much time to find someone else, but now she didn't have a choice.

The minute she closed the phone book, ready to call it

a day, her phone rang again. She stared at it, wishing the *Telegraph* had caller ID. If she answered that, she could be there for another hour, if not longer. Then again, it could be Quen calling back. She picked up the phone.

"Hello."

"Bobbi, were you busy?"

It was her mother, Wilma, and from the tone of her voice, Bobbi suspected something was wrong.

"No, but I was just about to leave. What's wrong?"

"I'm glad I caught you. Marcus came in here last night barely able to stand up. He reeked of liquor and cigarette smoke. I hate to see that boy waste his life away, but I don't know what to do."

Bobbi slid the phone book across her desk. "What is Marcus doing to himself?" she asked, exasperated.

"I wish I knew. Sometimes I can't get him to come out of his bedroom, then other times he won't even come home. I've talked to him until I'm blue in the face."

"Where is he now?"

"He's asleep."

"He didn't have to work today?"

"Of course he did. They're going to fire him if he keeps missing days. We've got to get him some help."

We. There goes that word again, Bobbi thought. It was time for Bobbi to the rescue. "Do you still have that card the policeman gave me?"

"I've got it around here somewhere. I can find it."

"Good. Give them a call and see what type of services they provide, and how much it costs. Then call me back and let me know." Somehow they'd have to talk Marcus into going.

"I'll call tomorrow. But give Marcus a call later this afternoon. Try and talk to him. Maybe he'll tell you what's going on. He sure as hell won't talk to me. And Lord knows I've tried."

"I'll try him back later. Did Aunt Alice see him?"

"She heard him stumbling around in the kitchen."

"What did she say?"

"She tried to whip his butt." Wilma chuckled. "You should have seen her."

Bobbi snickered at the thought of her elderly aunt chasing a seventeen-year-old twice her size. "I can see her now, with that thin black belt she hits you with."

"She whacked him good a few times. But he was so out of it I don't think he even felt it. Now when he sobers up, Alice is going to wear him out. If she can catch him."

"Speaking of Aunt Alice, are you ready for her party?"

Wilma sighed. "I'll be ready when the Fourth of July gets here. Everybody's coming but your uncle James and his new wife. They'll be in Florida, or wherever she's talked him into taking her."

"Doesn't he know it's Aunt Alice's birthday?"

"He knows. We hold a party every year. It's that prissy wife of his who's keeping him away from the family. I warned him, that woman's out for his money."

"Mama, Uncle James doesn't have any money."

"Well, he's found some to take that little . . . woman to Florida with."

"I'm sure your party will be fine without him. In the meantime, let's take care of your son."

"Once Marcus leaves here I don't want him living on the street homeless. I want him to be able to take care of himself."

"So do I. I want that for the whole family. I'll call back later and talk to him, don't worry."

Wilma let out a heavy sigh. "I'll try not to. I wish your daddy had been here today to help with that boy. I just hope he gets here before it's too late."

There she goes talking crazy again, Bobbi thought.

"Mama, I'm gonna hang up now. Call if you want me to bring anything for the Fourth."

"Okay, but, Bobbi, when you come home, we have to sit down and talk. There's something I need to tell you."

Bobbi swallowed the lump in her throat.

Eleven

Bobbi arrived a few minutes late for Thursday night's class. She slipped in the back door and slid into the closest seat. Professor Jennings glanced at her out of the corner of his eye and smiled. Busted.

"Ms. Cunningham, I'm so glad you could join us," he shouted.

Embarrassed, she nodded and said, "Me too." Everyone laughed.

"We were just going around the room giving status reports on our projects. Tell us . . . how's the prison society doing?"

Her bucked eyes roamed the room for Quen or Monica. Quen wasn't there, but Monica sat in the front row, smiling back at her. Bobbi had to think fast.

"It's coming along fine. We've broken our topic down into manageable sections, and each member of the group has a section to research. In a few weeks, we'll combine our findings and visit the state prison before completing the written portion of the project." She took a deep breath.

Professor Jennings nodded and smiled. "Good. It sounds like you guys have gotten off to a good start. Everyone's involved, and you plan to visit the facility. I like that. Thank you."

His smile reminded her of the very first A she'd ever brought home. Her father's proud smile had had her walking around town like a celebrity for a whole week. She'd been his smart little princess, and it had felt good.

The professor searched the room for another victim. "Butler, tell us how the health care society's doing."

Bobbi released a heavy sigh and asked herself, *Why in the world did he call on me?* Monica would have gladly told him in detail how everything was going. And where was Quen? She needed to catch him tonight to back out of the Prince concert.

Over an hour into the lecture, Bobbi rummaged through her purse for a mint or stick of gum. She needed something to keep her awake. Moments later, she was saved when Professor Jennings stopped for the usual fifteen-minute break. She grabbed her wallet and made a beeline for the vending machine. A can of Mountain Dew should keep her up for the rest of the class.

On the way back, she turned the corner and ran right into Quen. She braced a hand against his chest as they collided.

"Excuse me," she quickly said.

"Hey, I was looking for you." He grabbed her shoulders to steady her.

She took a step back. "Hi, I was hoping you'd show up."

He smiled. "You were? What's up?"

"About tomorrow night—"

"There you are." Monica strutted over and joined them. "Hey, Bobbi, that was nice the way you summed up our project earlier. I'm so glad he called on you instead of me. I have no idea what I would have said."

"You would have done better than me, I'm sure. I just thought of something on the fly. I have no idea how it sounded."

"Trust me, you were good." Monica turned and smiled at Quen. "Hey, Quen."

"Hi, Monica." He gave her a single nod.

"Are we going to meet for a few minutes after class, or wait until Saturday?" Monica asked, glancing around the hall.

"Since Gregory's not here, let's wait until Saturday." Quen said.

Bobbi nodded her agreement. She hadn't seen Gregory since last week, and she doubted he'd done any of his research either.

"Well, Quen, I ran into a few things I'd like to talk to you about if you have a few minutes?"

His gaze darted from Monica to Bobbi.

Bobbi waved him off. "Go ahead, we can talk later." She left them in the hall and returned to the classroom.

By the time Monica and Quen walked in, Professor Jennings had resumed his lecture. Bobbi wondered what Monica had to say that she didn't want her to hear; after all, it was a group project. Whatever she found out, she'd have to share with the group at some point.

At the end of the lecture, Bobbi again found herself standing beside Quen and Monica. And again, they discussed their research project. In the back of Bobbi's mind, she wondered if something could be going on between them. Tired of standing around, she decided to leave and let him realize the next day that she wasn't going. She turned to walk away.

She'd gotten two steps away when someone grabbed her by the arm. She looked back to see Quen smiling at her.

"No, you don't. We need to talk." He pulled her closer to him.

The blank look on Monica's face made Bobbi grin. There was absolutely nothing between Bobbi and Quen, but she knew what was going on in that brain of Monica's. Monica quickly finished her conversation with Quen and said good night.

"What did you do that for?" Bobbi asked, hitting Quen in the arm.

"What?" he asked. He rubbed his arm, grinning.

"You pulled me over here like that. She probably thinks we're up to something other than our research."

"So what. I don't care what she thinks. I want to know where to pick you up tomorrow night."

Bobbi shifted her weight from one leg to the other. "You know, I tried to find your number in the phone book last night—"

"It's under my company name."

"Yeah, well, I didn't know your company's name, but I wanted to tell you I can't make it tomorrow night."

"Why not? Something come up?" he asked, with a perplexed expression on his face.

"No." She shrugged. "I just can't." She couldn't have him thinking she'd ride anywhere with anyone.

He crossed his arms and gave her a sidelong glance. They didn't speak as students passed by them, leaving for the night.

Quen finally nodded. "Okay, I understand. Either you don't like me, or you don't trust me. Maybe you think I'll drive you off somewhere and hurt you. After all, you don't really know me." He held a hand to his chest and arched his brows.

She sighed and shifted her weight back to the other leg.

"I mean, I could be a geek computer killer, or the next Jack the Ripper, or—"

"Okay, okay, you don't have to be so dramatic. I didn't mean all that. But you're right. I really don't know you. We've been in class together, what, three weeks?"

He nodded. "I understand, and that's hardly long enough to invite you to a concert. Maybe we could have gotten to know each other during the hour-long ride.

Yeah, I guess that's too much to ask. I'll just pitch the tickets. It's too late to find somebody else to give them to."

"You're going to throw away Prince tickets?" she asked, amazed.

He shrugged. "Why not? I'm not going by myself. And I don't know another Prince fan. So, I'll just—"

"Okay, I'll go," she yelled to stop him. She hoped she wouldn't one day live to regret this, but she couldn't let him commit what she considered to be a crime. Although she'd only seen Prince in concert once, she dreamed about him often, and considered herself a huge fan. Her CD collection could easily back up that statement.

Quen smiled broadly as his eyes raked over Bobbi. He tilted his head and winked at her. "Thank you. I promise you'll have a great time, and you'll make it back safely."

"I better. And for your information, it's almost a two-hour ride." She crossed her arms protectively and grinned at him.

"Not if I'm driving. So, what's your address?"

"Can I meet you somewhere?"

He shook his head, smiling. "Not this time."

Bobbi tried on several outfits before settling on a denim lace-up bustier and jeans to match. To set the outfit off, she added a pair of earrings and a necklace made from an earthy material that her mother had designed for her. The stones shimmered around her neck, making her feel sexy.

She kept peeking out her bedroom window, looking for Quen. The minute she saw him pull up, she hurried out the door. She'd told Roz she was going out with a friend, which wasn't a lie, but may have stretched the truth a bit. She didn't want her to meet Quen and start asking all types of questions she couldn't answer. Bobbi didn't consider this a formal date. They were just two classmates catching a concert together.

He'd gotten out of the car and was halfway up the walk by the time she descended the stairs. She almost stopped breathing when she saw him standing there in all white, and a pair of tortoiseshell sunglasses. His shirt had an embroidery design down the front, and he wore the sleeves rolled up. He took off his sunglasses and stopped. She had to bite her bottom lip to keep from cursing. She quickly grabbed the railing to keep from falling on her face.

"All set?" he asked, as he walked around to open her door.

"All set and psyched for a good concert." She followed him to the passenger side of his car.

"You look great. That's the flair I'm talking about. I like that outfit." He opened the passenger door.

She looked down at herself. "Thank you. You're looking pretty good yourself." To her, he looked better than any of the men in those fashion magazines Roz bought all the time. Again, she reminded herself they were just two buddies going to a concert.

"Thanks." He smiled and held her hand, helping her inside.

She stepped up into the Land Rover and looked around. Everything was nice and clean, like new. His school papers weren't all over the seat like hers. And he didn't have an extra pair of shoes lying on the floor.

Quen climbed in and started the car. "Well, Ms. Cunningham. Ready for the ride?"

"There you go, sounding like Professor Jennings again."

He popped a Prince CD in the system. "Don't tell me you see me as some sort of a father figure?"

"Oh, no." *Hell, no* was more like it.

"Good. Because that's not what I had in mind." He pulled out of her complex.

She crossed her arms. "And what did you have in mind?" she asked in a playful tone.

He shrugged and glanced at her. "I don't know. I thought maybe after this concert I could talk you into a couple more dinners, maybe a trip to the beach, Disney World, who knows. Whatever you're game for."

"And I thought this ride was for us to get to know each other better. My, you work fast, don't you?"

"Are you kidding? It took me three weeks to ask you out." He smiled. "And you only said yes because you're a big Prince fan."

"And don't forget the tickets were free," she pointed out, laughing.

He shook his head. "Oh, yeah. Thanks, I'd almost forgotten that all-important deciding factor."

"Yep." She took a deep breath and exhaled. "That's what did it for me."

He glanced at Bobbi. "You know, you're great for my ego."

"Whatever I can do to help," she added, smiling.

They rode up the interstate talking and laughing about everything. Bobbi shared more stories from her childhood growing up in Douglas, Georgia. Then as usual, their conversation came back to the one thing that brought them together: sociology.

"So, does this cut into your study time?"

"No, I'm all caught up. I read during my lunch break to get ahead. What I haven't done is started my research for the project."

"Don't tell me you still haven't checked out those websites?"

She shook her head. "There's only so many hours in a day, you know. I'll start in the morning." She crossed her arms and shifted in her seat.

"Okay, look, let's not go down that road again. Not tonight. I promised you a great time, and I don't want to ruin it by talking about school all night."

"You won't get an argument out of me on that one."

"Turn around." He reached over and touched her necklace.

Bobbi's hand went up protectively and brushed his as he pulled away.

"Now, I like that necklace. Is it one of your mom's?"

"Yes. She made this for my birthday last year. It's one of my favorites."

"When's your birthday?"

"July seventeenth."

"That's next month. Got any big plans?"

"No. It's a Wednesday night, so I think I'll just chill."

"There's no class that night. Why not celebrate?"

She shrugged. "Maybe I'll rent a movie."

Quen shook his head and returned his focus to the road. Several minutes passed as they rode, listening to the music.

"So, do you plan on hanging around Macon when you finish school?" he finally asked, breaking the silence.

"Yep, I'll be right here. Leaving Douglas for Macon was a good move, but I don't want to get too far away from my family."

"You guys are pretty close, aren't you?"

"Yeah. As much as they get on my nerves, I don't want to move too far away from them."

"That's nice to have such a close family. Do you think you might move back at some point?"

"No way. Growing up in such a small town was cool, but that's because I was so young. For adults, there isn't a thing to do but leave town for fun."

"So, you're in Macon for good?"

"Maybe not for good, but for now. I can run home for

birthdays and summer barbecues, and crises—which there seem to be a lot of in my family."

"Oh, come on, your family can't be that bad."

"They're not bad at all; just a bunch of characters. From my quirky cousins who still have plastic all over their furniture and plastic runners throughout the house, to my uncle who's in his sixties and married to a woman half his age and trying to have a baby. When one's not in trouble, the other one is. And vice versa."

"And you? When you get in trouble, who bails you out?"

"Me?" She pressed a hand to her chest. "I never get in trouble. I lead a very careful, stress-free life. I go to work, go to school, go to work, back to school, I'm plain boring Bobbi."

He chuckled. "I find that hard to believe. You appear to be a pretty colorful person to me. Maybe not as colorful as some of your family members."

"Are you kidding? You just don't know me. I play everything safe. This concert is the most exciting and spontaneous thing I've done all year, and it's June."

"Get out of here." He gave her a look of disbelief.

She shook her head. "This is about it."

"Well, now, we'll have to do something about that."

"Oh, right, you're going to take me on a tour of a prison for fun." She laughed.

"Somehow, I don't think you'd find that exciting."

"Well, I'm glad we agree on that."

Bobbi's excitement grew as Atlanta's skyline came into view. In a few minutes, she'd be sitting down watching Prince on stage . . . watching him with Quen.

One of her favorite songs came on and she turned up the volume. "I love that song." She couldn't help but dance around in her seat.

Quen liked it, too, and they sang "Gonna Be a Beautiful Night" as they rolled into Atlanta.

An hour later, they were in the Civic Center enjoying the show when Perry walked past, taking the seat next to Bobbi.

Twelve

Quen stood outside the ladies' room, waiting for Bobbi. Along with the concert tickets were passes to a private afterparty. When he surprised her with the passes, he thought she'd jump out of her seat, she was so excited.

"I'm back." Bobbi tapped him on the shoulder.

He turned around, as excited to see her now as when he'd picked her up. "Come on, let's find a seat." The majority of the crowd hadn't arrived yet, so plenty of tables were available.

"This is a nice club," she commented as they walked through the first floor.

"Yeah, it's nice." He looked around at the contemporary decor, with its cozy booths and tables lit by candlelight, and found them a spot. He pulled out Bobbi's seat for her.

"When do you think Prince will show up?" she asked, taking a seat.

He shrugged. "I don't know. It's his afterparty, so the whole band should be here soon." He pulled his chair close to hers and sat down.

"Man, I've never been to a private afterparty before. This is great. Do you think we'll get to meet him?"

She was so excited, he hated to burst her bubble. He slowly shook his head. "I don't think so. I've been to a couple of his afterparties before, and you usually get to mingle and talk with the band, but not Prince."

She shrugged in a nonchalant manner. "That's okay, I don't have to meet him. Just hanging out here at the afterparty is cool."

A woman in a low-waisted skirt and midriff top walked past with a tattoo of Prince on the small of her back. Bobbi arched a brow, turning to Quen. "Okay, now, I'm not that big of a fan."

"I certainly hope not," he remarked, laughing.

The waiter came by and took their drink orders. As he walked away, Quen caught sight of Perry heading for their table.

"Oh, no."

"What's wrong?" Bobbi asked.

He took a deep breath and let out a heavy sigh. "Nothing yet."

Perry and a woman several inches taller than he approached the table. Her platinum blond hair and baby blue eyes set against coffee-colored skin reminded him of a drag queen he'd seen in Chicago. A man's woman said a lot about his taste, Quen thought.

"Quen, I thought that was your Land Rover outside." Perry turned to the woman beside him and winked. "See, baby, I told you that was his ride." He extended his hand across the table to Quen.

Quen stood to shake his hand, forcing a smile. He hoped they were just stopping to say hello.

"Hey, you guys left before the end of the show and I didn't get to introduce you." Perry pushed his date forward. "Baby, this is Quen, one of my buddies down at the agency. Quen, this is my lady, Loretta."

They exchanged greetings, and Quen noticed she had a ring on every finger except her index finger. "It's nice to meet you, Loretta."

She smiled. "Nice to meet you, too."

"This is Bobbi. Bobbi, Perry and Loretta," Quen

rushed through the introductions. Everyone exchanged greetings.

"Yeah, Bobbi and I met earlier," Perry revealed.

Quen looked from Perry to Bobbi, surprised. She hadn't mentioned anything about knowing him.

"He introduced himself during the show. He told me he was a buddy of yours," Bobbi explained to Quen, who sat there staring at her.

"Come on, baby, let's sit here." Perry pulled out one of the extra chairs at the table and gestured to Quen. "You two don't mind, do you?" He glanced around the club. "I don't think there's another table in here."

"Naw, man, have a seat," Quen relented, trying to mask his disappointment.

Perry unbuttoned his suit coat and sat down before Loretta, forgetting to hold her seat for her. Instead, he leaned back, eyeing Bobbi.

Once everyone was seated, the waiter arrived with drinks. Perry ordered something for himself and Loretta.

"Has Prince shown up yet?" Loretta asked.

"Not yet," Bobbi answered, with a broad smile.

"So, how did you get afterparty tickets?" Quen couldn't help but ask.

"Man, you know me." Perry leaned back in his seat with his chest puffed out. "I got ways of getting in anywhere. You might say I know people."

"You don't say." Quen knew Perry was resourceful, and once a con always a con, no matter how reformed he said he was. An educated guess would be he'd slipped the doorman some money.

"Quen, I think somebody's coming," Bobbi said, on the edge of her seat, looking back at him.

He nodded, diverting his attention from Perry back to Bobbi. Something was on Perry's mind tonight. He could tell from the shiftiness in his gaze.

"See, there goes the band," she pointed out.

He glanced toward the entrance, where some of Prince's band members were strolling in. Bobbi looked like she was about to bubble over with delight. She wanted to walk over and meet them, and he wanted her to. Concerts he enjoyed, but he'd never been overexcited to meet any band, not the way Bobbi was. Okay, maybe he could get excited about Sade, he thought.

Loretta stood and asked Bobbi to come with her to meet the band. Bobbi turned to face Quen.

"Do you want to go?" she asked.

"Uh, not really," he admitted. "But you go ahead. I'll be right here."

"Okay, I'll be back."

They made their way through the crowd until Bobbi stood next to the guitar player. Quen was proud of himself. She'd remember this night for a long time.

"Say, Quen, I've been meaning to ask you something. What did you do before joining the agency?"

Quen picked up his drink and took a sip. He'd wanted to forget Perry was still there. "The same thing I do now, run my computer business."

"I mean before you moved to Macon." Perry leaned onto the table, resting his elbows. "You know, you're pretty good with those ex-cons. What type of training do you have? I know you didn't go through the agency's training, but I don't remember what you said you did?"

What the hell was he getting at? "I didn't say."

"Oh."

Perry had a snide grin on his face that Quen didn't like. "But I trained with the Salvation Army in Chicago. We had about twice as many men come through there as I see in Macon."

The waiter delivered Perry's drinks. After paying for them, he glanced around the club, nodding. "So, what are your qualifications?" he asked, without looking at Quen.

Unable to hide the irritation in his voice, Quen asked, "Why are you so interested in my qualifications? I'm out having a good time, not applying for a job."

Perry threw up his hands. "Hey, don't get angry. I didn't mean to upset you. I'm just making conversation."

Quen shook his head. "Naw, you're doing more than making conversation." Or was he just being paranoid? If he'd wanted Perry to know all about his past, he would have told him. "What's up?" he asked again.

Perry smiled. "Just curious."

Loretta and Bobbi returned to the table as the house music turned up and the dance floor filled in.

"You shouldn't be so curious," Quen snapped. "Haven't you heard the phrase *curiosity killed the cat?*"

"What cat?" Bobbi asked as she took her seat.

Quen shook his head. "Nothing," he responded while staring at Perry.

"Yeah, I was just talking to college man here about his Chicago days. So, what else did you do in Chicago?"

Quen shrugged. "Nothing worth talking about." He swallowed the last of his drink and turned to Bobbi. "Let's dance." Before she could answer, he took her hand and helped her up.

Once on the dance floor, his mind was off Perry and on Bobbi.

"Your buddy's something else," Bobbi leaned in to say while they danced.

Quen narrowed his eyes at her. "He's not my buddy. We volunteer at the same place, that's all."

She laughed. "I can tell he gets your goat."

"He what?" Quen asked, laughing.

"You know. He drives you crazy," she translated.

"Yeah, that among other things."

After a few fast tunes, Bobbi thanked Quen and turned to leave the dance floor. But a slow song came on and he reached out and grabbed her by the waist.

"Not so easy. Can I have this dance?"

"I don't slow dance so well." She shrugged an apology.

"That's okay, just follow my lead." He placed one hand on the small of her back, took her other hand, and whirled her around on the dance floor.

At first she was embarrassed. Who did he think they were, Ginger Rogers and Fred Astaire? Then her body relaxed as he guided her into a slow jam.

She hummed along with the song, trying to ignore the signals her body gave off. She dipped and swayed with him as the rhythm of the music took her to a pleasurable spot. He held her close and she leaned in, resting her head on his chest. She easily followed his lead, until she stepped on his toe.

Quen pulled back, looking down into her eyes. She tried not to laugh, but a giggle slipped out. "Sorry about that."

"That's okay. You can step on my feet anytime. We'll get this down before the night's over."

He pulled her closer, and their bodies molded together like two pieces of a puzzle—a perfect fit. By the second song, the temperature in the room had risen a few degrees and her body sizzled. They danced as if they'd been dancing together forever. Then she felt the heat of his breath on her neck.

"You're doing great. I hope you're having a good time?"

I'm enjoying myself right now. "I'm having a wonderful time, thank you."

"You're welcome. Since you said this is the highlight of your year so far, I want you to enjoy yourself. If you want anything else, just ask."

"What could you do to possibly make the night any better?"

He looked down at her, smiling. "Do you really want me to answer that?"

His voice grew huskier than before, while his grip tightened around her waist. She looked up into his eyes, knowing full well what he was alluding to. "Maybe you'd better not answer that. Not tonight."

He pulled her back into the folds of his arms.

For Christ's sake, she had to see this man two nights a week for the next month and a half. Every time she looked at him, she'd think about this dance. She'd think about the way he held her, pressing her against him, how his breath against her neck made her feel warm, all the way down between her legs. She was headed for some hot summer nights.

A buzz came over the room as people started leaving the dance floor. When Bobbi looked around, Prince had entered the room. His bodyguards escorted him to a table where she had a perfect view of him. Unfortunately, partygoers weren't allowed to enter his sanctuary.

"Do you wanna stop and go over there?" Quen asked.

"Do you think I can meet him?" she asked, with a little less enthusiasm than before.

Quen gave a little chuckle. "I doubt it, baby. Sorry, but an introduction didn't come with my tickets."

She laughed. "No, I'm fine," she said, laying her head back on his chest. She hoped the music never stopped. Her body responded to him so well she wanted to be nowhere but in his arms. At the moment, Prince really didn't matter anymore.

After three slow jams in a row, the DJ changed the tempo. Quen took Bobbi's hand and they left the dance floor.

"I see your buddy's gone," she pointed out.

Quen narrowed his eyes at her.

She laughed. "I'm just kidding. He's out there." She pointed to the dance floor.

Quen turned around and spotted them. Never one to let a good opportunity go by, he leaned over to Bobbi. "Let's get out of here."

"Don't you want to say bye to them?" she asked, smiling.

He stood up and took her hand. "All I want to do right now is be with you."

He held her hand all the way out of the club. Bobbi's heart pounded and her head spun all at the same time. The whole night had been such a rush, and it wasn't over. If he hadn't held her hand, she would have never made it to the car. Tonight, she saw Quen in a whole new light. He was definitely interested in more than their research project.

After opening the door for her, he climbed in and started the car. Without either of them saying a word, he turned the air conditioner up full blast. The warm air hit her arm, not helping at all. She lowered the window a little, unable to wait for the cool air.

"You hot?" he asked.

She nodded, fearful that if she spoke he'd know he was the reason for her sudden hot flash.

"I'm sorry. I hope you didn't mind leaving. I just had to get out of there."

"No. I was ready to go, too." She shook her head.

He sighed. "But you didn't get to see Prince that good."

"It doesn't matter. I saw enough. Thank you."

He searched her face as if he were looking for something in particular. He reached over and, with the tip of his index finger, stroked the mole on the bridge of her nose. "You're welcome."

His touch was so light and sensual she had to turn her

head and look out the window. When she looked back, he pulled out of the parking lot.

Before leaving town, Quen stopped at a gas station and bought two bottles of cold water. She placed her water in the cup holder, but noticed Quen held his between his legs. They discussed the concert all the way back to Macon.

When they pulled up to Bobbi's apartment, she looked down at her watch. "It's almost four in the morning?" She gasped.

"You sound as if you're never up this late."

"I'm not," she said, yawning. "It's about five hours past my bedtime."

He laughed. "Well, I hope you had a good time."

"Oh, I did. It was wonderful. The concert, the after-party," *the dance,* "everything. You'll have to thank whoever gave you those tickets for me."

"Oh, I'll be sure and do that." He nodded and reached into the backseat. "Don't forget this." He grabbed her program.

"Oh, thank you. I'd forgotten it already." She flipped through the program, with its colorful publicity pictures of Prince and his band, "Well, I've got about five hours of sleep before I have to get ready for the library."

"Yeah, it is Saturday." He then said, more as a statement than a question, "What are you doing tonight?"

She shrugged. "I don't know. Why, you got some more free tickets to something?"

He laughed. "Don't tell me that's what it takes to get you out again."

She bit her lip. "No, I'm just kidding."

He turned in his seat and leaned closer to Bobbi. "Well, think about it and let me know later. I'd like to take you to dinner."

She nodded okay. He climbed out of the car and came around to open her door. Like the gentleman he was, he held her hand as she stepped down from the car. She took a step to walk away and he touched her arm.

"Was this still the most exciting night you've had this year so far?"

"Most definitely."

He smiled. "That's good. Now, I hope you'll let me top tonight, because I know I can."

"Are you sure?" she asked, placing a hand on her hip as her lips turned up into a generous smile.

He looked deep into her eyes. "Just as sure as I am about wanting to kiss you right now."

His declaration knocked the wind out of her. She tried to breathe, but she couldn't. Did he just say he wanted to kiss her? And was she going to play Miss Innocent and ignore him? Not tonight.

"So, what's stopping you?" She barely recognized her own ragged voice. Her lungs opened wide as she caught her breath.

He closed the car door and took a step closer to her. With his index finger, he slowly raised her chin and planted a soft kiss on her lips. She kept her eyes closed, hoping, praying there was more. His lips touched hers again for a more passionate kiss as their heads tilted in opposite directions. Her heart pounded so hard she thought it would leap from her chest.

He took another step, which forced her to back against the car. His hand slipped around the small of her back while his kiss grew deeper and hotter. This time Bobbi opened her mouth and her heart to him.

Quen stepped back, taking a deep breath and licking his lips. "I'll see you tomorrow."

Stupefied, Bobbi stood there, staring at his nose, his eyes, his lips, and his beautiful smooth chocolate skin glowing under the streetlight, again like a fine piece of Godiva chocolate. She fought the urge to reach out and touch his lips. What had he done to her? What was she doing standing under a streetlight at four in the morning, wanting a man she'd known for only three weeks?

He took her by the hand and walked her to the steps.

Bobbi pointed to her door on the second floor. "I'm just right there."

"Okay. Get some sleep. I'll see you later."

"Good night."

He backed away and stood by his car until she closed the door. She pulled back the curtain and watched him drive away.

"Wow, Bobbi, who was that?"

She jumped and turned around to see Roz standing in the hallway in her pajamas.

Bobbi's hand went over her chest and her knees buckled as she found the closest seat on the armrest of the couch. "Girl, you scared me to death."

Roz flipped on the hall light. "Good, that's what you get for not telling me about your date. Who was that good-looking brother you were standing out there with?"

"Just a guy in my class." Bobbi caught her breath.

"I saw you all kissing under the streetlight, so don't give me that just-a-guy line. I know you better than that; you don't just hand out kisses."

Bobbi slid off the armrest and fell onto the couch. "Roz, I think I'm falling in love."

Thirteen

Bobbi twisted and turned for hours, getting all tangled up in her sheets. She kicked the comforter off the bed and pushed the sheet down between her legs. Every night she dreamed of a life with some handsome celebrity as they traveled to unbelievable destinations around the world, made love in exotic places, and shared their deepest darkest secrets. This morning, the celebrity in her dream had been Quen.

She finally kicked the sheet off the bed and rolled over onto her back. Again she'd slept with her mouth open, because her throat was dry as sandpaper. She pulled at her soaking wet gown. *Who can sleep?* she thought as she climbed out of bed and shuffled sleepily into the kitchen for a glass of water.

Later this morning she'd meet Quen at the library, but what would she say to him? After that electrifying kiss last night he was so quiet and cool, while her body trembled like it was ten degrees out instead of a hot and humid ninety. He'd always seemed so confident and sure of himself, which scared her. Everything in his life was probably so perfect, while her life wasn't perfect by any means. He'd probably never let his AAA lapse. He owned his own home, his own business, and he probably even had a financial portfolio, while all she had was a one-thousand-dollar certificate of deposit, and three hundred dollars to her name. She'd never met a man like

Quen before. He was solid as a rock, in more ways than one.

The chill of the air conditioner caught up with her, and she hurried back into her bedroom to change pajamas. She opened her blinds as the morning sun began to rise. Since she couldn't sleep, she decided to turn her computer on and prepare herself for their library session. While she waited for the computer to boot up, she picked up her tablet and looked for the websites Quen had given her.

The first thing she ran across was the handout Quen had given them on prisoners and family communication. She picked up the paper and leaned back in her seat. He'd outlined how visitation improved the prison environment, and gave the inmate something to look forward to. Out of curiosity, she kept reading.

Quen rolled over in bed, kicking off the covers. He had a vision of his hands around a man's neck, while he kneeled over him, squeezing the life out of him. The man's bulging eyes gave Quen great satisfaction. All Quen needed to do was hold on a few seconds longer, and the man wouldn't be able to harm anyone ever again.

The vision was so real, Quen jumped up from bed gasping for air, then looked down at his trembling hands. Could he be capable of something so horrible? Could he really end a man's life with his bare hands? He shook his head, not wanting to think about it again.

He ran a shaky hand across his face and looked over at the bedside clock. Only two hours had passed since he'd climbed into bed, but he wasn't about to return to that hellish nightmare. He threw his legs off the side of the bed and sat there for a few minutes. After another sleepless night, he climbed out of bed and walked into the bathroom, where he tried to wash the nightmare away by running a cold washcloth over his face. He held the cloth there until every muscle in his body had relaxed . . . all except for one, and a cold cloth wasn't the answer.

By the time Bobbi walked into the library at eleven o'clock on the nose Saturday morning, Quen and Monica were already sitting at their usual table. Bobbi joined them, eager to present what she'd found in her research.

"Well, look who's on time." Quen pointed at his watch as Bobbi sat down. "How you doing?" he asked.

Their eyes met and the fluttering inside her stomach magnified tenfold. Suddenly, she could still taste his lips and smell his cologne, as if they were still kissing.

"I'm here, but that's about it," she said, tossing her tablet on the table. She forced herself to act as normal as possible. After all, it was just a kiss, she told herself. "And I checked out those websites you gave me, so I've got some questions for ya."

He leaned back with an astonished, but pleased, look on his face. "I'm impressed."

Considering the early hour they'd come in, she was impressed with herself as well.

She smiled. "You may want to hold off judgment until you hear my questions. I barely scratched the surface of what you gave me, but I have something nonetheless."

"Well, it looks like we're off to a good start," Monica said. "I've got a lot of good questions we can use, too." She turned to Quen. "Have you spoken to Gregory?"

"Not recently, but he did say he'd be here."

"If he doesn't show up, maybe we should divvy up his portion of the research. We don't want to be blindsided in case he's not working on it. I'd like to know everything I need to research before I delve too far into things," Monica added.

Quen pointed toward the stairs to the right of them. "Speak of the devil."

Bobbi and Monica turned to see Gregory coming down the stairs, scanning the room. Monica stood and waved until she caught his attention.

He moseyed over. "Hey, there you are. I've been looking for you guys all over." He pulled out the chair next to Bobbi and sat down.

"We're sitting directly across from the entrance. How could you have missed us?" Quen asked.

"Ah, man, I parked over on the side and came in that door. This is a big library, you know."

Quen, Bobbi, and Monica shared a knowing smile.

"Okay, what do you say we get started?" Quen took the lead as usual.

The next hour was spent discussing their research findings, and formulating some tough questions for prison officials to answer regarding transitioning ex-convicts back into society.

After that hour passed, Monica requested a bathroom break. Gregory used the break to step outside for a smoke. Quen and Bobbi used it to get caught up.

"Did you get any sleep last night?" Quen asked.

"A little. How about you?"

He shook his head. "My usual. I'm surprised you got up to surf the Web this morning. I looked for you to walk in here late crying you'd overslept."

She frowned. "I'm disappointed that you think I can't hang and get my work done, too. For your information, I couldn't sleep, so I figured I'd better get started. After all, I did tell you I'd have something by Saturday."

He smiled. "That you did." He hesitated a moment, then asked, "Did you think about what I asked you last night?"

She'd thought about how he'd kissed her but anything

beyond that was a blur. "I'm sorry, what did you ask me?"

"If you're not busy tonight, I'd like to take you to dinner, and then to the Comedy Zone."

"You tricked me into dinner once." She narrowed her eyes at him, smiling.

"Okay, shoot me for that one. But how about you let me make it up to you tonight?"

She hesitated, tapping her index finger against her lower lip. If she accepted, it would surely signify an interest on her part. "But I haven't been to the Comedy Zone in a long time," she said aloud.

"So that's a yes?"

She nodded. "It might be fun." Then she wondered why she hadn't kept that speculation to herself.

Monica and Gregory returned, and the group resumed business. Minutes later, Bobbi glanced up at Quen, and he winked at her. She bit her inside jaw and dropped her head so the others wouldn't know she was blushing all over the place. What did he want from her—a good time, a one-night stand, or a relationship? The latter was the only thing she would ever consider.

A ringing interrupted them and everyone reached for their cell phones. Bobbi then realized the battle cry was her phone, and pulled it from her purse.

"Excuse me," she said before answering, "hello."

"Bobbi, it's Mama. Gigi's in jail."

"What!" She jumped up from her seat.

"I just got a call from her. She's here in jail."

"I thought she went back to Chicago. What happened?" She grabbed her purse and made several attempts to pull it onto her shoulder.

"I don't know yet. She was too hysterical to tell me. I'm going to get her now. Can you come home?"

"I'm on my way." She hung up the phone and turned

to her society members. "I'm sorry, guys, I have an emergency and I need to leave."

"Are you going to be okay?" Quen stood and asked.

"Yeah, I'll be fine. I just need to run to Douglas."

"Want me to come with you?" he offered.

Touched by the concerned look on his face, she smiled. "Thank you, but I'll be okay. I'm sorry about leaving in the middle of things."

"You go ahead and take care of your business. We understand," Monica said.

"Here, take this." Quen ripped a sheet of paper from his tablet, wrote down something, and handed it to Bobbi.

She looked at his name and phone number on the page.

"Give me a call tonight so I'll know you're okay."

She folded the paper and shoved it into her pants pocket. "Okay. I'll see you all Monday night."

Bobbi hurried out of the library and to her car. She drove to her apartment and threw some clothes into an overnight bag. After explaining as much as she could to Roz, she took off.

The first thing Bobbi noticed was her uncle James's car in her mother's driveway. She pulled in alongside him. She'd called from the highway and found out her mother had gone to pick up Gigi, but her aunt didn't have any details.

Anyone who visited her mother more than once knew to use the back entrance, and not the front. Bobbi couldn't remember the last time the front door had been opened. She walked around back where her aunt Alice stood in the garden, watering the flowers. The garden was her favorite place, and the one thing Wilma and Alice enjoyed together.

"I knew you'd come," Alice said as if talking to the plants as Bobbi approached. "I told her not to call you, but I knew she would. Wilma can't handle anything by herself." She fanned the water hose toward another part of the flower bed without looking up.

Bobbi crossed the yard and walked over to her aunt, planting a kiss on her cheek. "It's good to see you, too, Aunt Alice. How's Gi?"

"She's fine, I guess. They're inside. I came out here to get some fresh air. Too much hot stuffy air in there."

Alice didn't like James, just as she didn't care for Bobbi's father, Mark Cunningham. "Well, I'm going to run inside and see how she's doing. Did Mama tell you what she got locked up for?"

Alice shook her head. "It's a shame what yo' daddy done to them kids. First Marcus, and now Glenda. He's a bad influence." She turned to acknowledge Bobbi for the first time since she'd gotten out of the car. "I tried to tell Wilma that, but she wouldn't listen to me. She claims that man was all she ever had and wanted." Alice shook her head. "You ever heard such foolishness?"

Bobbi wanted to say it was romantic, but she knew her aunt would say she was being foolish, too. Instead, she agreed with her. "Yeah, crazy, isn't it?" She turned and followed the walkway up to the house.

"You're my favorite, you know."

Bobbi stopped and looked back over her shoulder. She'd always thought as much. She'd just never heard her aunt say it before. They were kindred spirits.

"You remind me of myself when I was young. You don't take no stuff from nobody; you're tougher than yo' mama."

Bobbi looked at the long gray braid falling down her aunt's back. She was in a talkative mood this evening. "Okay, Auntie, I'm gonna go in right now. Don't stay out here too long, it's hot."

Alice continued watering the flowers and humming her favorite gospel tune. Bobbi shook her head, smiling, and continued up the walk. She'd give anything to know what her aunt had been like when she was young.

The minute she stepped into the kitchen, she realized why Alice had chosen to retreat to the garden. Loud voices were flying all over the room. Her mother was screaming at Gigi, and in return Gigi screamed back. Her uncle James paced around the kitchen on the phone, with a finger in his opposite ear.

"Bobbi, so glad you could make it."

She jumped when a hand slapped her on the back. She turned to find Marcus with a broad smile plastered on his face. The kitchen scene delighted him, to say the least.

"Marcus, what's going on?" she asked.

"Well, for starters, Gi here seems to be running with the wrong crowd. Looks like they got caught smoking a little"—he held two fingers to his lips and inhaled—"dope on the way to town."

Bobbi gave a startled gasp. She'd never known her sister to do drugs. Gigi was into men, not drugs. Wilma and Gigi stopped when they heard her.

Marcus continued. "And now Gi's trying to convince Mama she's not a pothead."

At the sight of Bobbi, Gigi stomped over to the kitchen table and reached into her purse. She fished out a cigarette and lit it. "And for the last time, I wasn't smoking dope. This is all I had, right here." She waved her cigarette through the air.

Wilma stood in the middle of the room with her hands on her hips, glaring at Marcus.

James hung up the phone and crossed the kitchen to greet Bobbi. "How you doin', baby?" He kissed her on the cheek.

"I'm fine, Uncle James."

He glanced from Gigi to Marcus. "Don't you kids

know nothing else"—he shook his head as if to say *too bad*—"but drugs? When I was a boy we didn't mess with that stuff."

"Shut up, James. These are *my* kids you're talking to, and you're *not* their daddy."

Bobbi looked at the keep-your-mouth-shut expression her mother had on her face as she glared at her younger brother.

"I think I better make myself scarce." Marcus walked around Bobbi and past everyone into another part of the house.

James pointed a shaking finger at Wilma. "Next time you need help, don't call me. As a matter of fact, I don't want you or that crazy woman outside to ever call me again." He stormed past Bobbi and out the back door.

Gigi laughed before blowing out a puff of smoke. "Ew, he's mad at you now."

"So what? That makes it three times this year. James can't stay mad at us. Let him run home to his little wife. That was probably her on the phone bad-mouthing me."

Bobbi closed the back door with a loud thud. "Okay, who's gonna tell me what happened?" She looked from her mother to Gigi.

Fourteen

Gigi repeated the story she'd told her mother and uncle when they'd picked her up from jail.

"I met Jeff and Denise through Roger. They were on their way to Florida with a couple other folks. They've got this big gig or something starting next week. I told them I had to get to Georgia, so they offered to drop me off in Douglas. No big deal. Since nobody pulled out any drugs until after we hit Georgia, I had no idea any of them smoked dope."

Wilma reared back in her seat, crossing her arms. "Huh, musicians and you didn't know they smoked dope?" she huffed.

Gigi rolled her eyes and took a deep breath. "Not all musicians are drug addicts, Mama. Roger doesn't do drugs. He just can't keep his penis in his pants."

Wilma shot up from her seat. "I wish you wouldn't talk like that. You say whatever's on your mind, good or bad. Think before you talk next time, girl, especially when you're talking to your mother." She walked over to the kitchen sink.

"Yes, ma'am," Gigi said with a sigh, looking toward the ceiling.

Bobbi couldn't believe Gigi's misfortune. She stayed in some type of trouble, but never anything involving drugs. This sounded like one of Marcus's stunts. "Let her finish, Mama."

"That's about it. After we crossed over into Georgia, I fell asleep. When I woke up, they were smoking pot. A few minutes later, we got pulled over and the cops found the drugs, but nobody owned up to it. I told the cop I had nothing to do with it, but of course he didn't believe me, just like you guys don't."

"I'm not saying I don't believe you' Wilma said from the sink as she washed the dishes. "I just don't understand how you'd wind up in a situation like that. You shouldn't ride nowhere with people you don't know. Why didn't you call me? We'd have found you a way home."

"I just wanted to get out of Chicago as fast as I could." Gigi slumped in her seat, crossing her arms.

"Did they charge you with anything?" Bobbi asked, still wanting more details.

Gigi shook her head. "Jeff finally confessed that the drugs were his, so they let us go. Come to find out, they only found two joints. So he was fined and he has to come back to court."

Bobbi had a better picture now, and the situation didn't seem as serious as she'd first thought. "You didn't have to be bailed out?" she asked.

Gigi threw her head back and ran her hands through her long straight red mane. "Nope."

"I can't believe they even carried you to jail for such a small amount. Who was the cop?"

Gigi shrugged. "Nobody I know, or I wouldn't have been down there, that's for sure."

"Well, you sure scared me calling here crying like they'd locked you up and threw away the key," Wilma recounted.

"Shoot, I've never been in jail before. I was scared. Mama, you're not going to tell Daddy, are you?" Gigi asked, sounding like a little girl in her mother's kitchen sitting in a high chair.

Bobbi recoiled at the mention of their father. What

did he have to do with this? He couldn't continue to be a father from prison.

Wilma turned and looked at her girls, twisting her lips as she contemplated what to say. "I'm not sure. If we don't, he'll eventually find out once he's here."

"But I don't want him to think I was doing drugs," Gigi protested.

"Then you'd better explain it to him yourself. He's going to be upset."

Bobbi snickered. "By the time he gets out, what can he be upset about? That they didn't buy the drugs from him?"

Wilma shot Bobbi a glare. "Don't you dare talk about your father that way. He committed a crime, and he's paying for it. But you remember, he was trying to put food on the table to feed his children when he got locked up."

"And because of that I'm not supposed to be ashamed? What happened to getting a regular job like everybody else's father? Gi's always worried about pleasing Daddy, when he never thought enough about us not to do what he did." Bobbi unloaded something that had been bothering her for years.

"Honey, you're trying to please him, too, in your own way, you just don't realize it. He always wanted you all to go to college and get a good education, just like you're doing now," Wilma informed her.

"But I'm not doing it for him. I'm doing it for me." Bobbi said with her chest out, proud of herself.

Wilma turned and smiled at her. "You're doing it. That's all that matters."

Bobbi looked down at the table, thinking back, but she couldn't remember one time when her father mentioned anything about college. When he'd left home, she'd been in junior high school, not even thinking about college.

"Bobbi, if you talked to Daddy sometimes, you'd see

he's a changed man. He knows what he did was wrong," Gigi added.

They were being so naive it was making Bobbi mad. "Yeah, I'm sure he's changed. He's had a long time to think about how he robbed us."

Wilma dropped a dish back into the soapy water with a splash. "Robbed you of what?" she shouted. "Did you grow up hungry? Did you not have a roof over your head and shoes on your feet?"

Bobbi slowly shook her head. She hadn't meant to imply that her mother hadn't done a good job. She'd done the best she could with her family's help. Bobbi had never realized their homemade dresses were all her mother could afford. She'd grown up thinking her mother was going to be a big fashion designer and they were wearing one-of-a-kind outfits, which she and Gigi loved.

"I'm sick of everybody putting Mark down. He's still the father of this family. If you went with us to visit sometimes, maybe you wouldn't feel that way. But you're a grown woman, and I can't make you go." She took her hands out of the dishwater and dried them off.

"I need to lay down. One of you finish these dishes for me." She threw the towel on the kitchen counter and stormed out of the room.

Bobbi and Gigi sat at the table, looking at each other for a few minutes. Ashamed of how she'd made her mother feel, Bobbi wished she could take everything back. The house was quiet, except for the faint sound of the television coming from the den. Marcus had evidently planted himself there, and she wanted to join him, maybe watch a little television and forget this whole conversation. But Gigi would say she was avoiding the issue again if she walked out.

"I'll fix something to eat if you finish up the dishes," Bobbi finally offered.

"Deal," Gigi said.

Bobbi found chicken legs in the refrigerator. "Fried chicken sound good?" she asked.

Gigi shrugged. "Yeah, whatever. I'm starved."

After Bobbi washed the chicken in one of the double sinks, Gigi worked on the dishes.

Bobbi seasoned the chicken and heated the skillet. "Okay, now tell me what really happened," she asked, turning to Gigi.

"What do you mean? I already told you." Standing at the sink with suds up to her elbows, she stared at Bobbi.

"If those folks were on their way to Florida, what made them offer to drop you off in Douglas?" she asked, sounding a bit skeptical.

"I guess they needed the extra gas money. The trip cost me fifty dollars."

"So, what happened between you and Roger? I thought you guys had patched things up?"

"No, we broke up instead. He's still screwing around."

"I guess you didn't get the job at *Vibe,* either?" Bobbi asked as she dropped the chicken in the skillet.

Gigi shook her head. "He was more interested in me than my photographs. And I ain't got time for no horny old man with no money."

Bobbi wondered if there couldn't have been a mistake when they were younger; she felt like the older sister. "Girl, you need to settle down somewhere before you really do get into trouble."

"I think I'm gonna stay here for a while this time." She shook the suds off and dried her hands before walking over to the kitchen table and picking up her cigarette.

"Besides, I've got something else in the works, but I

can't talk about this one, because I don't want to jinx myself."

The back door opened and Alice walked in, carrying a basket full of flowers and breathing heavily. "Lord, it's hot out there." She stood inside the door, staring at Gigi.

Once Gigi noticed her, she snuffed her cigarette out and reached for the basket. "Here, let me help you with these."

Alice blew as if she'd been working in the fields somewhere all day. "Now take those into the sunroom. I'm gonna put some vases together—brighten this place up a bit." She pulled out a chair and slowly sat down at the kitchen table. "Honey, hand me a glass of water."

"Yes, ma'am." Bobbi fixed the water while Gigi walked out with the basket.

"I love the way you always fill the house with fresh flowers," Bobbi said as she turned the chicken over. Afterward, she joined her aunt at the kitchen table.

"Did you girls talk about everything?" Alice asked.

"Yeah, kind of." Bobbi shrugged. "It sounds like a case of being in the wrong place at the wrong time, so she says."

"When is that girl ever in the right place? That boy in Chicago done put her out and she's got no place else to go. She don't have her own place, so now she's talking 'bout moving back in here. But that won't last. She's done got too big for Douglas. She won't be here for more than a couple of weeks."

"I'll give her one week," Bobbi added.

After dinner, Bobbi settled into her old room, now the craft room with an added futon. When she took off her pants, she felt something in the pocket. She pulled out a piece of paper and remembered Quen had given her his number. The thought of calling him made her nervous.

She hesitated a moment, then walked over and picked up the phone. She at least needed to let him know she was okay.

He answered on the second ring. "Hello."

"Hi, Quen, it's Bobbi."

"Bobbi, I thought you'd forgotten about me. Are you okay?"

"Yeah, I'm fine. My sister had just gotten into a little trouble, that's all." The sound of his voice made her stomach quiver.

"Bobbi to the rescue, right?"

She laughed. "They didn't actually need me this time. How'd the project go?"

"We wrapped up a little after you left. Monica's gonna email everybody a set of the questions we settled on. When do you think you'll be back?"

"Tomorrow. Everything here's under control." *For the moment anyway,* she thought.

"I'm glad to hear that. So, we can move our date for the Comedy Zone to tomorrow night?"

Our date. She liked the sound of that. "Sure, I guess so."

"You don't sound too positive. What's wrong?"

"I don't know. I feel like we're moving from classmates to . . . I don't know what we're moving to."

"Bobbi, from the day I met you I wanted to be more than just a classmate. I think you knew that. We may have gotten off to a rocky start, but some of the best relationships start off like that."

"Relationship! You're kind of jumping the gun, aren't you?"

He laughed. "No, I'm just using my clairvoyant powers and looking into the future. We're going to have one of the world's greatest romances. I can see us now."

She fell back on the bed, laughing. "That was hilarious. I bet you crack yourself up sometimes."

"All jokes aside, I want to get to know you better. I want to share more nights like we had Friday night."

Friday night was like something out of a romantic movie, she thought. Things like that didn't happen to her. She didn't think they happened to anyone. Most of her dates ended at some dive in town after somebody had too much beer and started a fight. "We did have a good time, didn't we?"

"Yes. Just like we're going to have tomorrow night, right?"

The sound of someone picking up the phone prevented her from answering.

"I'm on the phone," Bobbi said, irritated.

"Sorry. Is this Roz?" Gigi asked.

"No, it's not Roz," Quen spoke up.

"Ew, what a nice sexy voice. Who is this?"

"Gi, hang up." Bobbi sat straight up.

"Okay, okay, sorry." She hung up.

Bobbi let out a deep breath. "Sorry about that."

"Was that your sister?"

"Yeah." She didn't want to tell him about the morning's incident. "I better get off here. Looks like she needs to use the phone."

"You never answered me."

She stood from the bed and walked over to the dresser. She was afraid to answer him. Afraid of what might happen if she said yes, and if she said no. Then again, here was this incredibly good-looking man on the other end of the phone, wanting to spend time with her.

"You promise me a good time like Friday night?"

"Even better."

"Then I'll see you tomorrow."

Back in Macon, Bobbi walked into her bedroom Sunday afternoon, dropped her overnight bag, picked up the

phone, and dialed Quen. The urgency of her actions was
so foreign to her, she had to laugh. It felt good.

"I'm glad you made it back safe, and I hope you're
hungry," he remarked.

"I'm starved. Although I made fried apples, biscuits,
and country ham for breakfast."

"Man-o-man, sorry I missed that. Sounds like you've
got some cooking skills."

"Let's just say I know my way around the kitchen."
She wasn't ready for him to invite himself over for dinner like most men did.

"Well, breakfast happens to be my specialty. You'll
have to try my pancakes one morning. They'll melt in
your mouth."

She liked that he invited her over. God, she thought,
he was looking better and better every day. Where did
this guy come from? "Sounds like a breakfast date."

"Who knows, one date might run into another," he
added.

"Why, Mr. Brooks, if you ain't about the sneakiest
man I ever met. Always thinking ahead, aren't you?" she
said in her country girl voice.

"Hey, I'm a thinking man. And right now I'm thinking about tonight. So, I'll pick you up at five if that's not
too early?"

Bobbi thought for a moment. Roz was home today
and she'd definitely see Quen if he came by this time.
She didn't know if she was ready for her to meet him
until she knew he'd be around for a while.

"Can I meet you there?" she asked.

He sighed. "Okay, what's up with you always wanting
to meet me somewhere? You don't have a man hiding up
in that apartment, do you?"

"No, don't be silly." Although she felt like she was the
one being silly. If something was going to develop between them, Roz would have to meet him at some point.

"Then I'll pick you up at five. We'll eat first, then check out the Comedy Zone. Is that cool?"

She gave in. "Yes. It sounds good. I'll be ready."

"Great, and I'm looking forward to meeting your roommate."

Bobbi hesitated, then took a deep breath. "Okay."

Several hours later, Bobbi and Quen were laughing and talking over dinner.

"Too bad I didn't get to meet your roommate."

She tried to look disappointed. "Yeah, I'm sorry, too. She went to evening service."

"Maybe next time." He gave her a skeptical smile, tilting his head.

She nodded. "Why are you so eager to meet my roommate? I haven't met anyone you know. Other than Perry," she managed to say with a straight face, knowing how Quen felt about him.

"I want to make sure your roommate is a woman and not a man."

Her jaw dropped. "Now, if I lived with a man, don't you think I would have told you? As a matter of fact, I wouldn't be here with you."

He shrugged. "Maybe, maybe not. The last woman I dated lived with her boyfriend, but she didn't tell me until after about the third date."

"That's wild. What did you do?"

"I stopped seeing her. I don't get involved with other men's women. Call me old-fashioned, but I like to have my own woman. I never was good at sharing."

"So, you're not down with OPP?" She laughed at herself, while he appeared jolted by her words.

His laughter followed hers. "Definitely not. I'm not that kind of brother. And you don't strike me as the kind of woman who listens to Naughty by Nature CDs."

"I'm sorry, but I've always wanted to say that. I'm not so much a fan, but my brother is." She kept laughing.

He nodded, grinning. "I thought so. I bet you've been waiting for an opportunity to use that line for a long time."

Her laughter slowly subsided. "You just don't know how long. But trust me, Roz is a woman. I wouldn't do you like that."

"That's good. Because I like you."

"You do?" The sexy way he bit his bottom lip and smiled at her sent flutters through her stomach.

"Uh-huh."

She leaned back in her seat and suggestively crossed her legs. "But you don't even know me."

He leaned forward, resting his forearm on the table. "I know you better than you think. You're from Douglas, Georgia. You've worked for the *Telegraph* for at least seven years as a reviewer-slash-secretary. You have a sister and a brother, who drive you crazy. Your great-aunt lives with your mother—who makes jewelry. There's that nice little Honda I helped you out with once. You're a huge Prince fan. Roz, whom I've yet to meet, is your roommate, and you love roller coasters."

"So, I . . ."

He held up one finger. "Let me continue. You're also beautiful, smart, sexy, and an incredible kisser."

She blushed, drumming her fingernails along the table. "So, I see you're also a good listener." She shifted her weight in the seat. "Okay, Mr. Brooks. My turn. You're from Chicago, where your sister, brother, mother, and daughter live. Your father died when you were in high school. You run a computer business out of your home. You know, you never told me the name of your company."

"Netsource Solutions."

She nodded. "Okay, let's see what else." She looked

heavenward. "You volunteer with ex-cons, and you like amusement parks, too." She hesitated and had second thoughts before complimenting him on his good looks. Telling a man something like that could go to his head, she thought.

"You're very smart, a born leader, and a take-charge kind of guy." *Not to mention extremely handsome and sexy.*

He leaned back, nodding. "Well, looks like we know each other after all."

"You know a lot more about me than I know about you."

He shook his head. "No, I don't."

"Tell me about your daughter. You haven't talked about her much."

He smiled. "Kristy. She's your typical young lady. She's interested in shopping, music, boys, and traveling, thanks to her parents living in different states."

"I know this is a nosy question, but did you and her mother ever live together?"

He shook his head. "Nope. We sort of happened a little too fast. Seems like I met her one month and two months later she was pregnant."

"So, are you a good daddy?" she asked in a playful voice.

Quen looked down at his plate. After a brief hesitation, he nodded. "I try to be."

Bobbi detected a bit of sadness she hadn't noticed before. He looked troubled now, so she decided not to ask any more questions. She'd learn more about his daughter when he was ready to tell her.

He glanced at his watch. "Hey, we'd better get going if we want to catch the comedy show."

"Yeah, I could use a good laugh." She wiped her mouth and set the napkin on the table.

"Want me to take off all my clothes?" With a serious

face he reached for the button on his shirt, as if he was ready to undress.

"I don't think I'd be laughing. We'd probably never make it to the comedy club." She stood up to leave.

"Don't tempt me." Now smiling, he stood. "Where's the waiter?" he asked, looking around with his arm in the air.

"Over there." She pointed. "Why?"

"I want to see if he can use some comedy club tickets. I'm about to strip down in here."

Bobbi grabbed his arm, yanking it down. "Don't you dare." She grinned as the couple in the next booth smiled at them.

He laughed. "Come on, let's get out of here."

Fifteen

Quen and Dennis, one of the ex-convicts he was assisting, returned to the agency after a job interview.

"Man, I really appreciate this. If I get that job, I'll be able to get my car fixed," Dennis said.

"Once you get the job, not if. Think positive," Quen said, closing his car door.

"Oh, yeah. You're right. Once I get that job, I can put my Caddy in the shop and send my daughter some money." Dennis closed Quen's passenger door and followed him into the office.

"How old's your daughter?" Quen asked.

"She'll be thirteen next month, and I'd like to take her a little something when I go see her."

Quen opened the door for Dennis. "You'll get the job, don't worry. When's the last time you saw your daughter?"

"Shoot, man. It's been two years now. She used to come visit when she was younger, but you know teenagers. She probably caught a lot of flak from her friends."

Quen thought about that, and how close he'd come to putting Kristy through the same thing.

Olivia greeted them as they walked in. "How did it go, fellas?"

"Pretty good, thanks to Quen," Dennis said.

Olivia beamed. "He's one in a million. What did I tell you?"

"Stop it. I gave the man a ride, that's all."

"Man, you've been doing much more than that for me since I've been coming in here."

"Don't forget to fill out the paperwork. I left it on the back table," Olivia told Dennis. "Quen, Donald is here today. He'd like to talk to everyone if you have a few minutes."

"Sure." He turned to Dennis. "You can have a seat in the back if you want. I'll be right back."

"Okay. Ms. Olivia, I'll fill those papers out and bring them right back to ya."

"Thanks, honey."

She looked around as Quen headed for Donald's office. "Oh, you can't see him right now. He's talking with Perry. And they've been in there for a long time."

Quen stopped and looked back as Olivia came around from her desk. "If you ask me, he's up to something. He's not scheduled to volunteer today, so I don't even know why he came in."

"You think the board made up its mind, and he's got the staff position?"

She shook her head. "Uh-uh, I know that decision hasn't been made yet. And between you and me, he doesn't have a chance."

"Why not?"

"He's not qualified. If he gets that job, there'll be some trick to it."

Quen didn't know if Olivia was aware of how big a con artist Perry used to be—or still was, for that matter. But it sounded as if she was definitely onto him.

"Well, I'll be in the back working with Dennis. Call me when he's ready."

Before he could walk away, the door to Donald's office opened. Olivia cleared her throat and Quen glanced at her. She winked at him and walked back behind her desk.

"Thanks, Mr. Stewart, for the time and the opportunity. I'll get that report to you by the end of the week." Perry and Donald shook hands.

"Thanks, Perry." Donald looked up and saw Quen.

Quen stood back, waiting to see if Donald wanted to talk to him before he went to work with Dennis.

"Quen, got a minute?" Donald waved him over.

"Yeah."

As Perry walked away, Donald patted him on the back. "Perry, Olivia will get those files for you. Just tell her what you need." The phone in his office rang.

Quen hadn't seen them this chummy before. Maybe the agency was preparing to give Perry the job and Olivia didn't know.

"I'll get that." Olivia reached for the phone.

"I can get it. Go ahead and help Perry out for me. Quen, give me just a second." Donald gestured before turning back into his office.

Quen stood in the middle of the floor, not sure which way to go, when Perry came up to him.

"What's up, college man?" Perry and Quen exchanged handshakes.

Quen cringed every time Perry called him that. "Nothing, man, but sounds like things are going good with you." He pointed to Donald's office.

Perry nodded his head and turned up his lip. "I'm working on a little something-something"—he leaned closer to Quen—"you know, getting ready for things to blow up."

When he grinned and raised a brow, it gave Quen the willies. If nobody else thought Perry was getting the job, Perry did. "Yeah, well, good luck."

Before Quen could walk away, Perry tapped him on

the arm. "Man, what happened to you Friday night? We looked around and you guys were gone."

"It was turning into a long night. We decided to call it quits."

"Yeah. Your lady's cute. How long you two been together?"

"Man, she's just a friend." He reached over and patted Perry on the back. "Hey, don't let me hold you up. Olivia looks like she's ready for lunch. You'd better grab her while you can."

Perry turned around and Quen walked off to Donald's office.

Donald was still on the phone when Quen walked in, but he waved him over and pointed to a seat. Donald hung up.

"Quen, how you doing this morning?"

Quen crossed his legs and rested his hands on his thighs. "Everything's just fine."

Donald shuffled through a few papers as he appeared to be looking for something in specific. He looked up at Quen once. "That's good." He returned to his searching. "I wanted to talk to you about your proposal. There's been a few new developments since we last spoke."

Here comes bad news, Quen thought. He guessed he could use his counseling degree and get another job, but probably not working with ex-convicts in Macon.

Donald found what he'd been looking for and moved everything else over to the side of his desk. "I ran your idea about teaching soft skills past the board, and they liked it. But I need you to expand on some timelines for me. We're interested in starting something this fall. If you can rework your presentation with a September start date, I can re-present it and get the okay to approach Macon College."

"So they're giving the go-ahead?" Quen asked, surprised.

"Looks that away." Donald smiled.

"Then you got the funding you were hoping for?" Quen asked, still skeptical about this being good news.

"Some of it, yes. There's still plenty that needs to be ironed out. But for now, because of the cost savings, your proposal looked pretty good to them. I'm sorry, but I don't know anything about the positions just yet. I should know something in the next week or two." He slid Quen's proposal across the table as he stood up.

"If you can get that back to me next week, that would be great. And you know I'll try to make sure you get to head up the program. If you're still interested?"

That was better, Quen thought as he stood. "Of course, I'm interested. And I'd appreciate whatever you can do." They exchanged handshakes before Quen left.

When he walked out into the reception area, it was empty. Olivia had probably gone to lunch. He walked down the hall carrying his proposal. If Donald saw to it that Quen headed up the program, he'd have to be working full-time for the agency. Or so Quen wanted to believe. But he also realized anything could happen.

When he walked into the back office, Dennis and Perry were sitting at the table talking.

Dennis stopped and looked up when Quen entered. "Say, man, thanks for everything. My boy should be out front in a few, so I guess I'll see you next week."

"Call and let me know when you get the job," Quen said.

"Oh, most definitely. You'll be the first one I call." He walked over and shook Quen's hand while waving to Perry.

After Dennis left, Quen sat down at his desk and looked to see who was scheduled next.

"Is he still on parole?" Perry asked.

Quen nodded. "Yeah, and he needs this job he interviewed for today."

"I guess it's good he has someone with prior knowledge to help him out."

Quen looked up from his schedule and over at Perry. "What's that?"

Perry shrugged. "You know, you've already been through the system, so you can advise him."

So this *is what he's been getting at for weeks.* "I was on probation; it's not the same thing. But I don't remember having that conversation with you." One thing Quen didn't like was someone meddling in his personal business. Only the staff should know about his prior experience, and how he obtained it.

"Man, I know about everybody up in here. It's no big thing. All of us been through the criminal justice system in one way or another. That's why we're here. What was you on probation for?"

"If it's all the same to you, I'd rather not discuss it. I've put that behind me and now I'm out here trying to help guys get back on their feet."

"I feel you, man. You can sympathize. So can I. How about that little college friend of yours? How does she feel about it?"

Quen tried to play off a casual look as he realized he may have made a mistake. He'd avoided crossing that bridge because of her unsympathetic views toward ex-convicts. And now, he feared losing her if she couldn't understand. But he knew it was a bridge he'd have to cross sooner rather than later.

"I haven't told her." He gave a slight shrug.

"You plan to though, right?"

Quen nodded. He just hoped it wouldn't scare her away. He glanced over at Perry, wondering why he'd chosen to bring that up. He wanted to confront him about it, but someone walked in.

"What's up, my black brothers?"

Quen looked up to see another volunteer, Gary,

walking into the room. He shared a desk with Perry. Quen greeted him with a handshake.

Perry jumped up from his seat.

"You working today?" Gary asked.

"Naw, I just came in to talk to Donald about some things." He walked from behind the desk. "It's all yours, man."

After lunch Monday afternoon, Bobbi returned to her desk to find a large crystal vase holding a dozen perfect yellow roses. She slowly approached her desk with her mouth wide open. "What the . . ."

"Well, somebody's doing something right," Katherine teased her.

Bobbi pointed to herself. "Those are mine?"

"They're on your desk, aren't they? If you don't want them, just say so."

She walked up to the bouquet and sniffed. The smell of rose perfume put a smile on her face.

"Get the card, honey. I've been waiting for you to return because I didn't want to snoop. Who are they from?"

"Wait a minute." She had to think. It wasn't her birthday yet, or any other special occasion she could think of. And she'd never received flowers at work before. She pulled the envelope out of the holder and reached inside for the card.

"Well, who's it from?" Katherine rushed her.

Bobbi smiled as she read the card. " 'Thank you for a wonderful night. Let's do it again real soon. Quen.' "

"Nice. What did you do to that guy?" Katherine asked in a suggestive tone.

Bobbi frowned playfully at her. "Nothing. It's more like what he did to me."

"You go, girl. When are you going to see him again?"

"Tonight in class. Right after I drop these off at home." She sniffed the flowers again, smiling.

Tuesday afternoon Quen worked from his home office on a project for the Crown Plaza hotel. In the back of his mind he was working out a way to tell Bobbi about his past. He didn't actually regret not blurting it out the first time they met, considering that action would have surely scared her away. But Monday night when she'd repeated her distrust and discomfort with the prison system, although she knew she'd sometimes have to work within it, he felt like a jerk. Why hadn't he told her?

The phone rang, diverting his attention. He stood and stretched before reaching for the cordless phone across the room in an old leather armchair he'd held onto since college. "Hello."

"Hi, Daddy."

"Kristy. Hey, baby, how you doing?" He sat in his favorite chair, rubbing his eyes to take a much-needed break.

"Daddy, I'm all finished with my dance classes, so I can come see you now."

"Great, pumpkin. So, when's the trip to Las Vegas?"

"We're going to see Uncle Curtis the last week of July. Mama said I could come there the week before. When we get back, it'll almost be time for school to start."

"Good. Your mama and I just need to make the arrangements."

"You still gonna take me to a concert?"

He leaned back, scratching his head. "Baby, we'll have to see who's in town when you get here."

"They have concerts in Atlanta, don't they? It's not that far away. I know because we studied Georgia in geography class."

He laughed. "No, it's not that far away. I'll check and see who's coming and I'll let you know."

She squealed with joy. "Thanks, Daddy. Hold on, Mama wants to talk to you. I love you, Daddy."

"I love you, too, baby," he said, smiling at the words that touched him so deeply.

Then the Ice Queen got on the phone. "Quen, how you doing?"

He took a deep breath. "Fine, Arlene, how about you?"

"I'm blessed."

"Yeah." He never knew how to respond to that. She was truly blessed to have Kristy and live in the posh neighborhood where she resided. He realized she also didn't deserve the title "Ice Queen" any longer. Over the years she had mellowed, and they actually got along pretty well . . . not that the relationship was ever volatile.

"So, are you ready for your daughter?"

"I'm ready whenever she wants to come."

"She only has a couple of days. I'm sorry. I enrolled her in this advanced testing program, and then we're going to Vegas a little earlier than originally planned."

"So, what are we talking, a long weekend?"

"Yes, and we can make it up another time."

He snickered and shook his head. "Since I'm in school that's okay, but she really should have come down for a couple of weeks, you know."

"Who would keep her while you were in class?"

"I would have worked that out, or she could have come with me."

Arlene laughed. "Oh, I bet that would go over real well."

"Well, next year."

"Okay. For next month, how about sometime around of the seventeenth?"

He walked over to his desk and looked at the calendar.

The seventeenth was two weeks before his class ended, which gave him plenty of time to study for his finals. "That'll work. How's she been doing?"

"Great. She's having a good summer, and she's been dying to come down, so I'll get the ticket this week."

"Call me with all the details. I'll pay for the ticket. She's my daughter, too."

"It's no problem, I—"

"Arlene. Let me take care of this." She was still letting him know she made so much more money than he did. He hated when she reminded him of her Ice Queen days.

"Fine. I'll get back to you with the details."

"Thank you."

Quen hung up and returned to his work, but couldn't get Bobbi off his mind. He wanted to see her. He picked the phone back up and dialed her work number.

"Hello, the *Telegraph,* Bobbi Cunningham speaking."

"Hi, Bobbi. It's Quen."

"Hey, you, what's up?"

"Feel like doing a little shopping?"

"When?"

"This evening. I want to get my daughter a gift, and I could use a little womanly advice."

"If you want to make it 5:30, I can meet you at Macon Mall. I've got a movie to review this afternoon, so I'll be in the area."

"That'll work. How's your day going?"

She let out a heavy sigh that he felt through the phone.

"Today's not such a good day."

"Can I do anything to make it better for you?"

"That's sweet, but unless you can talk some sense into my boss, I don't think so."

"Is he giving you a hard time? You want me to come down there and rough him up a bit?"

She laughed. "No, he's just got this crazy idea about printing letters that come in from readers regarding my reviews. Today my assignment, should I choose to accept it, is to sort through stacks of letters for that perfect letter. We've never done this before, and I think he's looking to create a little controversy at my expense."

"Huh. That might not be all bad, depending on how you work it. Seems like you could make it work to your advantage."

"How?"

"I'll tell you what. Meet me in the food court at 5:30 and while we shop, I'll tell you ways you can turn this thing around to your advantage."

"Oh, that sounds good and sneaky. I'll see you at 5:30."

Bobbi found the food court and pulled out a small notepad to jot down some of her thoughts while the movie was still fresh in her mind. Another chick flick, but she liked this one. She was beginning to see that the movie didn't have to scare her to death to be good.

Minutes later, she looked up to see Quen heading toward her, dressed casual as usual in the sandals he'd worn the first time she'd met him. She closed her pad and put it back in her purse.

"How was the movie?"

"Surprisingly, pretty good."

He nodded. "You'll have to tell me about it. Ready?"

She nodded. "Let's go shopping. My favorite pastime."

She stood and pulled her purse strap up on her shoulder. "Where do you want to start?" she asked, looking around the mall.

He shrugged. "What's a good gift for someone who just finished a semester of dance classes?"

"What kind of dancing?"

"Ballet."

"Huh, something feminine. Does she like jewelry?"

He shrugged and looked around at the stores along the corridor. "I'll tell you what. Let's pretend we're shopping for you. Show me some things you like."

"But I'm much older than your daughter."

"I know, but it still might work."

"Okay then, let's start at Rich's."

As they walked toward Rich's department store, Quen tried to muster up the courage to tell her about his past. She seemed to be in a good mood; he just had to find a way to bring it up.

They started in the juniors department, where she pointed out some nice dresses, but he usually saw Kristy in jeans, so he passed on the dresses. As they passed the women's dresses, he talked her into trying on a few, thinking about her upcoming birthday. When she walked out of the dressing room in a little red number that had resembled a flimsy piece of material on the hanger, he was surprised in more ways than one.

"How does this look?" she asked, spinning around, causing the dress to slowly lift from her legs.

Quen smiled. He liked the way the dress hugged her body. It was simple, but on her body it came to life. He nodded his approval.

"That's you. What did I tell you? You have a flair for clothes. Everything looks good on you."

She shrugged. "I wouldn't say all that."

He kept admiring her body in the dress when he heard someone call his name. He looked up and almost stopped breathing.

"Quentin, is that you?"

A tall dimple-faced woman with deep-set tired-looking eyes smiled at him. He recognized her right away and tried to swallow the huge knot growing in his throat.

"Quentin Brooks?" she asked again.

He nodded.

The woman came around the clothes rack and walked over to give him a big hug. "How are you? It's been a long time."

"I'm great, and you?" He returned the greeting with an unaffectionate hug.

She stepped back. "You look great. I bet you don't remember my name, do you?"

He remembered. He remembered everything about her and the anger management class they'd been in together as part of his probation. If she mentioned that right now, he was dead meat.

Sixteen

"Jacque, with a *Q*. Right?"

"You remember." She smiled. "Yes, Jacque Russell. It's been a long time." She glanced over at Bobbi, smiling.

Bobbi had already noticed the dazed expression on Quen's face. He didn't look too happy to see Jacque, with a *Q*, whoever she was. Bobbi cleared her throat.

He glanced from Bobbi to Jacque. "I'm sorry. Bobbi, this is Jacque. We're . . ." He turned to Bobbi with his mouth open as if he were at a loss for words.

Jacque held out her hand. "I'm an old acquaintance from Chicago. Nice to meet you."

"Nice to meet you, too." Bobbi smiled and shook her hand.

"We took a stupid class together a few years ago," Jacque added.

Before she could continue, Quen jumped in. "Hey, I almost forgot. How's that son of yours? Didn't you say he was going into the service?"

"He did. But that's a long story."

"Excuse me, you two. I'm just going to get out of this dress." Bobbi excused herself while Jacque and Quen reminisced. The woman had some beauty to her. She reminded Bobbi of Angela Bassett in the Tina Turner story. She had a slightly hard face, but a pretty smile. It was evident in her tired eyes that she'd lived a rough life. Bobbi hurried out of the dress, curious about what type of class they'd had together.

When she walked out minutes later, Jacque was gone.

After Quen found the perfect gift, they left the mall. As they walked out, Quen stretched his arms over his head, looking around. "Thanks for the help." He held up his little blue-and-white shopping bag containing a necklace and earring set for Kristy.

Bobbi shrugged. "No problem." Since they'd run into Quen's *old classmate,* he'd been rather quiet. Seeing Jacque had surprised and maybe upset him. Bobbi wanted to know the story behind them, if there was one. Had he met her the same way he'd met Jacque?

"Are you hungry?" he asked.

"Yeah, I'm starved. All I've had since lunch is movie theater popcorn. With loads of butter."

"Want to grab something quick, like Jock's-N-Jill's downtown?"

"Sounds good. Want me to meet you down there?"

He shook his head. "Why don't I follow you home, and you can park your car, then ride with me."

"Okay." She nodded. "I'll see you at my apartment."

As they separated and walked to their cars, Bobbi smiled, thinking of his cleverness. He wanted to meet her roommate, and he'd found a way to get back to her apartment.

By the time Bobbi reached her apartment, Quen was already sitting in his Land Rover, waiting for her. He hadn't followed her; he'd left her. She climbed out of the car lugging her briefcase. By the time she walked up to the steps, Quen had gotten out of his car and reached out to help her.

"Let me take that." He took the bag and pretended almost to drop it from the sheer weight.

"Thank you." She gave him a slight roll of her eyes and noticed that the patio door was ajar.

"Looks like my roommate's here," she said, as she reached the top step and inserted her key into the lock.

"Good," he said, his tone conveying, *It's about time.*

She opened the front door and peeked in, making sure Roz was decent. In a pair of shorts and a white T-shirt with her college logo scrolled across the front, Roz lay across the couch watching television.

Bobbi stepped inside, holding the door as Quen walked in behind her.

Roz sat straight up when she noticed a man behind Bobbi.

"Hey, Roz." Bobbi closed the door and walked in.

"Hello, hello, hello." Roz smiled, looking pleased to see her roommate's guest.

"I'll take that." Bobbi took her briefcase from Quen. "This is my roommate, Roz." She pointed at Roz.

Quen took a few steps, making the short trip from the front door to the couch, and held out his hand. "Quentin Brooks, nice to meet you."

"No. The pleasure is all mine." Roz shook his hand with a curious look on her face.

Bobbi helped her out. "Quen's in my night class."

"Oh, right." She snapped her fingers. "The one who sent the flowers, after he took you to the Prince concert."

He smiled and nodded.

Bobbi caught Roz's attention and gave a hard roll of her eyes. She didn't have to sound so impressed with him. Bobbi threw her purse on a chair across from the couch.

"Quen, have a seat, I'll just go put this up and be right back." She held up her briefcase.

"Take your time." He sat on the opposite end of the couch. "What're you watching?"

Roz eased back down into her seat. *"Law and Order.* It's my favorite show."

He nodded. "Yeah, that's a pretty good one."

"You watch it, too?" she asked.

"I've seen a few episodes. I don't watch much television."

"Well, there's not much else to do around this town."

"You're kidding. There's plenty to do in Macon."

Roz turned to look at him with raised brows, as if he were a UFO. "You're not from around here, are you?"

He laughed. "Not originally, but I find enough to do to keep me busy."

"You guys are in school, so studying can take up a lot of your time."

"I volunteer down at the Lean On Me Agency, too," he added.

She twisted her lips up at one corner and glanced toward the ceiling. "I don't think I've ever heard of them."

"It's a placement center for ex-convicts. We help them make the transition back into society by finding job training, actual jobs, medical assistance, and whatever else we can."

"Oh," she said, with interest. "So you know a lot about men in prison, don't you?"

He nodded. "Yeah. Why, you know somebody in prison?"

"Not directly. But—"

"All set." Bobbi stepped into the living room.

"Hey, Bobbi, Quen was telling me he volunteers with ex-convicts. Did you tell—"

Bobbi clapped her hands together out of fear. "Roz, excuse me, I forgot to ask you something. Will you come back here with me a minute?" She pointed down the hall. "Quen, I'll be right back."

Roz stood with a perplexed look on her face and followed Bobbi.

Once in her bedroom, Bobbi closed the door and leaned her back against it, taking a deep breath.

"You didn't tell him, did you?" Roz asked.

"No, and I don't want you to either."

"Okay, so what did you say? Your father's on vacation in Alabama?"

"I didn't say. But I think Quen believes he's dead."

"Bobbi! You can't let him believe that. I thought you said you were in love with this guy? He'll find out eventually. And men don't like when they find out they've been lied to. He works with ex-convicts; he'll understand."

"I don't have a father." Her voice took on an icy tone. "And that's the way I see it. I'd appreciate it if you didn't say anything."

"Well, I won't, but . . ." Roz crossed her arms and shook her head, looking disappointed.

That look always sent shivers of guilt through Bobbi. "I'm sorry. It's just that I don't know everything about this guy yet, so I don't want to go telling him my whole life story."

Roz nodded and turned up her nose, as if she smelled trouble in the air.

Bobbi gave her a quick hug, and they returned to the living room. Roz went back to her seat on the couch.

"Ready?" Bobbi asked. "Now you have proof that my roommate is a woman."

Quen laughed.

"I'm what?" Roz asked.

"Every time I asked Bobbi out, she always wanted to meet me somewhere, so I asked if her roommate was her man. I thought maybe she was married or something. But now I see she isn't."

"That's right. I was just being cautious."

"Which is good," he added.

"Where are you guys going?" Roz asked.

"Downtown for a quick bite to eat."

"What? You mean Chef Bobbi didn't offer to cook something?"

Bobbi crossed her arms and pursed her lips, on the verge of rolling her eyes again.

"Chef Bobbi." Quen turned and gave her a raised brow and grin. "So, you've got those kinds of skills?"

Bobbi shrugged. "Some say I do."

"I thought you told me, 'Let's just say I know my way around the kitchen.' Sounds like you know more than that."

They shared a knowing smile.

"Why don't you guys stay here? I was about to run over to Belinda's anyway."

"No. We don't want to mess up your program," Bobbi protested.

Roz stood and waved at the television. "It's a rerun, and I've seen it already. I went to the grocery store earlier, so there's plenty in the fridge." She walked toward the front door, but stopped next to Bobbi. She whispered in her ear, "If you're gonna date him, get to know him."

She opened the front door. "I'll be across the hall, at Belinda's. Nice to meet you, Quen."

"Yeah, same here." He offered her a big smile.

The front door closed, and Bobbi stood in the middle of the living room, so outdone she didn't know what to say.

"So that's Roz," Quen said sitting back down on the couch. "I like her."

Bobbi walked over to the chair where she'd dropped her purse. She moved the purse and sat down. "That's her, all right."

They looked at each other, smiling. She shook her head and fell back in the chair.

"So, what's for dinner, Chef Bobbi?" he asked, rubbing his palms together.

Bobbi sighed and jumped up. "Let me go see what we've got." She walked into the kitchen and opened the refrigerator. "What to eat, what to eat," she chanted as she looked over the meats and vegetables.

A hand touched her waist, causing her to shriek. She jumped and turned around to find Quen standing behind her, looking over her shoulder.

"That feels good, doesn't it?" he asked in a slow seductive tone.

His hand circled her waist, pulling her closer to him.

"What feels good?" she asked, trying to catch her breath.

"The cold air from the fridge."

She didn't feel any cold air. Instead, the heat of his breath on her neck warmed her whole body, and one touch made her tremble. She didn't want him to know how nervous she was, so she leaned over, reaching for a package of meat on a lower shelf. Instead of the movement putting more distance between them, it pushed her backside into his crotch.

"And then again, that feels even better." He stood behind her, with his hand on her hip.

Bobbi jumped straight up and turned around. "I'm sorry, I didn't mean to do that." She held a hand over her mouth.

"Hey, no need to apologize, it was working for me. Did you find anything?"

"This." She held up the package, unable to say much more.

He took a step back and looked at the package in her hand. "Pork tenderloins."

She nodded and stood there with the refrigerator door open. She was so hot she found it difficult to concentrate, in which case, she'd never be able to cook a good meal. Instead, she'd leave a disastrous impression of her cooking.

"Earth to Bobbi." Quen reached out and ran his finger down the bridge of her nose, as he'd become accustomed to doing.

She took the package and whirled around, shoving it back into the refrigerator. "I'm sorry, I can't cook this. Let's just go grab something. Look, I'm starved, and it's already nine o'clock." She backed away from the refrigerator and closed the door.

"Do I make you nervous?" he asked, taking a step closer to her. Under heavy lids, his eyes focused on her lips.

She took a step back. "No. I'm not nervous. I'm just hungry and I get the shakes when I'm hungry."

"Oh, I felt you shaking, but I'm not talking about that." He stepped closer, reaching for her waist again. "I'm talking about this." He reached out and ran a finger down her nose again. "You're sweating."

"I am?" She ran a crooked index finger down her nose and felt the moisture. "It's hot in here."

He arched his left brow at her and smiled. "You were darned near standing in the refrigerator."

Why did he have to be so observant? She was on fire and he knew it. He stood so close to her, the smell and feel of him made her wet. They stood in the middle of the kitchen, as if afraid to move.

His hand found her chin and raised her head. "Forget cooking. We've still got time to run downtown."

His voice had deepened and his eyes became two balls of charcoal, burning into hers. His hand moved from her chin to her cheek. He brought up his other hand and slowly cupped her face in his palms.

The sound of their breathing took over the room. His was heavy and deep, while hers was soft and fast. Forgetting her hunger, she stretched her head forward until her lips found his, leaving a soft kiss. He returned with several hungry kisses.

Bobbi brought her arms up and circled them around his neck, causing her blouse to ride up. She wanted so badly to finish what they'd started after the Prince concert. His hands moved from her cheeks to her ears, then slid down her neck to caress her shoulders. Once his lips found their way to her neck, she tilted her head back, wanting to feel him all over her neck and breasts. And she probably would have, but the front door opened.

"Hello, I don't smell anything cooking in here," Roz called out as she reentered the apartment.

Bobbi jumped and pulled her blouse down. Quen took a step back, clearing his throat.

Roz poked her head into the kitchen. "Sorry." She quickly turned back and walked down the hall toward her bedroom. "I just came back to get my Angie Stone CD. Don't let me interrupt you guys," she yelled before entering her bedroom.

Bobbi walked over to the kitchen table and sat down, laughing. Quen lowered his head and started laughing, too. *This is ridiculous,* she thought, shaking her head. The moment reminded her of high school and sneaking around the stairs to kiss a boy. She wasn't in high school anymore, so why did this feel so juvenile? Then a loud growling noise came from her stomach.

Quen looked up, pointing at her. "Was that you?"

She nodded. "I told you I was starving." She held a hand over her stomach, laughing.

He reached over for her hand. "Come on, we're going downtown."

She stood and followed him into the living room to snatch up her purse. "Roz, we're going out," she yelled as Quen pulled her outside.

Roz walked out of her bedroom to catch Bobbi and Quen flying out the front door. "Okay. Don't leave on my account," she murmured to the closing front door.

Quen drove Bobbi down to the historic district of

Macon and they joined the late-night crowd at Jock's-N-Jill's.

Bobbi dove into her meal, limiting her conversation until she had her fill.

Quen followed suit, filling his belly, then he sat back and took a deep breath. "That's better."

Bobbi looked around. "And right on time. They'll be closing in a little bit."

He needed to talk to her, and tonight seemed like a good time. In his mind, he'd rehearsed his lines over and over, but aloud it wouldn't be as easy.

The waiter came back to clear the table and left the bill. Quen needed more time. However, seeing how the restaurant staff looked eager to leave, he didn't want to hold them up. He and Bobbi left.

On the way to his car, he had an idea. "It's a nice night, and we've just had a heavy meal. Let's take a walk."

Bobbi smiled, appearing to like the idea. "Okay, where to?"

"Right out here." They stood in the tourist district of Macon, but the street was short on tourists at eleven o'clock on a Tuesday night.

Bobbi agreed to the walk, and they strolled down the street hand in hand. The air was sticky and humid, but Quen hardly noticed it. He tried to figure out how to steer the conversation where he wanted it to go.

"Have you ever been in love?" Bobbi asked.

He looked at her, completely taken aback. Where did that come from? He nodded. "Yeah."

"What was it like?"

He forced his train of thought in another direction. "Like discovering your new favorite candy. For a little while, anyway."

"What happened?"

"She broke up with me."

"What did you do?" she asked, sounding sure he was at fault.

"I made a mud pie, and broke her Easy-Bake Oven."

Bobbi let go of his hand and started punching him in the arm, laughing. "I didn't say go that far back."

He shifted his left shoulder to dodge her fist, but a few punches landed. "Hey, you weren't specific."

"You know what I meant. As an adult."

He grabbed her hand and they walked together again. "Okay, it was like a roller-coaster ride at first, then in the end, it was like a roller-coaster ride again. After all was said and done, I was glad to get off, and I'm not sure why I got on in the first place."

"Who was that? Kristy's mother?"

"Yeah." He nodded. "What about you?"

She laughed. "It was like having the stomach flu."

Quen threw back his head and laughed at the top of his lungs. "Now, I've never heard love described like that. Are you sure it was love?"

"It had to be. I felt wonderful when we were together, but whenever he stood me up, or didn't call when he said he would, I felt nauseous. I couldn't stand to be away from him. It literally made me sick. That is, until I found out he was running around town impregnating everybody. I broke up with him, and my stomach flu cleared right up." She snapped her fingers.

Quen laughed. "I bet you were glad of that."

"You don't know how glad. I felt like I'd dodged a bullet."

She'd opened up the conversation to talk about their past. It was a perfect time for him to tell her about his.

"You know, sometimes you do things that later in life you're not particularly proud of."

"Tell me about it. He's married with a son, and paying child support to two other women."

"Everybody's past catches up with them at some

point in time. I bet he wishes he could take that time back, but he can't. I know I wish—"

Buzz, buzz. Quen's cell phone went off, breaking his train of thought. He unclipped it from his belt and answered in a rushed tone, "Hello."

"Quen, It's Evette. We've got a problem."

He took a deep breath and exhaled. That usually meant she had a problem she needed his help with. "What is it, Evette? I'm kind of busy right now."

"I'm at the hospital."

He let go of Bobbi's hand, detecting the nervous sound of Evette's voice. "With who?"

"Mama."

"What's wrong with her?"

She let out a loud sigh. "I don't know yet. The doctor wanted me to call you and Robert."

He walked over to lean against the front of a sandwich shop they were passing. He had to get back to his car.

Bobbi followed, reaching out for his hand. "Is something wrong?" she whispered.

He nodded and braced himself. "Evette, what did the doctor say?"

Seventeen

"She fell, and the doctor thinks she passed out. Mama doesn't remember, but she had blood on the side of her head when I got there. I asked her what happened. All she remembers is going into the kitchen to fix a cup of coffee. She said she went to put some bread in the toaster and felt a little dizzy. The next thing she remembers is the phone ringing."

He pushed away from the building and started back up the street, holding Bobbi's hand. "Does the doctor know what happened to her?"

"I'm waiting on the emergency room doctor now. They've run a lot of tests, but I don't have any of the results yet. The doctor wants to keep her for the night, and you know how she feels about that."

He ran a hand over his mouth and mumbled a prayer that she was okay. "If he wants her to stay, you have to make her stay."

"Oh, I will. She's scared. I can see it in her eyes. She just won't admit it."

They reached his car in a matter of minutes. He lowered the phone to his chest and opened the passenger door for Bobbi. "My mom's in the hospital. We're gonna have to go."

She shook her head. "Is she gonna be okay?" she asked, holding his arm and stepping up into the car.

He shrugged. "I don't know yet." He continued talking

to Evette as he started the car and left downtown to take Bobbi home. Evette hadn't asked him to come home, but his mom's situation sounded serious, so he needed to get home to his computer to find a plane ticket.

"I'm sorry, are you with somebody?" Evette asked.

"Yeah, but I'm on my way home now. I'll see when I can get a flight out."

"Quen, don't book anything until after I talk with the doctor. It might not be that bad."

He didn't want to take that kind of a chance. His mother was afraid of hospitals, because both her parents, after being admitted into hospitals, died there. She was petrified of hospitals. "Evette, don't leave her alone."

"You know I won't do that. No matter what she says."

Quen hung up and sat there thinking for a few minutes. If anything happened to his mother and he wasn't there, he'd never forgive himself He'd forgotten to ask Evette if she'd found Robert.

"Are you going to Chicago in the morning?" Bobbi asked.

Quen turned and looked at her. He'd almost forgotten she was in the car. "I might. I'm going to find a flight and wait for Evette to call me back."

"What happened to your mom?"

He recounted Evette's story to her. By the time he finished, they were back at her apartment. He pulled up and shut off the motor. "I'm sorry the night ended on a sour note."

"No, it didn't. Besides"—she looked down at her watch—"I do have to get up and go to work in the morning."

"Thanks for understanding. I hate that I cut our walk short."

"Go take care of your mother if you have to." She leaned over and gave him a kiss on the lips before opening the car door.

"Hold up." He jumped out of the car and ran around to her door. "I'm not so distracted I can't be a gentleman. Besides, you have a hard time getting in and out of here."

She held onto his hand and climbed down. "You know, I wasn't going to say anything, but why did you get a Land Rover? It's such a strange-looking car, SUV, or whatever you call it."

He laughed and closed the passenger door. "It came in handy in Chicago during the winter. Down here, I don't really need it, but it's paid for."

"I certainly understand that."

He walked her to the front door and kissed her good night. "I'll call you tomorrow."

Bobbi spent all day Wednesday and Thursday morning wondering if Quen's mother was all right. Since he never called the next day, she assumed he'd gone to Chicago. Then, Thursday night, he came strolling into class.

"Is your mother okay?" she asked during their first break.

"Yeah, she's better. They discovered she's got high blood pressure. That's why she blacked out."

"Did you go to Chicago?"

"No. I logged a lot of phone time, but I stayed here. I'm sorry I didn't call you yesterday. It was kind of a wild day. Kristy's mother called with her flight details, so I had to take care of that, too."

"Is she coming here?"

"Yeah, she'll be here in a couple of weeks for a long weekend visit. I want you to meet her."

She smiled. "Cool."

Professor Jennings and Monica walked up to them. "Excuse me, folks, but I need to let you know something."

"Yes, sir." Quen and Bobbi listened up.

"I was just informing Ms. Monica here that tomorrow is the last day to drop out and we've had one person drop out already. Your society partner, Gregory, turned in his paperwork this morning. So, it looks like the project is down to the three of you. I'm afraid I can't lower the percentage of your final or anything, but I will take into consideration that you had to take on more work late into the project."

Quen shook his head and let out a heavy sigh. "I had a feeling he'd do something like that."

"So did I," Monica spoke up. "Remember I asked about divvying up the work at our last meeting."

Bobbi and Quen nodded.

"I'll still expect a full report from the group." Professor Jennings's gaze focused on Bobbi. "Don't be afraid to buckle down and give this project all you've got. It's sixty percent of your grade, and can determine if you pass or fail the course."

Monica smiled. "We'll be prepared."

After the professor left, Bobbi started to panic. She'd procrastinated, and had only begun to do her research, but now she'd have to do even more. She needed this class and couldn't afford to fail, so she had to get her butt in gear.

"Guys, I've already looked over Gregory's questions and thought about how I would propose them, just in case he did something like this. He wasn't that prepared last Saturday at the library and it concerned me," Monica informed them.

"I've got an idea," Quen jumped in. "Instead of doing a lot more research through the Internet and journals, let's take a shortcut. If I can set up some interviews with actual ex-convicts, we can add that to our report. We'll have to tweak it a bit, but that might work." He gestured to them for an agreement.

"I like that," Monica spoke up. "We can find out

directly from the horse's mouth, so to speak, as to what they think they need to transition back into society. That's also a good way to see how they feel about the various programs being offered today."

"There you go." Quen pointed to her. "You've just added the next element to our project." He turned to Bobbi. "Like it?"

She shrugged. "Yeah, it's okay."

Monica reached out and touched Quen on the shoulder. "We can discuss it after class."

Professor Jennings continued his lecture. Bobbi sat through the second half mad at herself for not contributing as much as she should have to the project. Quen and Monica were so into the subject matter that she was starting to feel left out.

After the lecture, Professor Jennings caught her on the way out.

"Ms. Cunningham, how are your studies coming along?"

She smiled. "Everything's fine."

"Well, I hope you're going to take advantage of this opportunity given to you."

"What opportunity?" She looked at him.

"The added work. With one of our members dropping out, somebody will have to pick up the slack. I'm sure it will be divided among the group, but it's a perfect opportunity for someone like yourself to excel. Take on that added responsibility and run with it."

He was going to stay on her until she finished the course.

"I'm going to do my best to pitch in and help out. I'm a little more comfortable with the subject now. A little bit anyway." She smiled.

He patted her on the back. "That's good, because if you're majoring in public services, I'm sure our paths will cross again. I teach a lot of the graduate level courses. You are going to get your master's, aren't you?"

"I hadn't thought about that. If I finish the bachelor's program, I'll be happy."

"Think about it, then. To really get somewhere in this field, you need your master's. And if you do well in this course. I'm sure you'll be ready to continue."

It sounded good, but that meant she'd have to finance a master's, degree.

"Have a good evening."

He walked down the opposite hallway, leaving her confused, but determined. She'd wanted to get some-where with her bachelor's degree, but if it took a master's, then she'd just have to start saving for that, too.

When she reached her car, Quen was leaning against the hood.

"You're not trying to drop out, too, are you?" he asked.

"No. What made you think that?" She walked over and inserted her key in the door.

"I saw you talking to Professor Jennings, and tomor-row's the last day to drop out."

She laughed. "Don't worry, I wouldn't do that to you guys." She threw her books in the backseat and her purse in the passenger seat. "I told you. I like you."

He walked around and stood in the car door next to her. "Oh, yeah? Prove it." He gave her a quick kiss on the lips.

She thought for a moment. "What are you doing next weekend?"

"For the Fourth?"

"Yeah."

He shrugged. "I don't have anything planned, but I thought we could spend the day together. Maybe catch a fireworks show somewhere."

"Great. Then you can come to my aunt's birthday party with me."

"In Douglas?" he asked, surprised.

"Of course. Why? Do you have a problem with that?" she asked, crossing her arms.

"No, none at all. It sounds like fun. I get to meet the family?"

"The whole clan."

He smiled. "I guess you do like me." He leaned forward and kissed her again.

The first kiss was soft and gentle. Then his intensity increased with a hunger she'd never seen before. Holding the car door open, he stepped closer and lowered one arm to pull her closer to him. She let go of the car and, to keep from falling, held onto his arm.

"Hey, it's too hot for all that. Get a room." A man's voice came from the other side of Bobbi's car.

Bobbi and Quen turned to see one of their classmates waving and smiling as he climbed into his car.

Quen took a step back and they laughed at themselves.

For the next six days, Bobbi and Quen met for lunch, took long walks, and spent a lot of time together. She took him to review a couple of movies with her, and he treated her to every nice spot in town. They went to dinner, went dancing, and almost every waking hour they were in contact with each other.

Bobbi couldn't believe she'd found someone like Quen. He was everything she'd ever wanted in a man, but believed she had no hope of finding in Macon.

Thursday night, they had midterms. Her hand started to shake the minute she picked up her pencil. Over the past couple of days, she hadn't studied as much as she'd intended to. She hoped and prayed it didn't reflect on her test scores.

That night after class she went home to start packing. Roz was in the kitchen cooking when she walked in.

"Hey, girl, what's up?" Bobbi asked as she dropped her keys and purse on the kitchen table and picked up the mail.

Roz poked her head out of the kitchen. "I just got in, so I'm fixing some turkey cutlets. Want one?"

"Please. I'm starving." She dropped the bills back on the dining room table and walked into the kitchen. "Did you have to work late?"

"I didn't have to, I was just trying to get all caught up. I'm going to Savannah tomorrow, remember?"

Bobbi snapped her fingers. "Oh, yeah, I forgot. You guys are going over to Tybee Island."

"Yep. Too bad you have to miss out. It's going to be fun. Just hanging with the girls on the beach for a few days. You never know who you might meet."

Bobbi frowned. "If you were going to Myrtle Beach, I'd say you're right, but Tybee Island . . ." She chuckled. "Girl, you're not gonna meet any men down there. Not any black ones, anyway."

"You never know." Roz put the lid on the skillet and grabbed a bottle of water from the refrigerator. "But then again, you've already got your man," she teased, smiling and sipping her water.

Bobbi shrugged. "I don't know if I'd call him that. We're just hanging out and having a good time. That's all." She opened the pantry and grabbed a few cookies while waiting for dinner.

"Having a good time, my foot. You're taking him to Douglas with you on Saturday, and I've never known you to do that before. Not since I've known you, anyway."

"I want my aunt to meet him, and tell me what she thinks. I told you, she's pretty good at reading people. If he's up to no good, she'll let me know."

"And if she likes him?"

Bobbi sat at the kitchen table, chewing her cookies. "I don't know," she said between bites.

Roz joined her at the table. "Then you'll admit you've found your black knight?"

Bobbi laughed. "I wouldn't go that far."

"Girl, give it up. You've been walking around here with your head in the clouds ever since you met that guy. You used to hang around the house and cook all sorts of fancy meals, now he's always taking you out to eat. Every time you saw a romantic movie you came home ranting and raving about how they're destroying the young women of today. I read your review about that romantic comedy that came out last week, and I believe you liked it. What did you say, something about springing forth hope for a better tomorrow?"

Bobbi sat there with her elbow on the table and her chin in her palm. "You're right. I'm turning into a sap, aren't I?"

Roz laughed and walked over to check the stove. "You're in love, girl, and ain't nothing wrong with that. You just remember that love is blind."

Bobbi had said the same thing so many times. She thought about it for a moment. "You know what?"

"What?"

"I've never been over to his house." She sat up straight in her chair. "He made a big deal about coming over here and meeting you and all, but I've never been over to his place."

"You mean you guys haven't done anything yet?"

Bobbi turned and looked at her. "Anything like what?"

"Don't play with me. You know what I mean." She returned to the table. "Girl, he's fine. You mean you haven't crawled under the sheets with him yet?" Roz tapped her fingernails against the table.

"No, I haven't."

"Okay." Roz stood, clasping her hands together. "That's a good thing. You don't want to be too easy. Have you learned any more about him?"

Bobbi ran a finger down her water bottle, wiping at the perspiration beading up on the side. "Yeah, a little. He doesn't talk about himself that much."

"Then how do you know he doesn't live with somebody?"

"He doesn't. I call him at home every day. If a woman lived there, I would have talked to her by now."

"Have you met any of his boys? Everybody hangs with somebody."

"He didn't grow up around here, so he doesn't have a lot of buddies he runs with."

"But he's been going to school here for a while now. Don't tell me he hasn't made any friends or found any running buddies?"

Bobbi stood. "I honestly don't know. I like spending time with him, and I don't care to be around a bunch of his buddies."

"That's not what I'm saying." Roz walked over to the cabinet for plates. "This girl on my job, Angela, she fell for this guy who'd just moved to Macon. About a month later, she learned he was running from the police in New York. Now he's serving time somewhere and she could have gotten caught up in that mess. You have to check these guys out. Why did he move to Macon from Chicago? Have you asked him?"

Bobbi walked over to the stove and lifted the lid on the turkey. "Is this ready to turn over yet?"

"I've got that. You just answer my question." Roz set the table.

Bobbi dropped the lid, making a clattering sound. "He may have told me, but I don't remember. Probably to go to school."

Roz walked over and pulled a package of frozen

vegetables from the freezer. "Then you'd better ask a few more questions. Because they've got better schools in Chicago."

Usually Bobbi was the supercautious, supercareful one, but not this time. She thought about what Roz said, and the fact that she was taking Quen to her family's home. Maybe she'd rethink her offer.

Eighteen

Quen lay back in bed, talking to his mother on the phone, but thinking about Bobbi. Once he made sure his mother was feeling okay, he hung up and called Bobbi.

"Hello."

"Hey, baby, it's me."

"Hi there, you."

"Well, how'd you do?" He hadn't talked to her since before taking their midterms.

"I'm not sure, and you?"

"I think I did okay, but I would have liked to have done better."

"We'll find out Monday night. I just hope I did better than I think."

He chuckled. "Yeah, me, too. But we've got the final to make it up."

"Let's just hope we don't have a whole lot of making up to do."

He agreed with her. Quen had to talk to Bobbi about his past before their relationship went any further. It was too late to ask her out, and he couldn't do this over the phone.

"Bobbi, do you have any plans for tomorrow night?"

"I'm going to be pretty busy actually. I have to pick up my aunt's gift, then I have to run a few small errands before my hair appointment. And that usually takes hours. I won't see you until Saturday morning."

"Sounds like you'll be real busy."

"Why, is something wrong?"

"No, nothing's wrong. Tomorrow I'm going to ask some guys down at the agency about those interviews we discussed. I think I can set something up for next week, possibly Tuesday or Wednesday, is that okay with you?" Perhaps that would also be a good time for him to tell her what he had to. He could explain everything to her then.

"I guess it'll be okay. We have to get it over with. I could kick Gregory's butt for dropping out on us like that."

"We'll just have to work a little smarter, not harder."

"You've just got all the answers, don't you?" she asked.

He thought about how wrong she was, but didn't know it. "I wish I did. You don't know how much I wish I did," he stressed, regretting the things he hadn't told her.

They continued to talk on the phone until the wee hours of the morning. Quen loved listening to stories about her family and the crazy things she'd done growing up in a small town. By the time he hung up, he was looking forward to Saturday.

Quen had offered to drive, but Bobbi insisted on driving. She even offered to pick him up this time. Reluctantly, he agreed. He wasn't the only clever one. Now she'd get to see his place, and she could make sure he lived alone.

She followed his directions and found his house fairly easily. He lived in a nice two-story gray-and-white house with a two-car garage. She pulled into the driveway behind his Land Rover. At least she wouldn't have to be bothered with stepping up into that thing, she thought.

She blew her horn so he'd know she was outside, but

climbed out of the car and walked up to the front door. *Two can play this game,* she thought. "I'm going to check you out, Mr. Brooks."

He opened the front door wearing a pair of long khaki shorts and a white three-button shirt with the Polo crest on the front. "Well, don't we look all spiffy today?" she commented, walking inside.

"Spiffy. Come on, you can do me one better than that, can't you?" He stepped back as she entered.

Bobbi noticed his overnight bag sitting next to the front door. She scanned the foyer for any traces of a woman's touch. "I like the outfit. You've got a real flair for dressing, you know that?" She mocked the comment he usually gave her.

He closed the front door. "Real funny." He stepped over and kissed her on the cheek. "You look nice in those jeans," he complimented her.

She'd gained a few pounds eating out all the time like they did, and her jeans were a bit snug, so she knew what he meant: He liked the fit.

"Well, thanks. You ready?"

He patted his pants pockets. "Yeah, I just need to find my keys. You want some juice or something?" he asked, before walking into the kitchen.

"No, I'm fine," she answered, looking at the picture in the living room.

"I'll be right back." He went in search of his keys.

She left the foyer and entered the living room. It wasn't very large, but tastefully decorated. He had a white couch with two matching large white chairs. Almost everything in the room was white, except for the large piece of artwork over the fireplace. The picture was an abstract with splashes of vibrant color.

"Like that?" he asked from the doorway.

She turned around. "Yeah, it's nice. Where did you get it?"

"In Brazil."

"You've been to Brazil?"

He nodded. "A long time ago. I brought back a few pieces of artwork."

She turned back to the painting. "I like the way it sets off the room. I need something like this in my place. Next year, I'm going to the Black Arts Festival in Atlanta and buying some artwork."

"Cool. I'll go with you."

She laughed. *Who said you were going to be around next year?* she thought. "Well, we'd better be getting out of here. If I'm late, my mother will have a fit." She turned and walked toward the front door, still trying to look at the rest of the house. "You know, I've never been over here before."

He grabbed his duffel bag. "You haven't?"

"No, you've never invited me. Could it be because you've got a woman up in here somewhere?" she asked, craning her neck as if she were looking for someone.

He snapped his fingers. "Oh, that reminds me. You go ahead, I'm gonna run upstairs and tell my wife I'm leaving."

"Your wife?!" she asked, stunned.

He dropped his bag and started laughing. "Come on, girl, let me give you the ten-cent tour. Just so you'll know I'm only kidding."

They walked through the house, with Bobbi poking her head in every room looking for pictures or something to suggest someone else lived there. Instead, she saw nothing but pictures of his daughter and traces of masculinity all over the place. His bed wasn't made, and his office looked like a cyclone had just hit.

He cleared his throat. "Excuse the mess. I wasn't expecting company."

So, she'd finally found something Quen wasn't good at:

keeping a neat house. Everything downstairs looked good, but the second floor was another matter altogether.

"That's okay. At least now I know you're not from another planet. You seem so perfect to me."

"What? You've got to be kidding. I'm far from perfect. As a matter of fact, I don't even bear close resemblance."

They left the house and headed south to Douglas, Georgia. Bobbi had thought all night about Roz's comment regarding Quen going to school in Macon. They did have very good schools in Chicago. The minute he stopped talking about their prison project, she jumped in.

"Quen, I've been meaning to ask you: What brought you to Macon?"

"I told you before, didn't I? I was looking for a change of scenery."

"I'm curious why you didn't move to Atlanta? I mean, it's not as big as Chicago, but it's not as small as Macon."

"I know a few people who live in Atlanta, and all they do is cry about the traffic. I wanted to leave stuff like that behind me. Macon's cool. I like the university, too."

"It probably doesn't compare to any school in Chicago though."

"It's comparable."

"Is that where you met Jacque? In school?"

"It wasn't that type of class." He turned and looked at Bobbi.

"Oh" is all she said, hoping he'd care to elaborate.

"We met during a strange time in my life. I'll have to explain it to you some time."

"There's no time like the present."

He shook his head. "Not today."

"I'm not asking to hear about all your past relationships or—"

"Hold up. Jacque and I were never involved like that, if that's what you're getting at. We took a class together and that's all. I haven't seen her since the class ended. Which is why it was strange running into her here in Macon."

"Yeah, I got the feeling you were shocked."

"Only because I hadn't seen her in so long."

Bobbi kept her eyes on the road, but could see Quen tilting his head, smiling at her. She glanced over at him. "What's wrong?"

"Are you jealous?" he asked.

"What?" She laughed. "No. I was just curious, that's all."

He crossed his arms. "It bothered you that she said I met her in class, didn't it?"

"No," she lied.

"Okay," he said, nodding. "I don't want you to have the impression that I go around picking up women from all my classes."

"I wasn't thinking that at all," she lied again.

After a little less than three hours, they pulled into Bobbi's mother's driveway. Bobbi didn't know who looked more nervous, her or Quen. He looked up at her mother's house and commented on it. She'd never brought a man home with her before, so she was about the catch the third degree. The only person aware of Quen's visit was her mother. She'd promised to have the guest room all cleaned up and to be on her best behavior. If only she could get everybody else to do the same.

The minute they stepped out of the car, they could hear the music coming from the backyard. There weren't any cars in the driveway or parked along the curb, so nothing had started yet.

"This is a nice house. Nice and big. How many bedrooms?" he asked.

"Five. It was my grandmother's. After my parents bought it, they did a little remodeling. The kitchen's new, and bigger than the old one." She popped the trunk and Quen grabbed their bags.

"Well here goes," he said.

"Nervous?" she asked.

He shook his head. "Not really, you?"

"Very," she admitted, closing the trunk.

"Don't worry. I've got your back." He started up the driveway, then stopped. "Hey, before we get in there, how about a kiss for good luck?"

He leaned over and Bobbi raised her head to give him a quick kiss on the lips, but it turned into much more than that. They stood in the driveway kissing until Bobbi realized where she was. She backed away and frowned at him. "People can see us, you know."

He looked around. "So what? Let them find somebody to kiss. You're mine."

"I am?" she asked, starting up the driveway again.

"That's right. And we need to do something to make it official," he said, following her.

She looked back, smiling. "I didn't remember that discussion."

He grinned. "Then I'll have to do something about that."

They walked through the backyard, and everything looked ready for a party. The grill was smoking and the music was playing. Card tables were placed around the picnic bench and patio sets were up. Bobbi saw two coolers undoubtedly full of some type of alcoholic beverage and soft drinks.

The minute Bobbi opened the back door, Quen stepped inside a kitchen full of laughing women. All laughter stopped once they noticed him.

"Bobbi, girl, we didn't hear you pull up." A short woman with long braids walked from behind the counter to give Bobbi a hug.

"Hey, Aunt Doris. How you doing?"

"I'm fine, honey. You all come on in. Your mother's upstairs getting dressed."

"Hey, Bobbi," two other women spoke from their spots at the counter cutting up potatoes.

Bobbi waved. "Aunt Doris, this is Quen."

"How you doing, baby?" She held out her hand.

Quen shifted the bags to one hand and shook her hand. "I'm fine. Nice to meet you."

Bobbi introduced him around the room to her cousins. Then another woman walked in.

"Well, it's about time you got here. What took you so long? I thought you were going to help cook?"

Bobbi waved her off. "Quen, this is my sister, Gigi."

He shifted the bags again to shake her hand.

"So, this is the sexy voice on the phone the last time you were here?" She strutted over to him and shook his hand. "You have a wonderful voice."

"Down, girl," one of the cousins said, and everyone started laughing.

Quen thanked her and shook her hand. Now, this he hadn't expected. Bobbi's sister barely resembled her. He guessed her hair was red. Or was it orange? He couldn't tell. There were streaks of red, orange, and whatever color those two together created running through her head.

"Bobbi, don't make the man stand here holding your bags. Show him to the guest room," Gigi scolded her sister.

"I am. I'll catch you ladies in a few."

"Bye, Quen," they all said in unison.

He smiled and tilted his head toward them. He followed Bobbi through the living room to the staircase.

"Sorry about that. My sister's a little on the wild side."

"No problem. But let me ask you something." They reached the top of the stairs and she looked back at him.

"What?"

"Exactly what color is her hair?"

She laughed. "I have no idea. She's lightened it since last week. It was a real deep red. Now she looks like Carrot Top, the comedian."

Quen shrugged. "She's tall and thin enough to be a runway model, but I don't know about that hair."

"A model? No way." Bobbi opened the door to a room at the end of the hall. "This is the guest room. Make yourself at home." She stepped inside.

"Whose room did this used to be?" he asked, looking around at the flowery wallpaper and bedspread.

"I think it was one of my aunts. It's always been a guest room since we've lived here." She flopped down on the bed. "So it hasn't been slept in much."

He dropped his bag and stared down at her. "Let's see how well the mattress has held up." He walked toward her and placed his hands on her shoulders, easing her back on the bed. The mattress emitted a low squeak when he lay down on top of her. Before she could protest, he kissed her on the mouth. After several kisses and a few more squeaks from the bed, Bobbi pushed him over.

"Quen, in case you forgot, we're in my mother's house, and she can walk through that door any minute."

"Maybe we should shut the door," he suggested with a smile.

Bobbi jumped up from the bed. "Not right now. You know there's a kitchen full of women downstairs just betting on what we're doing up here."

"No," he said sarcastically.

"Trust me. I know my family."

"So, is this a hen party, or will some men show up?"

She laughed. "Of course there'll be some men here."

"Hey, I didn't know."

"Marcus is probably in his room. If he comes out, you'll get to meet him."

"*If* he comes out?" Quen phrased it as a question.

Bobbi nodded. "Sometimes it's hard to get him to leave his room."

"Oh, this is going to be a fun weekend." He sat back down. "Where are you sleeping?"

"Across the hall."

He raised a brow. "Like I said, this is going to be a fun weekend."

Nineteen

Several hours later, Quen found himself sitting in the backyard under a shade tree, drinking beer and having a conversation with Bobbi's uncle Sam.

"And that's Bobbi's cousin Will over there." Sam pointed to a man walking out the back door, stepping high. "He's drunker than a skunk. But that ain't nothing for him; he stays that way. And never misses a day at work. You ever known anybody like that?"

Quen took a swig of his beer and shook his head. "I don't believe I have."

"That bastard gets up every morning at six o'clock and goes to work. But, by six that afternoon"—Sam shook his head—"he's several sheets to the wind. That fool lives to drink. Now, does that make any sense?"

Quen shrugged with a helpless gesture. "I'm with you. Doesn't make any sense to me." Uncle Sam was talking Quen's ear off. He looked around the yard for Bobbi, but couldn't locate her in the sea of Cunninghams. The smell of barbecue had him practically salivating. He'd met every relative in the yard, and all he wanted right now was to pull a slab of ribs off the grill.

"Whereabout's you say you from in Chicago? I got some people there," Sam asked.

"Just south of Michigan," Quen answered, guessing Sam didn't know the first thing about Chicago.

The man scratched his head, as if he were trying to

remember where Michigan was. "Nope, don't think they live around that area."

Quen smiled and finished off his second bottle of beer.

"Let me get you another cold one," Sam offered.

"No, thank you." Quen stopped him. "I'm cool. Don't want to fill up before I get some of those ribs."

"Yeah, what's taking so long?" Sam looked around to see who was minding the grill. "Vernon, when we gonna eat? This man came all the way from Macon, he's hungry."

Quen wanted to reach out and strangle Uncle Sam. Several of the relatives at the card table turned around and looked his way.

"Don't ask me, ask Wilma. This ain't my house." Vernon returned to his card game, fussing at his partner for playing a bad card.

The back door opened and Wilma walked out with a large covered stainless-steel pot.

"Here we go, boy, watch this." Sam set his beer down and walked over to help Wilma. "Well, it's about time you all got that food ready. This man is starving over here." He pointed back at Quen.

Quen grabbed the closest chair and sat down. Uncle Sam was embarrassing him.

"As soon as Alice gets off the phone, we'll eat," Wilma answered.

"Tell that old broad to get out here so we can sing 'Happy Birthday' and get it over with. She makes us wait half the day to eat every year."

That was Cousin Will. Obviously not that drunk, Quen observed.

"He's a trip, isn't he?"

Quen turned to his left as a young man pulled up a chair and sat next to him. He set a bottle of beer down beside his chair, as if he were hiding it. "Yeah, I think he's had a little too much to drink."

"You ain't seen nothing yet. He just got started." The young man extended his hand. "Marcus. I'm Bobbi's brother."

Quen turned in his seat to face Marcus and shook his hand. "Hey, what's up, Marcus? Quen. Bobbi talks about you all the time."

He turned his beer bottle up, taking a gulp. "Don't believe a word of it. I'm innocent, man."

Quen laughed. "It was all good."

"Then we're not talking about the same Bobbi Cunningham. My sister's always on me for something."

"It's 'cause she loves you, that's all."

"Yeah, whatever." He took a few more gulps before pitching his bottle into a nearby trash can. "Man, I'm gonna sneak inside and grab me some meat. Want me to bring you something?"

"Yeah, bring me a piece, if you don't mind." He watched Marcus walk back in the house and wondered if his mother allowed him to drink beer at home. From the way he kept the bottle hidden beside his chair, he doubted it. He didn't look seventeen. To Quen, he looked older than Bobbi.

A cool breeze blew by and Quen welcomed it. It was three o'clock, the hottest part of the day. But the backyard was covered with overgrown shade trees, which kept the sun out. Earlier Bobbi had walked him through the flower garden; he hadn't expected it to be so big. Beyond what you could see from the yard, the garden extended several feet to what looked like a wooded area beyond the yard. Several chairs and benches were placed throughout the garden, for her aunt Alice to have a seat as she gardened, he was sure.

He saw Bobbi's older sister, Gigi, walking hand in

hand through the garden with a man who looked younger than Marcus.

"Here you go." A voice came from behind him.

Quen sat up as Marcus handed him a paper plate covered with a napkin.

"Eat up, because Bobbi's on my heels." He looked up at the back door, as if expecting her to come running out.

The barbecue smelled so good, he didn't have to tell Quen to eat up. He trimmed the bones in a matter of minutes. Somehow, Marcus beat him though. They threw the bones in the trash can and sat back, laughing.

"Thanks. That'll hold me for another ten minutes, anyway," Quen said.

"Want another beer?" Marcus asked, getting up.

"No, thanks." Quen wanted to tell him he shouldn't be getting any, either, but it wasn't his place.

Marcus walked over to the nearest cooler and fished inside for a bottle of beer. He pulled one out and closed the lid. Just then, the back door opened and Bobbi walked out. Behind her, Wilma and two more women carried trays of food.

Quen was happy to see Bobbi. After she set her tray down, she walked over to join him. She flopped down in the seat Marcus had vacated.

"Boy, am I tired. They're trying to work me to death in there. Are you okay out here?" she asked.

He smiled. "I'm fine. I was about to pass out from hunger, but Marcus helped me out."

"Is that what he was doing? I saw him sneaking around in the kitchen. I thought he was trying to swipe a bottle of beer."

"Oh, he's already been there. I didn't know if it was cool or not."

"It's not. If my mother sees him, she'll skin him alive." She leaned her head back in the seat and closed her eyes.

Quen walked behind her chair and began massaging her shoulders. She moaned and it made him want to take her upstairs to the guest room while everybody else was outside. No one would hear them once the party started, anyway.

"My aunt's on her way out."

Pop, pop, pop, pop. They jumped at what sounded like gunfire.

Quen let go as Bobbi jumped up from her seat. Several kids came running from the flower garden, laughing and screaming.

"Here, here. Get away from my flowers with those firecrackers." Wilma chased them out of the garden.

Bobbi sighed and dropped her shoulders. "That scared me to death. I thought somebody was crashing our party." She sat back down.

Quen returned his hands to her shoulders and continued the massage. "I almost forgot it was the Fourth. I should have brought some bottle rockets or something."

"Don't worry, Marcus will break his out later on. He usually does."

"Good."

A few seconds later, Aunt Alice walked out, preceded by another cousin holding a cake with candles and a sparkler in the center. As they walked across the backyard, the crowd began to sing "Happy Birthday." Bobbi and Quen joined in.

Finally, they ate. After the food came the music, and Aunt Alice got up to dance. She was pretty spry for an old woman, Quen thought, as he laughed at Uncle Sam trying to keep up with her. The dessert may have been better than the ribs. Quen had never had old-fashioned homemade ice cream before. Bobbi showed him the machine and how her aunt had made the custard the day before. He loved it.

As the sun set, Quen and Bobbi sat at the picnic

bench, having a discussion about police brutality toward black males since they'd witnessed a recent incident in the news. He straddled the bench while Bobbi sat between his legs leaning her back against his chest. The discussion was interrupted when a car pulled into the driveway with the stereo thumping loudly enough to shake the picnic table.

"Who invited him?" a cousin asked, gesturing toward the black Toyota in the driveway with tinted windows.

"Nobody," Bobbi said, getting up from the bench.

The car door opened, and Marcus got out. Someone turned the music down.

"Who's that?" Quen asked, sensing trouble.

"Peanut," another cousin said, getting up from the table. "I got it, Bobbi." He left the table and walked toward the car.

Marcus and two men leaned against the Toyota, talking.

"I'll be right back, Quen." Bobbi went in the opposite direction, toward the back door.

"Having a good time?" a woman asked.

Quen turned to his left to see Gigi sitting across from him. He brought his other leg around and under the bench. "Yes. I'm having a ball."

"That's good. You know, I'm gonna have to have a talk with that little sister of mine. She didn't tell me about you. When I suggested she bring a date, she looked at me like I was crazy."

Quen shrugged. "Well, I'm glad she changed her mind."

Gigi pulled a cigarette from her pocket and lit it. "So, Quen, where you from?"

"Chicago."

She froze, holding her cigarette in midair. "You're kidding?"

He shook his head and smiled. "No, why?"

She blew out a puff of smoke. "I lived in Chicago for a few years."

"Oh, yeah? What part?"

"Near North. Over by Monroe, close to Broadway."

"By Lake Michigan?"

"Yeah, one block."

He shook his head. "I know the area. It's real nice. I don't remember Bobbi telling me you used to live in Chicago. When did you leave?"

"Two weeks ago." She took another drag from her cigarette. "It's a long story."

He remembered Bobbi saying something about her sister being in trouble, but she'd never told him what had happened. What he really wanted to ask her was what had happened to her hair. It looked like a dye job gone bad.

"So, what area you from?" she asked.

"Southside, born and raised," he said proudly.

She shivered. "Rough over there, isn't it?"

"It's all in what you make it."

"So, you got a wife and kids in Chicago somewhere?"

He raised his brows at her. "You certainly don't waste any time, do you?"

"That's my baby sister you've been hugged up on. And you look a little older than her."

Quen laced his fingers on top of the table and studied Gigi. He hadn't pegged her for the protective big sister type. But he liked that. "I have a thirteen-year-old daughter in Chicago, but no wife."

"Have you ever been in jail?" she asked, sounding like a drill sergeant.

He shook his head, and hoped she stopped right there. "No. Have you?"

"Once, but they couldn't make it stick." She took another drag off her cigarette. "I was out in no time."

Tough girl. Or, that's what she wanted him to believe. He found it rather funny, but refrained from laughing.

Someone turned the music up, and Earth, Wind and Fire drowned out any conversation they might have continued to have. Quen turned in his seat to watch Bobbi's mother and another man dancing on the makeshift dance floor in the middle of the yard. Out of the corner of his eye, he saw Uncle Sam waving at him. He stood from the card table in the right corner of the yard. Two other people were sitting with him, and they all waved at Quen. He looked back at Gigi, to make sure they wanted him, and not her.

"Hey, better not take any money with you," she yelled.

"Why?" he yelled back over the music.

"You'll be going home broke. He plays for a living."

Quen nodded, thanking her, then climbed off the bench and crossed the yard. As soon as he sat down, Uncle Sam handed him another beer.

"Here, enjoy yourself." He laughed. "Yeah, it's a party, relax."

Quen and Sam made a good team. Before the evening was over, they'd beaten just about everybody in the backyard. The sun had gone down and the women were cleaning up the food. A few of the partygoers had left, but some family members were still there. Bobbi had come over and sat next to him, offering good-luck kisses while he played. He hadn't enjoyed himself this much in a long time.

The card game ended when someone put on the Isley Brothers' "Choosy Lover." Sam threw his cards down and grabbed his wife, yelling, "Ah, here we go. Now that's my song."

Before Quen knew it, just about everyone was in the backyard, slow dancing. He turned to Bobbi.

"My family's very old school. I should have warned you," she apologized.

"Hey, that's cool. I love old-school music." He put his

cards down and grabbed her hand, leading her to the dance floor.

He pulled her close to him and wrapped his arms around her. She fell in step and laid her head on his chest. The full moon provided the perfect setting for the cozy dance floor. A gentle breeze blew through the trees, cooling things off slightly.

Quen's body responded to having her so close. In the four weeks he'd known her, he'd grown to love her, and this was as close as they'd gotten. His body was hungry for her, and he didn't think he could hold out much longer.

The music stopped and he pulled her back just enough to kiss her on the forehead. "Thank you." He kept his hold on her, not wanting to let go just yet.

Assaulting rap lyrics came from the driveway, and everyone turned as the Toyota pulled back in. Peanut.

Bobbi pulled away from Quen when she saw her mother walking down the sidewalk toward the car. The car door opened and Marcus staggered out. Before Wilma could reach the car, it pulled back out of the driveway and off down the street.

Quen had wanted to grab Bobbi and keep her by his side. He hadn't liked the looks of Peanut when he'd seen him the first time. The party atmosphere was broken.

The three of them came marching back up the walkway with Wilma screaming at Marcus. As they drew closer, Quen could see Marcus's eyes were a bloodshot red. He'd had too much to drink, and possibly to smoke. He looked stoned. He wouldn't be shooting off any fireworks tonight.

"Boy, when Alabama gets back he's gonna have his hands full right there with that boy." A man's voice came from behind Quen.

"If it's not too late," a woman's voice said.

Quen wondered who Alabama was as he watched

Marcus go inside without saying so much as one word
to anyone. Bobbi tried to calm her mother down, but
Wilma was still yelling through the door at him.

Someone from the card table yelled, "Wilma, let
Alabama take care of him. Marcus is a grown man
now."

"Then I want him out of my house," she yelled back.
The party was over.

Later that night, when everything had calmed down,
Quen found himself sitting in the den, talking to Bobbi's
aunt Alice. It was as if everyone had left the room so
they could talk. He expected the third degree, but instead they had a nice conversation regarding life and
love.

Bobbi helped Gigi and her mother clean up the kitchen.
Wilma had calmed down, and Marcus had locked himself
in his room.

"I think the party was a success," Gigi announced.

Bobbi laughed. "Yeah, right up until the end."

"Well, Aunt Alice seemed to enjoy herself."

"As long as she has somebody to talk to, she's enjoying herself."

"Where is she now?" Wilma asked.

"She's in the den talking to Quen," Bobbi said.

"Good, because I need to talk to you a minute."

"Mama, if it's about him staying, you said it was all
right," Bobbi reminded her.

Wilma pulled a large box of aluminum foil from the
pantry. "It's not about him. He seems like a nice young
man, although he has octopus hands. Every time I look
at the two of you, you're hugged up or he's holding you
somehow." She covered the leftover meat.

"That's because she hasn't sexed him yet," Gigi blurted out.

"Shut up, Gi," Bobbi protested.

Wilma frowned at Gigi. "What did I tell you? Watch that mouth of yours."

"Okay, if it's not about him, what then?" Bobbi asked.

"I wanted your father to tell you this, but he said he's having a hard time contacting you. Which I don't doubt is true."

"Yeah, and?" Wilma was going to ruin her weekend by bringing up her father.

"He's getting out. He should be home in a few weeks."

Bobbi dropped the glass she was rinsing into the sink. It exploded and a piece of shattered glass cut her hand.

Wilma ran over to the sink and grabbed Bobbi's hand. She turned the faucet on and pulled Bobbi's hand over the other sink, holding it under running water.

"No!" Bobbi screamed.

Twenty

Quen excused himself after hearing Bobbi's scream come from the kitchen. He could hear the women fussing as he walked in from the den. "Bobbi, are you okay?" he asked, walking over to her and her mother, standing at the sink.

"I broke a glass and cut my finger," Bobbi said. She sounded annoyed with herself.

Wilma held Bobbi's hand up, examining it. "It's just a little cut. I'll take care of this and you'll be fine. Stop whining. You're lucky it wasn't deeper and you didn't sever a nerve."

Only a trickle of blood remained on her finger. The running water had washed most traces of blood down the drain. Quen took a deep breath. The way Bobbi had screamed, he'd thought something was seriously wrong.

Gigi put down her towel and walked over, grabbing Quen by the arm. "Quen, I didn't get to finish talking to you earlier. While Mama cleans Bobbi up, let's have a little powwow." She led him back into the den.

He walked away, looking back at Bobbi. Something about the stricken look on her face worried him.

In the den, Aunt Alice was getting up from the couch. Gigi had let go of Quen's arm and flopped down on the couch. He asked Alice if she needed any help.

"No, honey, you sit down and watch television." She cut her glance over to Gigi. "When you gonna wash that mess out of your head?" she asked, standing slightly bent over.

"It's dye. I can't just wash it out. It'll darken up in a few days." She ran a hand through her hair. "I went over by the mall and got my hair done. I should have done it myself."

Alice glanced at Quen and nodded her head toward Gigi. "It's a mess, isn't it?"

He shrugged, not wanting to get into the middle of things.

Alice started out of the room. "He's just being polite." She blew out a breath, appearing exhausted from the day's activities. "I'm going to bed. I'll see you folks in the morning."

Gigi jumped up and kissed her aunt on the cheek before she left the room. "Good night, and happy birthday, Aunt Alice. Love you."

Quen said good night and watched Aunt Alice waddle out of the room.

"So, Quen, what's on your mind this evening?" Gigi asked.

"I'm glad you asked. I've got something I need your help with."

"What?"

"Bobbi's birthday. It's coming up and I need a few gift ideas."

"Hmm, this is serious, isn't it?" she asked, with a raised brow.

Wilma sat Bobbi down at the kitchen table and took care of her finger. "You knew he'd be coming home someday, didn't you?"

"I guess so," she admitted.

"Bobbi, when Mark comes home, I want you to sit down and talk to him."

She shook her head. "Mama, I don't think I can. I don't even see how you can welcome him back after he pretended all that time to be going to work everyday, but he was out selling drugs. If he truly loved you, he would have never done that."

Wilma finished bandaging Bobbi's finger and set her hand on the table. "Baby, if I knew that's what he was doing, do you think I would have stood for it? I had no idea your father had lost his job. He was too proud to go downtown and ask for public assistance. He'd become desperate. He'd bought this big old house from my family, and didn't want anyone to know he couldn't pay for it. A friend of his offered a solution to his problem, and he took it."

"That wasn't a real friend, or a solution, in my opinion."

"No, it wasn't. But he had a mortgage, and three kids to feed and clothe. Let alone a wife who didn't work. From where he stood, it looked like a solution. His older brother, who you guys never knew, made a living selling drugs, until he died in a car wreck years ago."

Bobbi ran her other hand across her face and took a deep breath. In a few weeks, her father would be home, and her visits would never be the same. And what would Quen think of her? He thought her father was dead.

"So, it runs in the family, so to speak?" Bobbi asked. To her, it proved her theory and her whole reason for going to school. When people didn't know better, they repeated the sins of their elders. It was that vicious cycle all over again.

"I don't want to say that. Mark comes from a nice family, and you know that."

Bobbi nodded. She didn't have anything against her father's family, only him.

"So, when he comes home, are you two going to get along?" Wilma asked, reaching over to touch Bobbi's cheek.

Bobbi scratched her head and ran a few fingers through her hair. She couldn't commit to that, and she knew it. She hadn't had a real conversation with her father since she was in the ninth grade. "I'll think about it." That was as good as she could honestly do.

Wilma nodded, showing her understanding.

She looked so sad, but if Bobbi promised to get along with him, it would only create more friction once he showed up. She'd just have to start sticking around Macon more. She stood. "Well, I'd better rescue Quen from Gigi. Thanks," she said, holding out her hand.

Bobbi swatted at a mosquito before walking over to light another citronella candle. Quen had talked her into sitting outside alongside the garden with nothing but candlelight and the moonlight to see by. She walked back over to the bench and sat down. Quen straddled the bench and pulled Bobbi close to him. She leaned back, resting her head against his chest.

"I like it out here," he admitted.

"I can appreciate it now. But when I lived here, it was extremely boring."

He wrapped his arms around her shoulders and nuzzled her ear. She giggled and pulled away from him. "I'm extremely ticklish," she said through her laughter.

"Good," he said, before leaning down to tickle her ear with his mouth again.

All Bobbi could think about was that this would be a perfect time to let him know her father was indeed alive, and would be showing up one day soon. Although she'd never told him Mark was dead, she regretted letting him believe he was.

They sat there, talking and cuddling, into the night. She hadn't felt this content and happy in a long time. She hated to ruin the moment. Before she could say anything,

Quen held up her finger and kissed the bandage where she'd cut herself.

A warm fuzzy feeling ran through her body. His kiss was gentle and caring as he continued up her arm, tickling her again. She jumped away, but he pulled her back and clamped his arms around her in a bear hug.

"Okay, okay, I won't tickle you," he said.

"Don't, because I go crazy. I can't stand it."

"I can do better than that." He lowered his arms and grabbed her by the waist, turning her sideways. Once she partially faced him, he kissed the tip of her nose, then her mouth.

She opened up fully to him, wanting more than his hot kisses. Suddenly, he pulled up her top and she felt his warm hand against her stomach. She wanted him more than anything. Her body had waited long enough for him. Everything about Quen felt right, and his touch had a way of setting her body on fire. She twisted her upper body around, facing him, bringing her chest closer to his.

He pulled back a little, affectionately sucking at her bottom lip. She heard a hard moan escape from his lips. It was apparent he wanted her twice as much as she wanted him. His breathing was heavy and hot.

"Do you think everybody's asleep?" he asked.

Bobbi looked up at the house, dark except for a small light coming from the kitchen. "Probably so." She knew what was on his mind, and she was way ahead of him.

"Then let's go inside," he whispered in her ear.

His breath against her ear tickled. She lowered her head and heard a giggle, but it wasn't hers. She held her head up, and heard it again. Quen heard it, too. They looked at each other and he held a finger over his lips.

Seconds later, Gigi walked out of the garden with the same young man from earlier on her arm. Her flaming red hair was all over her head. Quen cleared his throat.

Gigi jumped and grabbed her young man's arm. "Hey, what are you guys doing sitting out here?" she asked, walking over to the bench with her young man.

Bobbi sat staring at her, slightly embarrassed. Her family was painting a picture of craziness for Quen. From her drunk uncle and stoned brother to her promiscuous sister.

"Just getting some air," Quen answered, holding Bobbi in his arms.

"Uh-huh, looks like you're trying to get a little more than air to me." She grinned and winked at Bobbi.

"Looks like you've already gotten more than air," Bobbi responded with a sarcastic grin.

Gigi threw her head back, laughing. Her young man kissed her on the neck. "Did I introduce you to Wayne?"

"No, I don't believe we've had the pleasure," Bobbi said.

"Wayne, this is my little sister, Bobbi, and her boyfriend, Quen."

Wayne stepped forward to shake their hands. Bobbi reached out, but didn't get up. He didn't look a day over twenty, she thought. Quen stood to exchange handshakes with him.

Gigi reach out and stroked his chin. "Now, doesn't he look just like Daddy?" she said, staring up into Wayne's eyes.

Bobbi shook her head. *She's sick*. The last thing she needed was Gigi talking about their father before she had a chance to inform Quen of his whereabouts. "Well, folks, I think we're going to call it a night." She stood and reached for Quen's hand.

"Good, we'll take your seat." They flopped down on the bench after Quen and Bobbi walked up the sidewalk toward the house.

"You two sleep tight," Gigi said, giggling.

Before Quen opened the back door, Bobbi reached out and stopped him. "I've got something I need to tell you."

He looked down, nodding his head. "So do I, but not tonight. We'll sit down and have a long talk when we get back to Macon."

Bobbi woke early Sunday morning, wanting to leave before her family left for church. She put water for coffee on for everyone, then sat down to a bowl of cereal until her Aunt Alice walked in.

"Did you enjoy your party last night?"

"I sure did. And I enjoyed meeting your young man, too."

Bobbi put down her spoon and helped her aunt. "What do you think of him? I mean, I know you can meet someone and see right away if they're a good person or not."

"And you want me to give you the okay on this young man?"

Bobbi shrugged. "If you can."

Alice sat down at the table to her cup of coffee. She shook her head and smiled up at Bobbi.

Bobbi hunched over her cereal bowl, peeking up at her aunt. "I mean, if you couldn't tell anything, I understand. You didn't get to talk to him for a—"

"He's a very nice young man. And I think he'll be good for you."

Bobbi sat back, smiling. "You think so?"

"Yes, I do. Bobbi, you've grown into a beautiful young woman and you deserve to be happy. Life is short, so very short. If you love this young man, and he makes you happy, I wish you the best."

Beaming, Bobbi got up and walked over to kiss her aunt on the cheek. "Thank you, Auntie. I love you."

Bobbi finished her cereal and put the bowl in the

sink. "I think I'm going to see if Quen's awake so we can head back."

"One more thing, baby."

Bobbi stopped and looked back at her aunt.

Alice looked up from her coffee. "He's got a heavy heart. I don't know what it is, but he's carrying something around inside of him that's more than he should have to endure."

Her aunt had a sixth sense that never missed. Bobbi nodded to let her know she understood and went to get Quen.

Twenty-one

Professor Jennings passed out the midterm grades with a solemn face. "I'm not pleased with some of these scores. Everyone's not studying the chapters."

He dropped Bobbi's exam on her desk facedown. She sat there, staring at the paper, afraid to turn it over. She could have read more and studied hardier, and she knew it. Instead of checking her score, she looked across the room at Quen. He smiled and shook his head, looking down. That was a bad sign.

She took a deep breath and flipped the paper over. She stared down at the big red C on her paper and exhaled. By a hair, she'd managed to pass. But that wasn't good enough.

On her way out the door, Professor Jennings waved her over. She walked over for what she was sure would be another pep talk.

"I'm disappointed in you, Ms. Cunningham."

She hung her head. "No more than I am."

"But you can turn things around with your final exam. I hear your group plans to interview ex-convicts as part of your research."

She looked up at him, hoping he wasn't going to shoot that idea down. "Yeah, Quen's set something up for this week."

He nodded. "Clever thinking. I'll be looking forward to your final presentation. I'm sure I'll be impressed."

All the way out to her car, Bobbi knew why she hadn't done so well on her test. She'd fallen in love and gotten sidetracked. Love was blind, and no more than a fantasy.

"So, how'd you do?"

She turned around as Quen walked up behind her.

"Not so good. I got a C. How about you?"

"Same here. We've got a lot of work to do in the next three weeks, you know?"

"Tell me about it."

"But first, how about dinner tonight?"

"Can we make it tomorrow night? I need to get caught up after being away for the weekend."

"Sure."

"I tell you what. I'll cook—since you've taken me to just about every restaurant in town."

He laughed. "You've got a deal. But we'll make it my place."

Good, she thought. She hadn't really gotten a good look at the place before. "Your place it is."

Bobbi served lamb chops with white beans and gremolata for dinner, and fixed iced tea to drink. For dessert, she'd purchased a lemon pound cake from a local bakery. After dinner, Quen challenged her to a game of Monopoly. She beat him, leaving him penniless before they called it quits.

"She beats me in the kitchen, she beats me at Monopoly, what else can you do better than me?" he teased.

"Hey, don't get mad at me because I purchased Boardwalk and Park Place. I'm the real-estate queen," she cheered, raising her hands over her head.

He turned up his lip to sneer at her, then smiled. "Okay, Ms. Thimble Tycoon. Give me all your riches so I can put this game up."

She handed over all her Monopoly money. "What time is it, anyway?" she asked, looking down at her watch.

"It's movie time," he responded.

She looked up at him in disbelief. "You're kidding?" What had she told him about dates and movies?

"Nope." He walked over and picked up the VHS tape. "It's something I know you haven't reviewed. It's vintage." He handed her the tape.

Bobbi's eyes opened wide. *"Freaks!"* She smiled up at him. "You weren't kidding, this is vintage—1932, to be exact. You know the same guy who directed the first *Dracula* did this one."

"Tod Browning, yeah, I know. He did most of the Lon Chaney silent films, too." He sat down next to her on the couch.

"Who told you I loved horror films?"

He shrugged. "A little birdie. Want some popcorn? I can make some."

Bobbi leaned over and kissed him on the cheek. "No thanks, I'm full. You're wonderful."

Quen's stomach felt queasy. How long would this last? Once he got up the nerve to tell her about his past, would she think him wonderful then? Tonight was a perfect time to have a talk with her. But that was the problem. The night was too perfect, and he didn't want to ruin it. He put his arm around her and returned the kiss.

Her proximity was giving him a hard-on. He stopped kissing her before he reached the point of no return. He crossed the room and popped the tape in. "Get set to be scared out of your mind," he said, with a sinister hint to his voice.

"Ew, I'm scared." Bobbi shivered, then kicked off her shoes and pulled her feet up on the couch.

Quen reclaimed his seat and held up his arm. Bobbi moved over next to him and snuggled close. He wrapped

his arm around her and inhaled the scent of fresh flowers.
He kissed the top of her head and settled in for the night.

Freaks may have been scary in 1932, but that night it
hardly scared Bobbi. All the same, she liked it. It was a
classic. The picture freaked her out more than scared
her. Several times she found herself burying her face
into Quen's chest.

By the time the film ended, she lay stretched out on
his couch with her head in his lap, dozing off. She heard
him stop the tape.

"Is it over?" she asked, coming out of her sleep-induced
fog.

"Yes, and you slept through most of it." He ran his
hand through her hair, pulling it back from her cheek.

Bobbi rolled over onto her back and looked up at
him. "I'm sorry. I guess I was a little sleepy."

"That's okay," he said, with a deeper voice than usual.
He leaned forward and kissed her on the forehead. "I
like to watch you sleep. You look so peaceful."

"Thank you. Just call me Sleeping Beauty."

"You're a beauty, all right." He reached down and
planted another kiss on her forehead, then another softly
on her lips.

His kisses were intoxicating. They traveled through her
body, stimulating her in places long left dormant. His soft
touches teased, creating a throbbing deep inside her.

Unable to stand the bashfulness and niceness of their
caresses, she reached out and wrapped her arm around
his head, bringing him down as she kissed him with a
hunger that surprised even her. She wanted him. She
wanted him to touch her in places that no one but she
had touched for months.

Soft music played in her head as he pulled her up from
his lap and positioned her back on the couch. He brought

his body down on top of her in one smooth gentle move. His hungry kisses traveled from her lips down the deep V-cut of her blouse and back up. His breathing was heavy and ragged.

When his warm hand touched her skin while unbuttoning her blouse, she jumped. It wasn't as if he hadn't touched her before; it was the anticipation of what was to come.

"What's wrong?" he stopped and asked.

"Nothing. Everything's right."

He kissed her again, keeping his head close, rubbing their noses. "Stay with me tonight."

His whispered words came out in a sensual tone that tickled her ears. She wanted him to make love to her so bad, it clouded her thoughts. "I don't know."

"Bobbi, I can't wait no more. All I want to do is make love to you. I tried to wait until summer school was over, but I can't. Whenever I look into your eyes, I see our future and our great romance."

"One of the world's greatest romances, right?" She mocked something he'd told her once.

"That's right." He kissed her again. This time their passion overflowed and his hot kisses led to the removal of her blouse and bra. He pulled his shirt over his head and tossed it on the floor.

He cupped her breast, and Bobbi arched her back, wanting to feel the heat of his breath on her body. She was dizzy with love and want for him. The minute she felt his tongue against her nipple, she wanted to explode inside. Something came over her and she shifted on the couch, reaching for his belt buckle. She wanted him out of his clothes. She wanted them out of their clothes.

Quen helped her out by rolling over onto his side, then caressing and sucking her other breast.

Bobbi managed to get his pants unzipped after running her hand down his chest.

"Hang on, baby." He eased up from the couch, taking Bobbi's hand. "I don't want you down here like this. I want you upstairs in my bed."

"Are you prepared for this?" she asked, hoping he knew she meant a condom.

He nodded. "I've been prepared for this for a long time."

She grabbed his hand and followed his lead. If love was blind, she concluded it was dumb, too. At that moment, she would have followed him off the face of the earth. Instead, minutes later she found herself nude in his bed, being ravished, and loving every minute of it. His hands were all over her, caressing and exploring every inch of her body.

She lay on the cool white sheets, trying to catch her breath, as Quen's hands moved down between her legs while he whispered in her ear. Thinking of nothing she wanted more, she opened her legs wider.

"Yes, I want all of you in me," she whispered back.

"And I want to give it all to you," he said, rising up from her. He reached over to the nightstand and opened the top drawer, pulling out a condom. He ripped the package open with his teeth, and she took the condom from his hands.

"Let me." Bobbi smiled up at him.

He smiled back.

Their lovemaking carried them deep into the night. Bobbi's body shuddered and quivered as Quen brought her toward climax over and over—then backed off. His fingers were like search-and-rescue soldiers, roaming between her legs, searching for the spot to rescue her from months of frustration. She did the same for him, each time loving the moans and pleas that escaped his lips. He begged her to stop before the volcano inside him erupted.

Unable to take the teasing any longer, Bobbi finally

pleaded with him, "Quen, please don't stop. I want to feel you inside me now. I want everything you promised." She could have pulled her hair out, she wanted this man so bad.

As promised, he lowered himself on top of her as they reached their final destination together. Night turned into early morning as they brought each other to climax again and again before finally collapsing into a state of fulfilled bliss. They lay across the bed, Bobbi snuggled into the crease of Quen's arm. She slept like a baby the rest of the morning.

She rose later that morning to the smell of food. She stretched her hand out across the bed, but Quen wasn't there. The bedside clock read seven A.M. She was going to be late for work. She climbed out of bed and found Quen's robe on the back of the bedroom door. Following the smell of food, she found Quen in the kitchen.

"What are you doing?" she asked, poking her head in. He stood by the stove in a pair of athletic pants, with no shoes or shirt on.

"I'm whipping up some of my famous pancakes. You hungry?" With spatula in hand, he walked over and kissed her on the forehead.

Bobbi held her hand over her mouth. "I'm starved, but I can't eat until after I brush my teeth."

"Upstairs, linen closet. Look inside and you'll find a few new ones." He went back to the stove.

"You just keep them on hand, huh?"

He turned and gave her his big Denzel smile again.

"No, they come with the toothpaste. And I've never had a situation arise where someone needed one—until now."

She smiled back at him. "Good answer."

He winked at her.

* * *

After Bobbi made arrangements to go into work late, she ran home and changed clothes. Later, she met Quen and Monica at the Lean On Me Agency to interview several ex-convicts. She kept thinking that one of these men could be her father. Once he was released, would he need a program like this in Douglas? Was there even something like this in Douglas? She had no idea, but whatever; she knew her mother would be there for him, whether Bobbi thought he deserved it or not.

The last interview touched her the most. When Bobbi asked Dennis what he thought he needed most, his reply moved her.

"No matter how many programs you find when you get out, nothing can replace me missing my little girl growing up. I was incarcerated when she was nine years old; now she's twenty-one, and I don't know her. I used to be her hero, but now I'm just this dude who calls himself her father. We're strangers, and that hurts the most."

The pain in his eyes reached over and squeezed her heart. He looked lost, as if someone had stolen his baby from him. She blinked and glanced toward the ceiling to keep the tears from rolling down her cheeks.

She sat in the reception area, looking over her interview answers and waiting for Quen and Monica, when Perry and another man walked in. She recognized him right away. And with one glance, he recognized her.

"College girl," he greeted her with a big smile, "how's it going?"

She smiled politely. "Hello. I'm just fine."

"Where's your boyfriend?" he asked, looking down the hall.

She didn't like his tone. It sounded like he was trying to put Quen down. "Quen's in the back."

The man with him continued down the hall, and Perry said good-bye. He turned his attention back to Bobbi and stood close to her seat. "I'm surprised to see you here."

"We're conducting interviews with some of the ex-convicts for a class project."

"Oh, yeah, I remember now. So, my boy must have told you everything?"

"Everything about what?" she asked.

Bobbi heard Monica's laughter coming up the hall and forgot all about Perry. Quen and Monica walked toward her, laughing at what seemed to be a private joke. All laughter subsided by the time they reached her. Following on the heels of their night of lovemaking, she couldn't help but feel a twinge of jealousy.

After Monica left and Perry walked back into his office, Quen and Bobbi walked out to her car.

"That wasn't too bad, was it?" he asked.

She shook her head. "No, actually it was an eye-opener."

A huge smile covered his face. "I'd hoped you'd learn something from it. That beats reading some books telling you what ex-convicts want, doesn't it?"

"It sure does." She reached inside her purse for her car keys.

"Am I going to see you tonight?" he asked, holding her car door open.

"Not tonight. I think I'd better do a little studying."

He understood and agreed. "Okay, then I'll talk to you tomorrow." They kissed again and she left.

Bobbi buckled down and focused on her class project for the next few days. When she came up for air on Saturday, Gigi called with shocking news. Their mother had talked Marcus into checking into a drug treatment clinic.

"That's great," Bobbi exclaimed. "How did she talk him into it?"

"She had a little help. Hold on, somebody wants to speak to you."

Bobbi walked into the kitchen with the phone cradled between her ear and shoulder. What was Gigi up to? Bobbi knew Marcus didn't want to talk to her, as much as she was always getting on him. She could hear a shuffling noise in the phone as Gigi set it down.

"Bobbi." A deep masculine voice came through the phone.

"Yes, who is this?" She hoped Gigi wasn't trying to introduce her to some new boyfriend over the phone, as she'd done before.

"It's Daddy, baby. I'm home."

Twenty-two

Speechless, Bobbi had to sit down. The day she'd dreaded was here. Her father had been released from prison. For some reason she wasn't as mad as she would have been weeks ago, but she couldn't be overjoyed to hear from him, either. Deep down inside, she was still a mad little girl.

"That's okay, you don't have to say anything. I just want you to know I'm here and I'd like to see you." He cleared his throat. "Whenever you're ready, anyway."

"Okay—now I know." It hurt. Talking to him hurt, but knowing she had to see him eventually made it worse.

"I know you're mad at me, baby. I can wait, but we're going to talk."

Gigi got back on the phone to let Bobbi know how disappointed she was with her. Bobbi needed to think, and she needed some air. She hung up and went for a walk.

Bobbi spent the weekend at Quen's house, and he couldn't have been happier. He was expecting Kristy in the next few days, and Bobbi had a birthday coming up. After she met Kristy, he'd sit her down and tell her about his past. Hopefully, it wouldn't matter now that they'd grown closer together. His plan was to take Bobbi and Kristy to Justin's in Atlanta for dinner and to see a free concert in the park. As far as a gift was concerned, he'd made his mind up to get her a couple of nice dresses, but he didn't know her size. From his cell phone outside the mall, he tried to call her roommate, Roz, but when she wasn't in, he called Douglas and got Gigi.

"Well, isn't that nice. I'm jealous," she said after he explained his plans. "She's a seven-eight in dresses, and I think a size-seven shoe."

He jotted it down. "Thanks, Gigi. I meant to ask her in a way so she wouldn't know what I was up to, but I forgot."

"I'll tell you what. Why don't you hold off and give her the gift this weekend. You all can come down for Daddy's party. We're throwing him a little welcome-home bash."

"*Your* father?" he asked, in a surprised tone.

"Yeah. I know Bobbi probably didn't tell you since they don't get along too well, but he's here and we're celebrating this weekend. You're welcome to come. Maybe you'll be the only way to get that sister of mine here."

Quen sat there, shaking his head in confusion. "Do you guys have different fathers or something?" he asked in an attempt to clear things up.

"No. We all have the same dad."

Quen wanted to say *I thought he was dead?* But he didn't. Instead he sat there in disbelief, shaking his head. Her father was alive.

"She probably didn't tell you about him, did she?" Gigi asked.

"No. She didn't." He felt like a fool.

"Well, he's been in prison for the last twelve years, and they don't have the best of relationships."

He kept shaking his head, unable to digest this shocking new information. No wonder Bobbi had a hard time with their project. Why she hadn't told him, he didn't understand. Especially since she knew he worked with ex-convicts and would be able to understand her feelings.

"Quen, you still there?" Gigi asked.

"I'm here."

"What did she tell you about him?"

He couldn't tell her what he'd been thinking. "She never actually said anything. I just assumed . . . . I don't know what I assumed."

Her tone changed to a more cheerful one. "Well, we're throwing another party this weekend. If you're not doing anything, come on down."

"Thanks, Gigi. And thanks for the dress information."

Quen picked Kristy up at the airport Tuesday morning and tried not to think about Bobbi's father. He had Kristy for the next four days, and he didn't want to mess up her trip by being in a bad mood. He stored the information in the back of his head and promised not to bring it up until after Kristy went home. The next day was Bobbi's birthday, and he had most of the day mapped out.

He spent his first day with Kristy driving around seeing Macon, then stopping at the mall. Like all girls her age, she loved to shop. While at the mall, he told her about Bobbi and asked if she wanted to meet her. He wasn't sure how she'd react, but it didn't seem to bother her.

"What's her name?" Kristy asked.

"Bobbi Cunningham. I think you'll like her." He tried to read the expression on her face. She shrugged and didn't appear to be really paying attention.

"Okay, when do I get to meet her?"

"Tomorrow. It's her birthday, so I thought we'd take her out to dinner."

"Is she pretty?" she asked, holding up a skirt that looked like it was for a toddler.

Quen took the skirt from her and replaced it on the rack. "She's beautiful."

The morning of July seventeenth, Quen called Bobbi to wish her a happy birthday. The conversation was short at best. He invited her to dinner that night. She accepted the invitation, but kept asking him if everything was all right.

Several hours later, Bobbi called Quen on his cell phone.

"Does Kristy have a bathing suit?" she asked.

"I don't know."

"Ask her."

He asked, and Kristy had come prepared. "Yes, she has one, why?"

"I've got a better idea. Why don't you guys come over, and let's go swimming. I'm only working half the day today, and I thought I'd relax by the pool. I'll even throw something on the grill."

Since he didn't have a pool in his subdivision, and he knew Kristy loved swimming, he agreed. So much for his dinner plans.

Bobbi and Kristy spent the entire afternoon by the pool. They pranced around the pool, rubbing suntan lotion all over themselves like two little prima donnas. He supposed he should have been happy they were getting along, but all he thought about was if he could trust Bobbi or not, and how many more secrets she had.

Quen had done everything he needed to do to pave the way for the news he was about to deliver. Bobbi had met his daughter, and over the course of the summer, her views toward the prison system had somewhat improved. He'd waited for her to tell him about her father, but she hadn't. Tonight, he'd have to discuss that with her, and tell her about his past.

She met him at the Lean On Me Agency, to return two of Kristy's CDs she'd left at Bobbi's apartment when they'd gone swimming. When she walked through the door, Quen was talking to Olivia. Bobbi had on a cute pink dress with matching sandals.

He walked to the door to greet her. "Thanks. She'll be calling me about these as soon as she misses them." He hadn't forgotten that he was still irritated with her.

"I know. That's why I decided to swing them by. You can mail them to her."

"Yeah, I'll do that."

"Quen, you're not gonna introduce me to this lovely young lady?" Olivia asked, getting up from her seat.

"I'm sorry." He stepped aside. "This is my lady, Bobbi. And Bobbi, this is the woman that holds this place together and keeps me in line."

Bobbi walked up to her desk and offered her hand.

Olivia waved her hand at him as if to say *never mind him.* "It's nice to meet you, honey. If this guy ever gives you any trouble, you just call me. I know how to handle him."

Bobbi nodded. "I'll have to remember that."

"So, where are you two going to lunch?"

Quen shook his head. "We're not. She came down to return these CDs."

"Oh, why not? It's such a nice day."

Bobbi looked at him. "What do you say, you got time for a quick lunch?"

Any other time, he would have jumped at the chance to take her to lunch, but today he was a little too upset with her. "I can't. I've got a busy day," he lied, knowing his shift was over and he was free for the afternoon.

"Oh, okay then. I guess I'll catch you later?"

"Yeah. I'll be by tonight."

Olivia had turned back to her computer, but obviously had caught most of their conversation. After Bobbi walked out, she turned to Quen. "Somebody's not in such a good mood."

"If you mean me, yeah, I'm in a foul mood today."

"What's wrong with you?"

He shook his head. "I guess I just woke up on the wrong side of the bed." He tapped the CDs against the palm of his hand and avoided Olivia's eyes. He was walking around mad at Bobbi without her knowing what he was upset about. That was wrong and he knew it. He wasn't being fair to her, and he had to do something about that.

Bobbi sensed something had changed about Quen. He hadn't been his same touchy-feely self since his daughter had shown up. And now that Kristy was gone, he still seemed to be in a funk. He'd only kissed her once or twice in the past few days. She walked out the outer doors of the agency and started down the stairs.

Perry came around the corner just as she stepped off the last step. They almost bumped into each other.

"Oh, excuse me." Her mind was somewhere else as she stopped short.

"That's okay. Hey, college girl." He pulled his hands out of his pants pockets and held out a hand to steady her. With one finger, he pulled his shades down on his nose to get a better look.

"I guess I better pay attention to where I'm going."

"No problem. Where's your man at?"

"He's inside."

"I didn't get to ask last week, but how'd the interviews go? Two of the guys I work with volunteered."

"Oh, they were great. It was a learning experience for sure."

"Yeah. What your boy should have done was added something about probation in that report, then he could have done all that firsthand. Just like you talked to the cons firsthand."

"What would Quen know about that?" she asked. Perry had said firsthand; did he mean what she thought?

"He didn't tell you? Before he came down here he was on probation."

Bobbi froze. A knot was forming in her throat, making it difficult for her to say another word.

"Yeah, seems like he would have used that to his advantage." He shoved his hands back into his pockets, jingling his keys and change, while staring at Bobbi. "Are you okay?"

"Uh-huh." She nodded and tried her best not to look so stunned.

Perry shrugged. "I thought he would have told you by now. It's no big deal."

"What for?" was all she could get out.

Perry grinned. "Now you'll have to ask him about that. I've probably said too much already. Quen's kind of a private guy."

It couldn't be true. Bobbi wanted to run back in the building and ask Quen herself. But why would Perry lie? They worked here with ex-convicts, and he'd probably told them all about his probation. He'd probably told everyone—but her.

"Well, I gotta go." She hurried to her car, fumbling for her keys.

"Yeah, catch you later. Hey, keep that under your hat, why don't you?"

She'd already taken off for the car, and didn't really hear everything he said. She felt a headache coming on. What had he done? Was he a drug dealer, too? Or, maybe he'd hurt someone? What she couldn't get over was why he hadn't told her. She'd had sex with this man, and he hadn't said one word about that part of his past.

"Bobbi," Quen's voice called out to her.

She looked up and saw Quen coming out of the building's front door. She hurried to open the car door and get in.

"Hey, hold up." He bumped into Perry, rushing inside the building.

She started her car and backed out of the lot. She saw him waving, but kept going. He wasn't who she'd thought he was.

Twenty-three

Quen had tried to catch Bobbi, but she'd kept going. He was sure she'd heard him calling. Once in his car, he tried to reach her by cell phone, but she didn't have it turned on.

"Well, I tried."

He stopped and grabbed some fast food for lunch, then headed home. As soon as he got in the house, he tried Bobbi at work. She never answered. He knew they didn't have caller ID, so he kept trying, hoping she would pick up eventually.

Around six o'clock, he started trying her house. No answer there, either. At 7:30, he decided to pay her a visit. If she was mad at him about something, they could talk it out; if not, he could ask her about her father.

He parked his Land Rover next to her Honda. Good, she was in. He knocked several times before she finally answered the door with her arms crossed. She looked pissed.

"What's wrong? You're not answering the phone." He walked past her into the living room.

She left the front door open and took on a stance of defiance. He pretended not to notice and went to sit on the couch. She didn't follow him.

"Okay, what's up? You look like somebody stole your bike."

She reached out with one hand and slammed the front door closed, then returned to her stone-faced stance.

"We need to talk." Her words were like daggers aimed at him.

Before she jumped down his throat for something he probably hadn't done, he decided to beat her to it. "Yeah, we do." He stood. "Why didn't you tell me your father was alive?"

Her folded arms slowly lowered to her sides. "What are you talking about?"

"I talked to Gigi the other day."

She took a few steps back and lowered herself into a dining room chair.

He crossed back through the living room to stand in the dining room doorway. Bobbi slowly ran the palms of her hands over her face. She looked stressed and tired. Quen realized he shouldn't have blurted it out like that. He walked over and pulled out the chair next to her.

"Why didn't you tell me? Of all people, you know I would have understood."

She lowered her hands and leaned back against the seat. "Why? Because working with ex-convicts was part of your probation?"

Quen shot back in his seat. He felt all the color drain from his face. He couldn't believe what she'd just said. "Who told you that?"

She didn't answer. She only stared at him. The pained look on her face was killing him. He wanted to get down on one knee and beg her to forgive him. Instead, they sat, staring at each other for a while before he lowered his head.

"Is it true?" she asked.

God, this was what he hadn't wanted. It was his fault for not telling her himself, and telling her sooner. In slow motion, he nodded. "Yes."

She stood and pushed her chair in to the table.

He stood to meet her. "But you have to let me explain it to you."

She held up her hand, palm out.

He wasn't about to talk to the hand, so he reached out and grabbed her hand. She snatched it away from him.

"Bobbi, please, I was going to tell you—"

"When? After summer school was over? Was I just a little summer fling to you? Is that what you do, move around taking classes and picking up women?" She threw her hands through the air, gesturing. "I know that's how you met me, and it's how you met Jacque, with a *Q*." She rolled her head on the *Q*.

He kept shaking his head. "Stop it. It's not like that."

"Oh, that's right, it's a long story," she said sarcastically.

She was going off the deep end, and he had to reel her back. "I met Jacque in an anger management class. A class I was forced to attend by the court. And I told you, I've never been intimate with her."

Bobbi threw her hands up and stomped past him.

Quen tried to reach out and grab her arm, but she leaned and pulled away from him. She opened the front door. "I don't know you anymore. Get out!"

He shook his head and laughed to keep from crying. This had to be a joke, or another bad nightmare.

"Get out!" she screamed this time, as the first tear rolled down her cheek.

He walked over to the front door and slammed it shut. He had to plead with her. "Baby, look, I was going to tell you tonight. I've been walking around for weeks with every intention of telling you. You just don't know how I've agonized over what your reaction would be. I kept putting it off because I was afraid you'd react just like this. But you have to let me explain."

She reached to open the door again, but he held his hand against it and stopped her. "Bobbi, please let me talk to you. Come on, it's no different than you not telling me about your father. I should be mad at you for that."

The tears started to roll down her cheeks as she reached for the door again. He wanted to stop her, but he couldn't stand the sad look on her face. He'd hurt her enough, and she needed some time.

"Get out," she repeated, in a softer tone.

Reluctantly, he walked out the door. He couldn't stand to see her cry, knowing he'd caused it. He didn't even turn around when he heard it slam behind him.

Bobbi fell back against the door. The pain in her chest was so bad, she thought her heart would break. The floodgates opened and she bawled. A river of tears streamed down her face. *Probation, anger management class . . . what had he done?* She was so horrified, she couldn't even talk to him about it right now. She just wanted him as far away from her as possible. He should have told her he'd been on probation the first time they'd met. Instead, he'd wined and dined her, all the while pretending to be something he wasn't . . . just like her father.

Bobbi spent most of the weekend in bed, until Roz barged in Sunday evening, dragging her out.

"Come on, get dressed." Roz grabbed a T-shirt from the foot of Bobbi's bed and threw it at her. "We're going for a walk."

"A walk!" Bobbi sat up for a moment, looked around, then fell back into the pillows. "I'm not walking anywhere."

"Yes, you are. Look at your room. It's a mess." She sorted through the clothes laying around the room.

When she found a pair of jeans, she threw them at Bobbi. "Put those on."

Bobbi pushed the stack of magazines she'd been reading to the side and threw the covers back. "But I don't feel like taking no walk. Can't you just leave me alone?"

"No, I can't. If that was me sulking over a *man,* you'd have a fit. You'd be yelling at me to snap out of it, so that's what I'm going to do to you. Come on." She walked back toward the door. "I'm going to get my tennis shoes on and I'll be right back."

Bobbi's legs were like two lead pipes. It took all of her energy to throw them over the bed. She sat there, realizing Roz was right. She was acting stuped. All this childish behavior was giving him power over her. It had been fun while it lasted, but like most of her relationships, it was over before it started good.

"You're not ready yet?" Roz stood in the doorway with a hand on her hip.

Bobbi threw back the covers. "No, but I'll be ready in a few. You're right. I'm not going to let him get me down like this."

"That's right. You might as well get ready, since you have to face him tomorrow night."

Bobbi cut her eyes at Roz. "Don't remind me."

They walked around the large complex twice, talking out everything that was on Bobbi's mind.

"Bobbi, I told you to check him out good, didn't I? I felt like he was hiding something from you. Look how long it took him to take you to his house."

"I should have guessed he was keeping something from me when, like you said, I never met any of his friends."

"Yeah, but when you think about it, you can't really get too mad after the secret you kept."

"It doesn't matter. Something like that he should have told me."

"Yeah, you're right there. But think about it—you may not have made it easy for him to tell you."

"What do you mean? He could have told me at any time."

"Bobbi, as much as you fussed about working on anything that dealt with the prison system, I'm not surprised he didn't tell you."

"That should not have mattered. If anything, that should have made him tell me right up front. Then I wouldn't have gotten involved with him if I'd known."

"Bingo! That's probably why he didn't tell you."

Bobbi shrugged. "God, I hate complications." They made it back to the apartment and Bobbi took a shower, then called Gigi. She hoped her father wouldn't answer the phone.

After several rings, it picked up. "Hello," her aunt yelled into the phone.

"Aunt Alice, are you okay? It's Bobbi." Her aunt hardly ever answered the phone.

"I'm fine. I don't know how come nobody answered the phone."

"Is Gigi there?"

Alice hesitated, and Bobbi could picture her looking around the room, wondering where everybody had gone.

"No, she's not here right now. Your mother's at work, and I think Mark went off with Marcus somewhere."

"I'm going to strangle Gigi when I see her."

"What did she do now?"

"She told Quen about Daddy."

"What do you mean she told him? Told him what?"

Bobbi took a deep breath and exhaled. "I never told him Daddy was in prison. He just assumed he was dead, until he called and talked to Gigi."

"Uh-uh-uh. That's Gigi being Gigi. That mouth of hers is going to get her in trouble someday."

"Yeah as soon as I get ahold of her."

"Well, that goes to show you should always be truthful. How's that young man of yours, anyway? What's his name?"

"It's Quen, but I'm not seeing him anymore."

"Oh, no. What happened? He seemed so right for you."

"Remember when you told me he had a heavy heart?"

"Yes."

"Well, he was keeping something from me. Back when he lived in Chicago, he was on probation."

"My goodness. What for?"

"I don't know, but just that fact that he was on probation is good enough for me. I don't want to be involved with a man like that."

Alice started laughing. "Honey, you stopped seeing the young man and you don't even know what happened?"

Bobbi didn't see anything funny. "The court also ordered him to take an anger management class. He must have done something pretty bad, don't you think?"

"You know your daddy's had an effect on all you kids. I thought it was just Gigi and Marcus, but looks like he got to you, too."

"How did it affect me? I'm not running around like a loose cannon." That was how she saw her sister and brother.

"Baby, you're about to leave that young man without knowing what he did, all because something in his background reminds you of your father's situation. Bobbi, he's not Mark. Don't do that to that young man. At least find out what he did, so you don't live your life regretting it. It might not be as bad as you think."

Bobbi paced in her bedroom. Her aunt was right. She didn't want to admit it, but she knew she was right. Her father had messed them all up in one way or another.

"Well, that's why I don't want to see Daddy. I can see what he's done to this family."

"I know you're mad about it, but he's still your father, and he appears to be a changed man. I think he found Jesus or somebody in that jailhouse. At least he's had an effect on Marcus already. That Peanut won't be coming around here anymore."

"Well, that's good for Marcus."

"It's going to be different for all of us, but we'll pull through this. He's home now; nothing can prevent you all from being a family again."

"I thought you didn't like him," Bobbi said. Her aunt was turning on her.

"I don't like what he did to this family, I'll admit that. And I never thought he was the right man for your mother. But my feelings should have nothing to do with how you feel about your father. We don't pick our parents. And life is so short, you don't want to leave this world having any bad feelings toward anyone."

"Yeah, well, you all have to live with him, but I don't. I'm sure Gigi is beside herself."

"Gigi is Gigi."

"And she's going to be mine when I catch up with her."

Quen left Bobbi another message. He didn't want to explain anything on her answering machine. He wanted to talk to her. He'd already left several messages at her job, but she hadn't returned any of those, either.

When the phone rang, he quickly reached out for it, hoping it was Bobbi.

"Hello."

"Quen, this is Donald Stewart."

"Mr. Stewart, hello." He tried to hide his disappointment. He was a little surprised. Donald had never called him at home before. Quen hoped it wasn't bad news.

"I'm glad I caught you at home. I wanted to let you know the board has given the okay to meet with the faculty at Macon College."

"That's great. So, they like the revised proposal?"

"Very much. And they'd like you to run the program."

"In what capacity?" Was this the job offer he'd been waiting for?

"We'd like to offer you a full-time counseling position."

All right. He pumped his fist through the air. "That's good news. When does it start?"

"How about late August? That gives you plenty of time to finish school."

"Sounds good."

"Well, I wanted to give you the good news today. We can go over all the details when you come in.

"Thanks, Mr. Stewart."

Quen hung up and wanted to call Bobbi. He tried her apartment again, knowing full well she wouldn't answer the phone. This time, he left a message. "Bobbi, it's Quen. I know you're not taking my calls, but I got some good news about a job today and I wanted to share the good news with you." His tone softened and he lowered his voice. "I miss you and I wish you'd let me explain. I don't want to do it over this machine. Maybe I can talk to you Thursday night." He took a deep breath. "If you change your mind, please call me tonight."

He hung up, wanting to hit himself in the head. Why hadn't he told her already? He'd had a million chances, but he hadn't been able to do it. Now they had three more classes and a prison visit before the semester was over, and he'd never see her again.

He needed Bobbi. Thanks to her, he could now sleep through the night. No more waking up in the middle of the night doing homework or watching infomercials. He hadn't even had a nightmare in a while. He'd come to terms with what he'd done, and knew for sure he would never do it again.

Thursday night, he half expected Bobbi not to show up for class, but she walked in about fifteen minutes after class started. He tried to make eye contact with her, but she did a pretty good job of avoiding him. When Professor Jennings gave the usual fifteen-minute break, Quen watched Bobbi hurry out of the room. He walked down the hall for a soda. When he returned, Monica was waiting for him.

"Are we all set for next Tuesday?" she asked.

"Everything's all set." *Unless Bobbi changes her mind,* he thought. They were scheduled to visit Macon State Prison as the last part of their project. I guess we need to talk about"—he looked around him as Bobbi came back into the room—"when and where to meet."

Monica waved Bobbi over. "Bobbi, come on over, let's talk right quick."

Bobbi came, but Quen could see she did so reluctantly. She glanced at him once, then focused on Monica. His heart sank.

"What's up?" Bobbi asked, approaching with her arms crossed.

"We were just discussing our little trip next week. Let's try to meet up."

"How about I meet you guys in the parking lot before we even go in?" Quen asked, looking at Bobbi. She nodded, but still didn't look at him. "Bobbi, is that cool?" he asked, trying to force her to look at him. It worked.

She looked him directly in the eye. "Sounds good to me. I'll be there." She didn't uncross her arms, but cocked her head slightly. He could see fire in her eyes.

"Is everything okay here?" Monica asked, gesturing

from Bobbi to Quen. "I sense a little tension," she teased.

"We're okay," Quen answered.

"Why do you ask?" Bobbi turned her angry stare from Quen to Monica.

Monica held up her hands. "Hey, I'm just asking. Because last week you guys were acting like kissing cousins, and now you look like Superman and Lex Luthor. I'm just trying not to get caught in the middle."

"Everything's cool. Right, Bobbi?"

She looked toward the ceiling with her tongue pressed against her cheek. "Uh-huh."

Twenty-four

Tuesday morning, Bobbi arrived at the Macon State Prison after working all weekend to finish her research. Over the past several weeks, she'd accumulated enough information to put Monica to shame. She'd checked out every website Quen had given her, and found more. Her ex-convict interviews were integrated into her section of the written report, and the only things missing were the prison official answers. Their usual Saturday session had gone off without a hitch. She found out she could work with Quen in a professional manner without bringing up their relationship.

Monica and Quen arrived shortly after she did. The three of them were ushered inside, and she was surprised to see a few more students from another local college there taking a tour.

How exciting, she thought, *a field trip to tour a prison.* This place wasn't her idea of a fun trip.

After a brief tour of the facility, where every time the iron doors closed, Bobbi jumped, they were ready to sit down and talk with a prison official. Quen acted as the spokesperson for the group. He explained the intent of their visit and started taping the session.

Officer Jerry Samuels, a slim man who looked to be in his early forties, with a receding hairline and what looked to be a nervous twitch, willingly answered all their questions.

Bobbi couldn't keep her mind off her father this morning. She'd seen two older men in their prison uniforms in the hall earlier, and thought about how much her father had aged. He'd sent her numerous pictures that she hadn't wanted to look at, but she always did. She wasn't sure why, she just did.

"I'll tell you what, come with me. I've got some people I want you to meet." Office Samuels stood and gestured for them to follow.

They walked down a long corridor to several offices at the end of the hallway. Officer Samuels opened the door and motioned for them to go in. A black woman with short spiky hair sat behind one of the desks, talking on the phone.

"This is Joanne Lopez. She comes in about three times a week and works with the inmates who are about to be released. It's something we just started last year. I'd like for you to talk to her. She graduated from Macon State College a few years ago."

Joanne hung the phone up and walked around her desk to greet them with a huge smile. "Hello, I'm Joanne Lopez. It's a pleasure to meet you."

Officer Samuels introduced them and asked Joanne to spend some time telling them about her program, then return them to his office.

Bobbi noticed how Joanne was so enthused talking about her job. She acted as if she had the best job in the world. She showed them around her office and explained what she tried to do for the inmates before their release. Bobbi also learned that they had the same major, which meant working at a prison would be an option for her if she ever chose to explore it . . . which she never thought she would.

"Whenever possible, I try to get the family members to come in for at least one meeting. I try to set expectations as to what they're going to be up against upon release.

Without a good support system, it can be very difficult. Many of the men without support wind up right back in here. I don't want to see that happen. Another part of my job is to refer them to outside programs geared towards the transition process."

Quen told her about the Lean On Me Agency, and she was very familiar with it.

"That's one of the best programs in Macon. How did you come about volunteering there?"

"Several years ago I got into an altercation with a man and was sentenced to two years' probation, and five hundred hours of community service. I did my community service at a halfway house for ex-convicts. That's where I learned about the transition process. And I've been working with them ever since."

"That's wonderful. A lot of people get caught up in their community service and become permanent volunteers after their time is done. Some even later go to work for the companies. That's good, because we need dedicated people willing to give up a little of their time in order to make a difference in other people's lives."

Monica looked shocked. She stared at Quen with a questioning look, probably wondering the same thing Bobbi was. Why hadn't he told them before?

What he'd just described sounded like more than an altercation, Bobbi thought.

After their tour and interviews were all over, the three of them stood outside on the prison steps.

"Quen, why didn't you tell us you'd been on probation before?" Monica asked.

He shrugged. "It's not something I like to talk about."

"Trust me, we would have understood. Wouldn't we, Bobbi?"

Bobbi just stared at him. *An altercation of what type?* she wanted to ask. "Yes, I think we all would have understood. Had we known the details earlier."

"I don't mean to be nosy, but what happened?" Monica asked.

"This jerk tried to rape my daughter," Quen answered, focusing on Bobbi.

"Oh my God, that's awful. I would have tried to kill the bum," Monica exclaimed.

"I did."

The way his lips turned down slightly when he answered and he looked as if he were in pain made Bobbi's heart ache for him.

"And you got probation for that?" Monica seemed rather shocked.

Quen shook his head. "I kind of went off. It's a long story." He looked at Bobbi. "I'll have to tell you all about it sometime."

Bobbi wanted to reach out and hug him. Just last week she'd witnessed how much love he had for his daughter. She couldn't imagine the pain and horror something like that must have caused all of them.

"Wow, I'm real sorry to hear you had to go through that. It must have been a bummer," Monica said, looking sad.

Quen laughed. "Yeah, it was a real bummer."

"I'm sorry to hear about that, too." Bobbi didn't want him to think she was some heartless witch. She had empathy for him, Kristy, and Kristy's mother.

"Thank you. That's what I was trying to explain to you."

Well, he'd messed up. He shouldn't have waited so long to tell her. If he held that back, what else could he be holding back? And he'd said it was a long story— what else had he done?

"Well, guys, I've got to run. My boyfriend is in town this week and I'm meeting him for lunch."

Quen glanced at his watch. "Yeah, and I'm meeting a new client in thirty minutes. So, this Saturday is our last meeting. We can put the final touches on the project and rehearse our oral presentation, if that sounds cool."

"Sounds good to me," Monica offered.

"Yeah, me, too," Bobbi agreed.

"Okay, I've got to run, but can I call you later?" he asked Bobbi.

He'd put her on the spot, right there before Monica. How could she say no? "Sure." He could call, but that didn't mean she'd see him.

He left her and Monica standing on the prison steps.

"So, what's going on between you guys? Are you officially a couple now?" Monica asked.

"We were," Bobbi responded.

"What happened? Quen is such a nice guy. But, boy, I would have never guessed he'd been on probation. He's a pretty big guy, too, I wonder what he did to almost kill that guy?"

Bobbi watched him pull way. Had he shot him? Stabbed him? Or almost beaten him to death? He'd been forced into anger management. He was certainly big and strong enough to do any of those things. "Yeah, I wonder, too."

Bobbi worked late Tuesday to make up for being out that morning. Rich had called her in and given her the responses from the reviews on the Web. After talking with Quen, she'd been able to talk her boss into putting the readers' letters only on the website. They'd created a section for site surfers to send e-mails and she would respond, posting one a week on the website. The reader response had been overwhelming. She was receiving positive fan mail in droves.

"You know, the idea of trying this out on the Web first was brilliant. We're getting over five hundred hits a week, not to mention reader mail has increased. See"—he pointed at her—"it wasn't such a bad idea after all, was it?"

Not after I tweaked it a little, she wanted to say. "I guess it wasn't such a bad idea. But now, along with my secretarial duties, I've got loads of letters to answer. I'll be here all night. Are we talking overtime pay?"

He laughed. "Maybe I'll see what I can do about an increase."

"Yes, now you're talking."

She stepped out and brought her dinner back to work overtime and answer some reader fan mail. She loved that term, *fan mail.* Her phone rang several times, but she ignored it. She knew it was Quen, but she couldn't talk to him at the moment.

Quen and Monica sat at the library on Saturday morning, ready to prepare their oral presentation. After thirty minutes, Quen dialed Bobbi's number. He didn't expect her to answer, but tried anyway.

"You don't think something happened to her, do you?" Monica asked.

He shook his head. "I think she's still mad at me."

"But this is for our final exam. She has to show up."

They proceeded without her. Quen couldn't believe it. He'd feared Bobbi would get this upset, but to blow off her final exam . . . He didn't understand.

He'd gone from waking every night reliving a horrible nightmare, to sleeping through the night with her beside him, back to waking in the middle of the night, fearful of losing her. He was afraid his worst fear had come true.

Bobbi sat across the table from her father, resisting the urge to glance at her watch. He had insisted she come have lunch with him. Then he'd shown up early.

"Bobbi, I know you're pissed at me."

She snorted and laughed.

"Okay, maybe pissed isn't a strong enough word. And I know you feel like you don't know me right now, but I know you. You're still my baby girl. And I know you're hurting. I just want to talk to you a minute."

"Do you know what you did to us?" She fought to keep from crying.

"I know, baby, and I want to try and make it up to you guys, in whatever way I can."

"How do you make up twelve years of parenthood? It can't be done."

"I know that. But I'd like to start trying by taking you to lunch today. We can talk and get better acquainted."

"I hardly think a lunch can do it."

He nodded. "You're right. It can't. And I don't blame you for being mad at me. I did a stupid thing. And in the process, I hurt my family very much. I couldn't stand it if I'd lost you guys. And I feel as if I've lost you."

She shrugged.

"Come with me. We need to have a long talk."

She grabbed her purse and forgot all about her library session.

Quen listened to the health society give their final presentation and wondered where Bobbi was. He looked at his watch. They were up in fifteen minutes. Monica looked over at him and he shrugged.

The door squeaked open and he turned to see Bobbi walk in. She tiptoed over to them and sat down.

"I'm sorry," she whispered.

"Where have you been?" Quen asked, unable to keep his voice down.

"Let's step out." Monica motioned for them to follow her.

Once they stepped out the door, Bobbi began apologizing. "I'm sorry. I've been really messing up, but I'm prepared and can give my portion of the oral presentation. Quen, I owe you an apology, but for right now, let me get this presentation over with and we can talk."

He took a deep breath. "You missed Saturday."

"I know, I'm sorry. My father came to see me. We had to talk."

Quen understood what she meant. She'd made up with her father. He hoped that meant she had room to forgive him. "Okay, let's go in here and give them what we've got." He looked over at Monica, who seemed confused.

"I'll explain it to you later," Bobbi offered to her. "But for right now, let's go in here and pass this final."

The prison society turned its written report and presented its oral presentation in three parts. The class stood and applauded when the members finished. Professor Jennings was visibly pleased and applauded as well. He focused his smile on Bobbi and gave her the thumbs-up.

As soon as the final presentations were over and the prison society received accolades, Bobbi and Quen walked out together.

"You did pretty good in there," he offered.

"Not as good as you, but I owed it to the group to pull my act together. I'm sorry for my behavior these last few weeks."

He stopped. "No, I'm sorry. I should have told you everything the first time I asked you out."

"I understand why you didn't. I wasn't able to handle it then. Now, I think I can. Or I know I can sit still long enough for you to explain it tome."

He smiled at her. "Great. Want to go grab something to eat?"

She shook her head. "No. I'm not hungry right now. Let's talk. There's no time better than the present."

He nodded. "Okay, let's have a seat." He pointed to a bench he'd seen her sitting on once before when they'd been early for class.

She sat down and crossed her arms. "I'm ready."

He took a deep breath. "Well, I served two years' probation for trying to kill the guy right outside the courthouse.

"You might say I flipped out in front of everybody. If no one had been there, I think I might have succeeded. Because of the circumstances, I was given probation. The anger management class was thrown in to make the cops feel good. I didn't really need it. Or I don't think I did."

"Quen, why didn't you tell me? I thought all types of things."

"Believe me, I wanted to. Is that something you can handle?"

"I know I can. I talked to my father Saturday, and we worked through a lot of issues. I'm not totally over everything, but I did sit down and talk to him. We're working through it."

"I think I need to take you to Chicago to meet my family. I want you to see that I'm not some type of a killer or madman."

"Deep down, I knew that. I was just hurt that you didn't tell me and I found out from Perry."

He let out a sigh. "I had a feeling that's who told you. But I'm not worried about him. Since Donald's given me the only job they had for the fall, I don't expect Perry will be a thorn in my side any longer."

"I got your voice mail. I think that's great. It's what you were hoping for."

He nodded. "Yeah, that was a moment I would like to have shared with you."

"I'm sorry. I shouldn't have been so stubborn. You'll be happy to know that your helpful insight about the reviews on the Web helped me out a lot."

"What happened?"

"I'm getting fan mail in droves now. Eventually, I'll be able to branch off into my own column. Or maybe even something bigger."

"Bobbi, that's great."

"Will you ever forgive me for how I've behaved?"

He leaned over and kissed her on the forehead. "You're forgiven."

"Let's start all over. This time, let's be up-front about everything. No more secrets. So, if there's anything else I need to know, tell me now."

"That's it. I don't have anything else that I haven't shared with you. How about you?"

"Oh, my dad wants to meet you. I told him about your volunteer work."

"That's good, because I'm looking forward to meeting him. I want to meet everyone in your family that I haven't already."

She laughed. "Are you sure about that?"

"Yes. I need to know who all my relatives are going to be."

"Excuse me?"

"I told you, we're going to have the world's greatest romance. Mr. and Mrs. Quentin Brooks."

"It must be hotter than I thought out here." She laughed, fanning herself.

"Baby, you're not half as hot as you're going to get." He wrapped his arms around her, pulled her close, and gave her the biggest kiss. Quen held onto Bobbi as if she were his life support.

"Hey, why don't you guys get a room or get married this time?"

They stopped long enough to see a classmate wave at them, laughing.

"We plan to," Quen yelled.

"Yeah, we plan to," Bobbi whispered.

ABOUT THE AUTHOR

Pinnacle/Arabesque books published SOUL MATES, Bridget's first novel in 1997. It was also nominated as best paranormal romance by *Affaire de Coeur* magazine. Her novella, IMANI, part of the MOONLIGHT & MISTLETOE holiday anthology for Pinnacle books was also nominated by *Affaire de Coeur* as best ethnic romance for 1997. Her third Arabesque romantic suspense RENDEZVOUS, was released in 1998, then re-released when it was turned into a made-for-television movie by BET Networks, and aired November 1999. Her other Arabesque books include: LOST TO LOVE, April 1999; REUNITED, September 2001; A KWANZAA KEEPSAKE (a reissue of IMANI), October 2001; ALL BECAUSE OF YOU, May 2002.

Born and raised in Louisville, Kentucky, Bridget holds a degree in counseling and guidance. Her writing career began in 1987 when she moved to Atlanta, Georgia. Along with her writing career, she works a full-time job. You can contact her at P.O. Box 76432, Atlanta, GA 30339, or Banders319@aol.com.